CONFESSIONS OF A BANGKOK PRIVATE EYE

D1487336

CONFESSIONS OF A BANGKOK PRIVATE EYE

True stories from the case files of Warren Olson

monsoon

monsoonbooks

First published in 2006
by Monsoon Books Pte Ltd
71 Ayer Rajah Crescent #01-01
Singapore 139951
www.monsoonbooks.com.sg

This edition published in 2012 (6th edition)

ISBN: 978-981-05-4832-2

Printed in Singapore
15 14 13 12   6 7 8 9

For Natalie

CONTENTS

THE CASE OF THE
DOUBLE-CROSSED DUTCHMAN

There are a whole host of things I love about living in Thailand: the gorgeous women, the climate, the food, the beaches. But right at the top of the list of things I hate is being pursued at high speed by two motorcyclists with gun-toting pillion passengers. The guys out to put a bullet in my head weren't flashing the smiles that Thailand is famous for—they were glaring at me with murder in their eyes. I swerved over to the right, trying to clip the rear wheel of the bike nearest to me but he moved away easily. The pillion passenger was caught off balance and he grabbed the waist of the driver. I took a quick look over my left shoulder. The second pillion passenger had his gun aimed at my head. I slammed on the brakes and the bike roared by, the passenger's hair whipping in the wind.

I cursed, spitting out pretty much all the swear words I knew. I was in deep, deep shit, and it had all been the fault of my brand new digital camera.

The case had started easily enough. I'd received a phone call from a Dutch detective agency in Amsterdam that I'd done business with a few times. They were good payers and good payers are like hens teeth in the private-eye business. They were acting for a well-known Dutch businessmen who'd married a girl from Bangkok five years earlier. The businessmen had started taking his wife to a local Thai restaurant and was worried that she might have started a relationship with a young waiter. The Dutch detectives had put the wife under surveillance but so far hadn't caught her misbehaving, but now the wife was planning to fly to Thailand for Songkran, the Thai new year. It's the traditional time for Thai families to get together, and the businessman was too busy adding to his millions to go with her. A red flag was raised when the Dutch detectives discovered that the Thai waiter had booked onto the same flight to Bangkok. It could have been a coincidence, of course, but the Dutch guys wanted me to mount a surveillance operation once they'd arrived in Bangkok.

The girl's parents lived in Chiang Mai, in the north of Thailand, so the first thing I did was to check if she had booked an onward flight from Bangkok. She hadn't, but she might be planning to buy the ticket once she'd arrived, or even travel up by train or bus. I asked for a description of the jewellery and watch she usually wore, because photographs were often surprisingly unhelpful for identifying people and there would be several dozen young and pretty girls, all with black hair and brown eyes, getting off the KLM 747 from Amsterdam. The information, along with her passport number and a copy of her Thai ID card, came over with her pictures, plus a photograph of the waiter, and a sizeable retainer was transferred into my account with Bangkok Bank.

She was due to arrive at Don Muang at eleven o'clock in the morning in two days' time. The problem was, I had no idea what she was going to do once she'd arrived. I bought Business Class tickets on the three flights that were due to leave for Chiang Mai after her flight had arrived, just in case she decided to head up north straight away. But if she took a car into Bangkok, I had a problem. I'd have to be in the terminal to check that she arrived, but that would mean parking my car in the multistorey. If she hopped into a cab I'd lose her before I got back to my vehicle. If she was picked up by a friend then the friend would have parked in the multistorey and by the time I'd identified their car it would be too late to get to my own vehicle. I couldn't use motorcycles to follow her because motorcycles aren't allowed on the country's expressways, and the route from the airport to the city was all expressway. I didn't have the money to start paying half a dozen guys to stake out the airport to cover every eventuality so I decided to nab a taxi driver at the airport and offered him 2,000 baht for a four-hour hire. He practically bit my hand off and I gave him 500 baht up front and told him to wait outside the terminal for me. He had a mobile phone so that if the girl headed to the car park I could follow her and then call the taxi to pick me up. If she hired a cab then I was ahead of the game, I just had to get into my taxi and follow her. And if she walked over to the domestic terminal and bought a ticket to Chiang Mai, all I'd have to do would be to get on the flight with her. I was feeling pretty pleased with myself as I sipped a cup of coffee in the arrivals area.

The terminal was packed, as hundreds of thousands of Thais rushed home in time for the New Year celebrations. There were lots of tourists too, who think it's fun to douse each other with water as a way of celebrating Thai New Year. Frankly, after ten years of having water thrown in my face every April, I celebrate the festival by staying at home and ordering pizza and beer over the phone. But that's just me.

The flight landed bang on time and it took them just over an hour to pass through Customs and Immigration. I spotted the girl among a group of Thais. She was pushing a trolley piled high with suitcases and bulging nylon bags, presumably gifts for her family. The waiter was a few paces behind her, pushing his own trolley. Nothing suspicious about that, they would have been sure to have met on the plane even if they hadn't been planning to travel together. The photographs that the Dutch agency sent didn't do the girl justice. She had waist-length hair, high cheekbones, and was model-pretty with curves in all the right places. She was tall for a Thai, five-seven or thereabouts, and she was wearing a short denim skirt that showed off a gorgeous pair of legs.

There were four people waiting to greet the girl, two were a few years younger than her and they quickly waied her, pressing their hands together and placing the tips of the fingers against their chins. Showing respect. That tends to be how Thais greet each other, even after long absences. No great show of emotion, no hugs or kisses. A nice, respectful wai. The girl first waied the two older members of the group, then returned the wai to the girl and boy who had waied her. Then she introduced them to the waiter. He waied them all, then they pushed their trolleys towards the car park. That answered two questions right there. She wasn't flying to Chiang Mai and she was definitely travelling with the waiter.

I kept my distance but the terminal was so crowded that I doubted they would have spotted me even if they'd looked my way. They walked to the car park and started putting the bags into the back of a Toyota van. I made a note of the registration number and hurried back to the waiting taxi.

I was feeling even more pleased with myself as the van pulled out of the multistorey car park. I told the taxi driver to follow the van and settled back in my seat. All we had to do was keep the van in sight on the expressway and make sure that we took the same exit. The fact that I was tailing the van in a Bangkok taxi meant that there was virtually no way they'd spot me. Taxis account for about ten per cent of the cars on the roads at any time.

The van started to pull away from us and I told the driver to step on it. He nodded enthusiastically but we didn't go any faster. I told him again, this time in Khmer, but that didn't seem to sink in so I repeated myself in the Isaan dialect that many taxi drivers speak. He nodded again but the van continued to disappear into the distance. I peered into the footwell. The accelerator was flat against the floor. I groaned. The engine was juddering like a heart-attack victim and we hadn't even broken sixty kilometres an hour. The driver grinned and gripped the steering wheel so tightly that his knuckles started to turn white.

We lost the van before we reached the first turn off so I told the driver to take me back to my office. I gave him half the fee we had agreed on but he threw a temper tantrum and started waving his mobile phone at me and threatened to call his friends. Most taxi drivers have at least a crowbar or baseball bat in their vehicles, and guns aren't unknown, and one of their favourite pastimes is roughing up troublesome farangs, as they call us foreigners, so I gave him the full 2,000 baht. The Dutchman would be covering my expenses anyway so it was no big deal.

I phoned the Dutch agency and spun them a story about knowing the general area where the subject was, but that I wanted a recent phone bill from the client to see if there were any Bangkok numbers that the girl had called before arriving in Thailand. An hour later and a phone bill was faxed through to me. I was in luck—there were four numbers with Bangkok's 02 prefix. I fed the numbers into a reverse directory I use and the computer gave me the addresses. Three were offices and one was an apartment in the Bangna area of the city. I drove out to Bangna in a rental car and sat outside the apartment block for the rest of the day.

The apartment was in a small side road and it was difficult to get a view of the main entrance without sticking out like a sore thumb so I parked the car and went and sat in a small chicken restaurant opposite the block. I ordered some kow man gai, steamed chicken and rice with a tangy sauce and a bowl of watery soup. There was a British soccer game on the television set in the corner and after muttering 'Man U *channa nanon* (Manchester United are sure to win) I was pretty much ignored by the half dozen male customers sitting at a Formica table drinking Singha beer. After about an hour I saw the waiter walking towards the apartment block. Bingo. He went inside.

I phoned my contact in the Dutch agency and explained that the waiter was definitely staying with the girl and there was no indication that they were heading up to Chiang Mai. My contact was pleased, but said that his client wanted a photograph of the girl and the waiter together.

I had a brand new digital camera in the boot of the car, so I parked as close to the apartment block as I could and sat with the camera on my lap. It had a telephoto lens and the salesman had assured me that it was state-of-the-art. Being digital, I could use my computer to email the pictures without having to wait for film to be processed. I as starting to feel pretty pleased with myself again. I had found where they were staying, there was only one way in and out, all I needed was a photograph and the fee was in the bag.

Time passed. It got dark. I had a couple of bottles of water in the car and I drank them both. Midnight passed. I was thinking about abandoning the surveillance for the night, figuring that perhaps the girl and the waiter were having too much fun to go out, when I saw movement in the lobby. I wound the window down and got the camera ready. It was the waiter. He held the door open and the girl walked out. 'Yes,' I hissed triumphantly. I brought up the camera lens and took a couple of quick shots. Just then there was a double flash of lightning. It looked as if my luck was changing for the worse—the weather had been fine all day and now that I had them in my sights a tropical storm was starting. I fired off another two quick shots and lightning flashed again.

Click. Flash. Click. Flash.

Then it hit me. My state-of-the-art digital camera with its onboard smarter-than-a-human-being computer had decided that as it was dark I should be using the flash. What the bloody thing hadn't realised was that the last thing a private detective on a stakeout needs is a flash going off, computer-controlled or otherwise. The girl and the waiter looked in my direction and hurried along the road away from the car.

I cursed and fumbled with the camera, trying to find the control that turned off the flash.

Something smacked against the bonnet of the car and I looked up to see a muscle-bound Thai man glaring at me. He had a thick gold chain around his neck and a wicked scar across his left cheek that cut through a crop of old acne scars. He thumped on the bonnet again.

'*Tham arai*?" he screamed, which means 'I'm sorry old chap but what exactly are you doing?' or words to that effect.

I put the camera on the passenger seat and hit the central locking switch. The thuds of the locks clicking into place antagonised the man even more and he slapped the windscreen. A second man, just as heavily built, ran over and began pulling at the passenger door handle.

I looked around. Two more men were walking purposefully out of the restaurant and one of them was swinging a large machete. I didn't know what I'd done to upset them but they didn't look like the sort of guys who were going to respond to reason. I had the engine running to keep the aircon cold so I put the car into gear and moved forward, slowly enough to give the guy with the scar a chance to get out of the way. A foreigner running over a Thai would end only one way and sleeping on the floor of a Thai prison wasn't how I was planning to spend my retirement.

I pushed harder on the accelerator. The guy kept hold of the passenger side door handle and jogged to keep up. I cursed. I didn't want to drag him down the road, but I was equally unhappy at the prospect of the guy with the machete doing a remodelling job on the rental car.

Machete Guy shouted something and started to run. I stopped worrying about the man on the passenger side and pushed the accelerator to the floor. The wheels screeched on the tarmac and the car leapt forward. I roared down the road, snatching a quick look in the rear-view mirror. The four men were standing on the pavement, screaming at me. I grinned and took the first right turn, onto a major road. I was just starting to relax when I saw the motorbikes.

As they got closer I recognised one of the drivers—it was Machete Guy. I had no idea what I'd done to upset the guys, but figured they had obviously been up to something iffy and thought that I'd been taking photographs of them. Drugs maybe, or gambling. There might have been an underage brothel above the restaurant for all I knew. In an ideal world I'd have just explained that I had been taking pictures of an unfaithful wife, but Bangkok wasn't an ideal world and it was probably too late for any explanation.

There was a fair bit of traffic around and I had to slow down. The motorcycles quickly gained on me. Machete Guy's pillion passenger brandished a pistol and motioned for me to pull over to the side of the road. Yeah, right. I shook my head, braked hard, and pulled a left, cutting across a bus and feeling the rear end fishtail as I floored the accelerator again. I knew there was no way I was going to be able to outrun the bikes in the city. It would only be a matter of time before I hit traffic or a red light.

I could feel sweat trickling down my neck. Life is cheap in Bangkok. That's not a cliché, it's an economic truth. The going rate for a professional hit is 20,000 baht for a Thai, 50,000 if it's a farang.

But amateurs were also happy to use bullets to solve a quarrel because most murderers end up serving seven years at most, and that was in the unlikely event of them being caught. All of this was running through my mind as I drove through the streets at high speed. Along with wondering why I hadn't chosen another profession, why I'd moved to the Land of Smiles in the first place, and why I hadn't read the manual for the camera before taking it on the job.

The best I could hope for was to run across a police patrol car but even that was no guarantee that I'd be safe. For all I knew, the four guys in hot pursuit could well be off-duty cops.

The second bike drew up on my passenger side and the pillion passenger waved a large automatic at me. I swung the car to the right. I had a really, really bad feeling about the way this was going to play out. They were getting madder and madder and all it would take would be one shot to a tyre and it would all be over.

Suddenly I saw a sign for the Pattaya Expressway and realised that it was my best hope: bikes aren't allowed on the expressway and even if they ignored the law and followed me I'd be able to get the car up to full speed and with them being two up on small bikes they wouldn't be able to keep up with me.

I kept on going straight, accelerated, then as the ramp approached I slammed on the brakes and pulled the car hard to the left, just missing the concrete dividing wall that separated the ramp from the road. The bikes continued to roar down the road then I saw the brake lights go red as they realised what had happened. I sped towards the line of toll booths, pulling my wallet out of my pocket and flicking through the notes. The toll was forty baht but I flung a red 100-baht note at the toll booth attendant and yelled at her to keep the change as I sped on through.

As I accelerated down the expressway I kept looking in the rear view mirror but there was no sign of my pursuers, and after twenty minutes barrelling along at more than 140 kilometres an hour I started to relax. I left the expressway at the third exit, then parked up and had a bowl of noodles and pork and a bottle of Chang beer at a roadside vendor to calm my nerves. My hands stopped shaking by the time I'd put the third bottle away.

I waited a couple of hours before driving back to the city, and I caught a few hours sleep after emailing a full report to the Dutch agency along with the photographs I'd taken.

I was woken by the phone ringing. It was one of the Dutch operatives—the client had booked himself on the next flight to Bangkok and he wanted to confront his wife, ideally while she was in bed with her lover. I've never understood that, but it's happened time and time again. It's not enough for the wronged guy to know that his wife has been unfaithful, he wants to rub her face in the fact that he knows. If it was me, I'd just up and leave. Okay, I'd clear out the bank accounts first and maybe take a razor blade to all her clothes, but I wouldn't bother with a confrontation. That's just me, though, and in this business the client is always right. Even when he's wrong.

I got up and showered, then returned the rental car. The guy who ran the rental company was an old friend and he agreed to swap my paperwork with that of an American tourist who'd just flown back to Seattle so I was covered just in case the bike guys had taken my registration number.

The Dutch agency had told me to take good care of the client so I booked a Mercedes and driver and got to Don Muang Airport an hour before the flight was due, holding a piece of card with his name on it as I sipped my black coffee. The man who walked over to me and introduced himself was just about the fattest guy I had ever set eyes on. He wasn't big. He wasn't even huge. He was obese and must have weighed at least 400 pounds straight out of the shower. He was in his early forties, with slicked back hair and half a dozen chins. He was wearing a light blue suit that was stretched like a sail in a high wind; I figured he must be at least five times the weight of the his wife and I couldn't imagine how they went about having sex. We shook hands. His was the size of a small shovel but the fingers were soft, like underdone pork sausages. He had no luggage and hadn't shaved on the plane, but he said he wanted to head straight out to the apartment. I sat upfront as we drove out to Bangna. The client didn't say anything and only grunted at my attempts to start a conversation so after a while I just let him sit there in silence.

It isn't unusual for a pretty young Thai girl to marry an older guy. Like girls all over the Third World they want someone to take care of them and their families and there's no doubt that a few thousand dollars in the bank can help add to a man's attractiveness to the opposite sex. But there was no way on earth that the match between the lovely girl we were going to see and the blimp I had in the back of the Mercedes was a marriage made in heaven. He must have known that. Every time he caught a glimpse of the two of them in a mirror it must have hit home that he was simply too big for her. If it had been me, I'd have just been grateful for the fact that I was allowed to sleep with a woman as beautiful as her, and if the downside meant that she had the occasional fling with a man nearer her own age, well then I'd just put that down to the price I had to pay. The Dutch guys hadn't managed to catch her being unfaithful in Amsterdam, which meant that she was probably only fooling around in Thailand. I wanted to tell the client that he'd be better off turning a blind eye to the occasional indiscretion and that the best thing he could do would be to go straight back to Holland, but I kept quiet.

I had the driver park around the corner from the apartment block, and pulled on a pair of shades and a Singha beer baseball cap before I got out of the car. The client was obviously used to sitting in the back of expensive vehicles because he didn't make a move to open

21

his door himself, he just sat staring straight ahead until I opened it for him. He wheezed as he hauled himself out of the car, and I swear the suspension sighed with relief. 'I burn easily,' I said, explaining away the cap and sunglasses, but the real reason was that I didn't want to risk being recognised if Machete Man and his gun-wielding buddies were back in the restaurant. They weren't, and I relaxed a little when I saw that the restaurant was closed.

A receptionist buzzed us into the apartment block and a purple 500-baht note got us the room number. We rode up in the lift in silence to the fourth floor. I looked around to see if there was a weight limit for the lift, and I kept having visions of the cables snapping and us both plummeting to our deaths.

There were a couple of dozen rooms on either side of a long corridor. We walked slowly along to the room. I waited at the side of the door as the client knocked, twice.

The door opened. The girl was there wearing a white T-shirt and blue denim shorts. She stared at him sleepily, then her jaw dropped as she realised who it was.

'Darling …' she said, but then the words dried up and her mouth open and closed silently.

'Don't "darling" me, you whore!' hissed the client, and he pushed the door open. It was a studio apartment and the waiter was lying on the double bed, wrapped in a towel. The waiter leapt to his feet as the big guy strode into the room and rushed out, his bare feet slapping on the tiled floor as he bolted down the corridor.

I stayed where I was. The client had left the door open so I could hear everything that was being said. The girl began pleading that there'd been a mistake, that the waiter was just a friend, that she was only staying in the room until she could get a flight to Chiang Mai. The client let her beg and plead, then silenced her with an outburst of expletives that suggested he'd had an army career in his younger, and probably thinner, days.

'You were a whore when I met you, and you're a whore now!' he shouted once he'd finished swearing. 'I gave you everything. I gave you the clothes on your back, the watch on your wrist. I gave you money for your parents, I paid for your brothers to go to school. Anything you needed, anything you wanted, I gave to you. And you do this to me? You fuck around behind my back.'

She started to cry.

'You're dead to me, you bitch!' he shouted. 'When I get back home I'm destroying everything of yours. Every dress, every handbag, every shoe; everything I ever gave you, I'm burning. Every photograph of you, I'm destroying. You're dead to me. I'm divorcing you and you won't get a penny. The best lawyers in the country work for me, and if I get my way you'll lose your Dutch citizenship.'

There was a dull thud and I took a quick look into he room just in case she's beaten him over the head with a blunt object but she was the one on the floor, slumped down next to the bed, her hands over her face, sobbing her heart out.

He waddled over to a dressing table and grabbed her handbag. He pulled out a Dutch passport and ripped it into several places, went over to the toilet and flushed away the pieces. Then he threw the handbag into the toilet for good measure.

'Please, darling ...' sobbed the girl.

The client sneered at her and walked out of the room, his ham-sized hands clenched into fists. I followed him back to the lift. I saw the waiter in the stairwell, anxiously looking in our direction, his hands clutching the towel around his waist. I waved for him to keep out of the way.

The lift doors opened and we rode down. 'Bitch,' said the client, venomously. His face was bathed in sweat and there were damp patches under the arms of his jacket.

I said nothing. I could see his point, but I figured that of the two of them, he'd lost the most. She'd lost a sugar daddy, but then she wouldn't have to satisfy the sexual urges of a man big enough to crush her if he rolled over in his sleep. And a girl as pretty as her wouldn't have to look too hard to find another husband. He'd lost a beautiful young gold-digger but now he'd have to sleep with nothing more than his right hand for company. Swings and roundabouts? I didn't think so. If ever there was a Pyrhic victory, this was it.

We walked out of the block and over to the Mercedes. 'I don't need you any more,' he wheezed. 'I can take care of myself at the airport. Thank you. For everything.' He handed me a fistful of euros which I guessed was my cab fare home.

I opened the rear door of the Mercedes and he hauled himself slowly into the back. The suspension groaned in protest. I closed the door behind him and the car moved away from the kerb. I got one last look at the client as the car drove off. There were tears streaming down his fleshy cheeks.

THE CASE OF THE
CHRISTIAN CONMAN

Khun Bua was a lovely woman, a decent middle-class Thai lady who kept dabbing at her eyes with a lace handkerchief as she told me her story. She was my first real client. I'd done a few bargirl investigations for friends but Khun Men was to be my first paying customer. She'd read my one and only advertisement in a tourist magazine that was delivered free to Bangkok hotels. I was surprised to be contacted by a Thai because the advert was aimed at tourists and visitors. I'd assumed that any Thai would prefer to deal with a Thai detective. But as Khun Bua told me her story as we sat together in a Kentucky Fried Chicken outlet close to her home, it became clear why she wanted a farang.

She had a copy of the magazine with her. Not the one that contained my advert, hers was from almost a year earlier. It was open at a page with an article about a Thai marriage agency. There was a photograph of a man in religious attire conducting a marriage ceremony between a middle-aged farang and a young Thai girl.

As I read the article, Khun Bua sniffed and dabbed at her eyes. She was wearing a small gold crucifix around her neck. It was unusual for a Thai to be Christian. Thailand is a Buddhist country and Christians are a small minority. The man in the picture was the Reverend Marcus

Armitage, and he had founded the Canadian–Thai Christian Dating Agency with the aim of finding wives for good Christian men back in Canada.

Between sniffles, Khun Bua explained that she worked for the magazine. A friend of hers, a wealthy politician's wife, had put up the money for the publishing venture, but Khun Bua had been hired to do most of the work. She sold advertising space, wrote many of the articles, liaised with the printers and arranged to have the magazines delivered to the city's hotels. Khun Bua had never married and had worked hard all her life, putting all her spare money in a savings account for the day when she retired. There's no Government pension scheme in Thailand, it's every man, and woman, for themselves. Thai parents have their children to support them in their old age, but Khun Bua was alone in the world and would have to take care of herself. But she lived frugally, saved every baht she could, and once she was retired she planned to build herself a small house in Phetchabun and spend her time reading and sewing. But the Reverend Armitage had brought Khun Bua's plans crashing to the ground.

Armitage had met Khun Bua at the magazine's office. He had agreed to pay for a half-page colour advertisement and in return Khun Bua had agreed to write an editorial, extolling the virtues of the new agency. He had been charming, and impressed Khun Bua with his knowledge of the Bible, often quoting passages at length. He had taken her out for dinner, he had sent her flowers when the article had appeared, he had given her a leather-bound Bible on her birthday. As she dabbed at her eyes, she told me that she had fallen in love with the smooth-talking Canadian. There had never been anything physical, she added quickly, not even a kiss on the cheek. He was the perfect gentleman. She had told him everything, her hard early years on a farm in Isaan, the one man she had loved who'd been killed in a road accident when she was twenty-one, and that fact that she was saving to build her own home.

During one dinner at a well-known Bangkok seafood restaurant, the Reverend Armitage told Khun Bua about his plans to start a new business in Thailand. His marriage agency was working well, he said, but what he really wanted to do was start a flower business. He planned to export flowers, especially orchids, to churches back in Canada to use in funerals and wedding ceremonies. The only thing that was holding him back was the fact that all his capital was tied up in the marriage agency and in his home on the west coast of Canada. If only there was some way he could find a business partner to help him get the new venture up and running. With his church connections back in Canada, the money would come rolling in.

Khun Bua took the bait. She offered to back the Reverend Armitage in his new venture. At first he declined, saying that he didn't want to jeopardise their friendship by going into business, but Khun Bua insisted. She trusted the man of the cloth, and he was offering her a way to fund a very comfortable retirement. The Reverend allowed Khun Bua to persuade him that she was the perfect business partner, and he went with her to the bank where she drew out all her life savings in a cashier's check. Armitage gave her a legal-looking document which stated that she was a partner in the Thai–Canadian Christian Orchid Company and that she would be entitled to fifty per cent of all future profits.

There were no profits, of course. At first there were excuses. Lots of excuses. There were problems with permits, with visas, with suppliers. Then his mobile phone number was disconnected. Khun Bua went around to the offices of the marriage agency in a run-down tenanted high-rise in Asoke. The only employee there was a young secretary who hadn't been paid in two months. Of the Reverend Armitage there was no sign.

At this point in the story, Khun Bua broke down and began

sobbing. I started to get angry looks from the diners in KFC, who obviously thought that I was the one making the middle-aged lady unhappy. I patted her on the back of the hand and told her that I would do what I could to help, and she blew her nose loudly and took a deep breath.

'I'm so sorry,' she sniffed. 'But I have nothing now. That man, that evil, evil, man, took everything I have.'

The secretary told her that the rent hadn't been paid, and that the electricity and phone were about to be cut off. She had Armitage's home address but he wasn't answering his phone. Khun Bua went around to the apartment in Soi 39 and found the landlord there. All Armitage's personal effects had gone and he owed a month's rent.

Khun Bua collapsed in the landlord's arms. He advised her to go to the police, but they said there was nothing they could do: Armitage hadn't broken any laws. Khun Bua had taken a week off work. She was getting heart palpitations and had developed a nervous tic. While at home she'd picked up the latest copy of the magazine and saw my advertisement. As we sat in the KFC outlet, she threw herself on my mercy. I was her last hope. Her only hope. And she had no money to pay me. Nothing. Nada.

Like I said, she was my first real case and I really did feel sorry for her, so I agreed to work on a commission of ten per cent of any funds recovered. If I could find the elusive Reverend Armitage, I stood to make 40,000 baht, which wasn't at all shabby.

My first stop was the marriage agency's office. The secretary was still there, but she was packing her things into a cardboard box when I walked in through the door. Her name was Nid and she was a typical young Thai university graduate, eager-to-please and working for a pittance. The average university graduate in Thailand earns less than 8,000 baht a month. Young Nid had been promised twice that but had only been paid for two months. She had no idea where her employer had gone and had problems of her own. Her rent was due that week and she hadn't been able to send any money back to her family upcountry. Her only hope was to find another job and that wasn't going to be easy as Bangkok was awash with newly qualified graduates.

I promised to do what I could to get her back pay, so she let me rummage through the desks. There were no clues as to where the elusive Reverend Armitage might have gone, but on one of the desks was an old computer. I plugged it in. It was password protected but Nid had that so I was able to get into the email programme and pull out his contacts list. There were two Armitages on the list, which I figured would be close family. I showed the names to Nid and she confirmed that they were both his brothers. One was in Montreal, the other lived in Singapore.

Nid also told me that her boss had a girlfriend from Udon Thani but she didn't know the girl's name. From the description—tall, leggy, long hair and a tattoo of a scorpion on one shoulder—it sounded as if the Reverend Armitage was either rescuing wicked women or he'd fallen for the charms of a bargirl.

I headed off to the Canadian Embassy but they were in no mood to help. I explained that Armitage had left a decent middle-class Thai woman penniless but the young Canadian guy behind the glass window just shrugged and told me that they didn't give out information to third parties. I went to an internet café where I downed a couple of strong coffees and fired off emails to the two brothers.

I knew that both guys received the emails but neither got back to me. I didn't have an office back then, I worked out of my apartment and used computers in local internet cafes. I'd pop in every few hours to see if there was a reply but after a couple of days it became clear that they were ignoring me. The one person who kept calling me was

Khun Bua, who was becoming increasingly frantic. I tried to calm her down but I knew that it wasn't going to be an easy case to crack. I had no idea where he was, and even if I did find him, I was only a private eye. To force him to hand back Khun Bua's money I'd need the backing of the police, and that was easier said than done.

Thai police precincts don't cooperate especially well with each other. They prefer to operate as separate entities. As the money had been taken in Bangkok, I'd have to register the complaint at the Thonglor police headquarters. But it looked as if Armitage had fled Bangkok, and that being the case the Thonglor cops wouldn't go out of their way to pursue him. Equally, if he was picked up outside Bangkok for anything else, it wasn't a foregone conclusion that the upcountry cops would check back with Bangkok. I needed an arrest warrant, and for that I needed a judge. Then I had a stroke of luck. Khun Bua was on the edge of a nervous breakdown so I offered to take her for a coffee. I was shocked when I saw her. She'd aged a good ten years since our first meeting. She'd developed a stammer and I swear her hair was now streaked with grey. I explained the position to Khun Bua, and she told me that one of the owners of the magazine company was related to a Supreme Court Judge. Bingo! Getting things done in Thailand is all a matter of who you know and who you're related to. As a farang, I was short of top-level contacts, but Khun Bua had come up trumps.

I took Khun Bua to the police station and made an official complaint. As part of the deal Khun Bua agreed to pay the station a small percentage of any money recovered. Par for the course in Thailand. The cops gave us a copy of the complaint and Khun Bua went with her boss to see the judge who happily signed an arrest warrant. Now all I had to do was to find the elusive Reverend Armitage. I remembered what Nid had said about Armitage having a girlfriend from Udon Thani. It was a fair bet that if he was still in

Thailand he'd gone back to her home town. That being the case he'd have to do a visa run every few months, and most long-stay expats in Udon Thani crossed the border at Nong Khai to visit Laos, get a new visa and then return to the Land of Smiles.

I took a train to Nong Khai—twelve hours on a hard seat on a rattling train that at times rumbled along at barely more than walking pace—and then paid a motorcycle taxi to drive me out to the border. On the way we stopped off at a local supermarket and picked up two bottles of Johnnie Walker Black Label—the universal sweetener.

My Thai was good enough to get me ushered into the local immigration chief's office and I handed him the whisky and the warrant. I told him the full story, how Armitage had ruined the life of a sweet little old lady, and that I was pretty sure that he'd be crossing the border at some point. I told him that Khun Bua was well in with a Supreme Court Judge and, naturally, promised him a share of any money recovered. And that was all I could do. I caught the next train back to Bangkok and waited. Khun Bua kept calling me but I explained that it was now in the hands of the immigration officers at Nong Khai. She promised to pray for my well being, and for Armitage to be apprehended.

The private-eye business is all about waiting. You wait for clients, you spend hours, sometimes days, waiting outside a building for your target to appear, you wait at airports, you wait outside hotel rooms, you wait to get paid. You need the patience of a saint, and I was never a particularly patient guy.

I first arrived in Thailand in the late eighties. I was born in Cambridge, a small town in New Zealand that produces most of the country's thoroughbred horses. Most of the town's 5,000 or so population are involved with horses in one way or another, so it was no surprise that I became a trainer. Hand on heart, I wasn't averse to bending the rules, if not exactly breaking them, something that stood me in good stead when I later became a private eye. If a borderline legal painkilling injection meant that a horse of mine stood a better chance of winning than not, then I'd give the injection. I trained for a few Asian owners and with them, winning was the only thing that mattered. If I didn't come up with winners, they'd take their business elsewhere. I'm not making excuses, I'm just telling you the way it was. Thing is, word got around that I was sailing close to the wind and all my winners began to be tested and the chief steward started making frequent trips to the centre where I trained my horses. It was time to look for pastures new.

One of my Asian clients told me he was going to visit his mia noi—a minor wife, or mistress—in Thailand and offered to take me with him. We flew into Bangkok and it was an eye-opener. While my client enjoyed himself with his mistress, I made full use of the city's go-go bars, massage parlours and nightclubs. After almost forty years in New Zealand and Australia, I was like a kid in a sweetshop.

In between watching girls dancing around silver poles I decided to take a look at the local horse scene. My client took me to a huge stable in Siricha owned by a wealthy Thai who, as it happened, had gone to university in New Zealand. He loved horses but spent so much time building hotels and office blocks that he had no time to manage his stock and they were a pretty rough collection of horseflesh. In no time he offered me a job, and I moved to Thailand.

I hit the ground running. I trained during the week, we went to the Bangkok racetracks every Sunday, and on Monday—my day off—I stayed over in the Grace Hotel with a succession of temporary girlfriends plucked from the hotel's disco. Spending so much time with jockeys and bargirls, neither of whom spoke much English, my Thai language skills improved by leaps and bounds.

The client's horses were okay, but in most cases were just a few generations removed from Mongolian ponies and they weren't a patch on the thoroughbreds I'd worked with in New Zealand. The problem was, for a horse to race in Thailand, it had to be born in the country. It didn't take me long to spot the loophole in that regulation, so I flew over a pregnant mare and trained up her foal. She was a little beauty and on her first big race she was a firm favourite. Then, in typical Thai fashion, disaster struck. A jing jok, a tiny lizard that loves to climb across ceilings, fell on top of our jockey. The Thais regard that as just about the worst possible bad luck, equivalent to a farang breaking a mirror or walking under a ladder. The jockey rushed of to the local temple on the back of a motorcycle but crashed on the way back. He was still able to ride but crashed his horse into the back of one of the front runners and shattered her knee. She had to be put down and my client came in for all sorts of flak from his friends along the lines of 'you've got an expensive farang trainer but your horse still dies'. Needless to say it was a massive loss of face and the only solution was to let me go.

By then I was pretty much addicted to the Thai nightlife so decided that I'd stay in the country. I decided to put my newly acquired Thai language skills to use and landed a job as marketing manager of a hotel in Surin, a largish town not far from Cambodia. I was mainly teaching the staff basic English, updating brochures and menus, and marketing the hotel around the world. It was a monster of a hotel, the biggest in Isaan, with 600 rooms, a ballroom, a nightclub, karaoke bar, three restaurants and two enormous conference centres, where most regional government and police meetings were held. And the kicker for me was the massage parlour with eighty beautiful girls. Forget the sweetshop. Now I was the kid in the sweet factory.

The Surin job meant that I also picked up Khamen, the Cambodian language spoken in the Thai border provinces of Surin, Buriram and Si Saket, and that came in handy when I started working as a private eye as many bargirls come from those provinces, and it's a big advantage being able to speak to them in their own language. Then, once again, disaster struck, in true Thai fashion. My employer's family were openly known as Isaan mafia and had a nice sideline importing Russian prostitutes with the help of the local head of police, who had his own suite at the hotel. Back then middle class Thais had money to spend and they'd only ever seen big blonde women on the movie screen. The girls were charging 3,000 baht for short time and there were queues down the corridors all day. My bosses were planning to bring in more girls and send them on a tour around the region's hotels, splitting the profits with the other hotel owners. Anyway, two of the family members became infatuated with the same Russian girl. One was an old guy, the other was much younger, but both were rich and neither wanted to back down. Eventually the younger guy had the older one murdered and the shit hit the fan. The local police chief had no chance of keeping a lid on the scandal, the family sold the hotel and moved to the United States, and I found myself out of a job. I went back to Bangkok and booked into a cheap hotel on Sukhumvit Soi 8. I took a long, hard look at myself. I didn't want to work with horses again, and I was fed up with the hotel business. I was fairly proficient at speaking Thai and Khamen, and I knew pretty much all there was to know about bargirls. I didn't fancy running a bar, but after a few tourists asked me to check up on their temporary girlfriends after they'd gone home, I had the idea of setting up a private detective agency. I figured that way I'd be paid to do what I did best: to hang around with bargirls and drink Jack Daniels.

When I'd set up as a private eye, I had no idea that my first paying customer would be a middle-aged Thai lady who wouldn't dream of setting foot inside a go-go bar. But I was determined to do my best for her. The problem was, all I could do was to wait. And wait.

It was a month before the Thonglor police phoned me to say that the Reverend Armitage was in custody in Nong Khai and that they'd sent a pick up truck to bring him back to Bangkok. I phoned Khun Bua to give her the good news, then I went down to an internet café and fired off emails to the two brothers, telling them that Marcus was in custody and that he would be facing serious jail time. I gave them a few details of what life was like in a Thai prison—based on my own experience, since you ask—and told them that the only way to avoid a long spell in a cell with an open toilet and wall-to-wall mosquitoes was for Marcus to pay back the money he'd stolen.

The next day Armitage was in a holding cell at Thonglor police station. I went in to have a look at him. He didn't look like a man of the cloth. He was wearing faded blue denim jeans, a Chang Beer T-shirt and a baseball cap, and there were shackles on his legs. He was complaining to anyone who would listen to him that he was going to complain to his embassy, that he was a Canadian citizen, that they had no way to treat him like this, and so on. The fact that the three guys he was sharing the cell with and most of the officers at the station spoke absolutely no English meant that he was wasting his breath. And even if he was able to make himself understood no one there would have given a damn. Armitage was a farang and the Thai legal system showed farangs no favours. Innocent until proven guilty had no standing under Thai law. He would stay in custody until his trial. He would be found guilty for sure, and he'd get three years in the Bangkok Hilton—the infamous Thai prison—unless he bought his way out.

At first Armitage thought I was from the Embassy but as soon as he heard my New Zealand accent he started getting cagey, telling me that he wouldn't speak to anyone but his lawyer. I told him that Khun Bua was well in with a Supreme Court judge and that there wasn't a lawyer in Thailand who could keep him out of prison. And once the court heard how he'd defrauded a good Christian woman they would throw away the key. Thai prisons are seriously nasty places. Up to forty men sharing a cell with an open toilet, the lights on all day and night, prisoners sleeping like sardines on the floor, no airconditioning, rampant disease and god-awful food. Armitage was facing a long sentence and I told him that I didn't think he'd survive more than a few months.

There was only one way he was going to stay out of prison, and that was to pay back the money he'd stolen. Immediately. At the moment he was in a holding cell. Police could be paid off, Khun Bua could be persuaded not to press charges, and Armitage could walk away. But once Armitage was charged he'd be in the system and there would be nothing he could do to save himself. It was his choice, I told him.

He started to say that he didn't have the money, that his bank account was almost empty, his companies had all been losing money, but I held up my hand to silence him.

'I don't care either way, pal,' I said. 'The only reason I'm even wasting my breath on you is because Khun Bua is a nice lady and I don't want her living out the rest of her years in poverty. If it was up to me you'd rot in prison, but that's not going to help her. The guys in here will let you use a phone. Call one of your brothers and get them to fly over with the cash.'

Armitage's face tightened but I could see that he had taken on board what I'd said.

'If you're going to make that call you'd better do it today,' I said, tightening the screw. 'You'll be charged tomorrow then it's off to the Bangkok Hilton and they won't let you near a phone there.'

Armitage made the call and the next morning his brother flew over from Singapore with enough money to pay Khun Bua what she was owed, plus sweeteners for the police and the immigration officers up in Nong Kha. Plus my fee, of course.

Once the money had been paid and the police had pocketed their sweeteners the atmosphere changed. The shackles were taken off, Armitage was given a coffee and croissant and taken to Don Muang Airport in the back of the police chief's Mercedes where he and his brother were escorted on to the next plane to Singapore. Armitage's passport was stamped persona non grata and he was told never to darken Thailand's doorstep again.

My first case, and I'd come out smelling of roses. I'd made money and I'd helped someone; a private eye couldn't ask for a better result.

THE CASE OF THE
RELUCTANT VIRGIN

It was love at first sight, at least that's how the client described it. He'd seen her across a crowded dancefloor in a trendy Phuket nightclub. She was slim and sexy, long black hair, great legs, and was one hell of a dancer. The client was an accountant from Glasgow in Scotland with an accent so impenetrable that I had to keep asking him to repeat himself. He was in his late forties, which made him almost twice the age of the love of his life. He was average looking, definitely not movie-star material but he had his own hair and most of his own teeth and the gold Rolex on his wrist suggested that he was making good money and that alone would make him attractive to the average bar-going Thai girl. Not that Joy was a bargirl. She worked in a hair salon in Patong, the island's major tourist area but she liked to let her hair down in the evenings.

The client, Bill MacKay, had offered to buy Joy a drink as she rested between bouts of dancing, and the following day she'd acted as a tour guide, showing him around the island. MacKay showed me photographs of them at a monkey show, riding elephants, posing on beaches. The perfect couple. MacKay had gone to Phuket with three golfing buddies, but after he met Joy he didn't spend much time on the links. He and Joy became inseparable and by the time his three-week vacation was over he'd proposed to her, on bended knee in a crowded seafood restaurant as the band played 'My Way'. He'd asked for the theme from Titanic but something had got lost in translation. Not that MacKay cared. Joy said yes and that was all that mattered.

They went to Joy's home town of Chiang Mai and he met her parents. They were a middle-class Thai couple with six children of whom Joy was the second youngest. They owned a small noodle shop and seemed thrilled to have MacKay as a potential son-in-law. They'd discussed the sin sot—the Thai dowry that's usually paid to a girl's parents—and they'd agreed on a very reasonable 100,000 baht. Reasonable for a farang, that is. Thais usually paid about 20,000 in poorer families.

MacKay was sure that his bride-to-be was a good girl and not involved in the island's thriving sex industry. Estimates of the number of prostitutes working in Phuket vary from 4,000 to 20,000, but Joy had never danced in a go-go bar or worked up a lather in a massage parlour. But even good girls can be won over by handsome strangers so he didn't want her to stay in Phuket while he was back in Scotland. I guess he figured that if he could win her heart in just a few short weeks, another visitor might just be as lucky. He had given her 50,000 baht and told her to quit her job and stay with her parents while he was away. MacKay planned to be in Scotland for two months, and then return with his parents for a big Thai wedding. He'd do the paperwork with the embassy and if all went well he and Joy would return to Glasgow to start a new life together. He owned a big house on the outskirts of the city and planned to set Joy up with her own beauty parlour and then live happily ever after. But he'd heard all the horror stories about men being ripped off by Thai brides, taken for a ride while a husband or boyfriend waited in the background, maybe with a kid or two. So the day before MacKay was due to fly back to Scotland, he came around to my office and plonked down the holiday snaps and a 30,000-baht retainer on my desk.

'I want to know if she's got any skeletons in her closet,' he said.

'Like a husband?' I said.

'Anything,' said MacKay. 'I'm sure I've got nothing to worry about, but better safe than sorry, as my mother always says.'

'Forewarned is forearmed,' I said. 'Has she ever given you any reason to suspect that there might be a problem?'

MacKay shook his head emphatically. 'She's never asked me for money, never given me any reason to suspect that she might be hiding anything.' He leaned across my desk and lowered his voice to a whisper. 'And so far as I know, she's still a virgin.'

My eyebrows headed skyward. Joy wasn't a sex worker but she'd clearly had no reservations about going out with a farang, and that suggested she had at least some sexual experience. I'd never met a Westerner before who'd claimed that his girlfriend was a virgin. But I've never seen the Taj Mahal and everyone tells me that exists, so I was prepared to give him the benefit of the doubt.

'You haven't slept together?'

He flashed me an embarrassed smile. 'We've slept together loads of times, but we've never ...' He nodded like a woodpecker getting busy on an oak. 'You know ...'

I nodded. I knew. But it sounded unlikely. Lots of Thai girls were virgins when they married. In Thai society, it was pretty much the norm. But Thai girls weren't usually so coy with Westerners. And real virgins generally didn't share a bed with their boyfriends.

'She does things ...' he said. 'You know ...' He nodded encouragingly. 'Things.'

'Things?'

'You know. Oral.'

I winced. More information than I needed.

'She loves oral. It's just that she says she doesn't want to go the whole way, not until we're married.'

'Right,' I said. 'I get the picture.'

'She's really good at it. I mean, the fact that we haven't had sex yet doesn't worry me. She says she loves me.'

'Got it,' I said.

'Spends hours going down on me, that's not a problem, but she won't allow, you know, penetration.'

Far more information than I needed. I stood up and shook his hand and ushered him out of the office, promising to call him once I'd run a check on the lovely Joy.

First things first. I bought a Thai Airways ticket from Bangkok to Phuket, Phuket to Chiang Mai, and Chiang Mai to Bangkok, then flew down south and wandered into the beauty parlour where she worked. There was no sign of her and when I asked for her I was told that she'd gone back home, to Chiang Mai. So far, so good.

I had a haircut and a face massage, a manicure and a pedicure. All at the client's expense, of course. I walked out smelling like a tart's boudoir with the full background on Joy. She'd met a farang called Bill, fallen in love with him and had gone back home to stay with her parents until they got married. So far as the beauty parlour girls knew. Joy had never had a serious boyfriend and had never been married. She'd always enjoyed dancing and discos, and had gone out with several farangs, but there had been nobody regular and she didn't have anyone sending her money from overseas. It was starting to look as if Joy really was on the level and that Bill had found the rarest of jewels, a Thai girl who was a virgin and who loved him.

I caught a taxi to the airport and got the next flight to Chiang Mai. It was late evening by the time I arrived so I checked into a small hotel and drank the best part of a bottle of Jack Daniels before retiring to bed. Three times during the night small cards mysteriously appeared under my door offering visiting massage services but a good nights sleep was all the relaxation I needed.

Joy had told Bill that she was from Chiang Mai, but in fact she'd been born in a small town about forty miles away. There is nothing unusual or suspicious about that, most Thais would give the nearest big city as their place of birth. But it meant that I'd have to go to the local municipal office rather than the big one in Chiang Mai.

I had the hotel's buffet breakfast and then went out on to the street to negotiate with a taxi driver. I promised him 500 baht for a half day, plus another 200 to take me to the airport once I'd finished.

For starters we took a drive past the house where Joy was living. I didn't stop because a farang visitor would have attracted too much attention. It was a three-storey shophouse with the noodle shop in the ground floor. I saw a Thai man in his sixties, who I guessed was the girl's father, ladling soup into a line of chipped bowls, but there was no sign of Joy.

The driver took me to the municipal office, the Tee Wah Garn, a grey concrete building with two Thai flags and a life-size painting of the King above the main entrance. On the way we stopped off at a supermarket and I bought two bottles of Johnnie Walker Black Label whisky, making sure that I kept the receipt.

The driver offered to go inside with me but I told him to wait outside. There are times when it pays to play the naïve foreigner, so I wasn't planning to let on that I spoke pretty fluent Thai and I didn't need an interpreter. The information on the government computers is supposedly confidential but a couple of bottles of imported whisky and a lot of smiling tends to get me what I need.

There was a reception desk that stretched across the main room behind which were a couple of dozen men and women tapping away at computer terminals. On the public side of the room were lines of plastic chairs where a handful of farmers waited patiently for whatever business they were hoping to transact. Overhead a couple of fans tried in vain to stir the stifling air.

I caught the eye of a middle-aged man with slicked-back hair and circular glasses, gave him a beaming smile, and went into my prepared speech. My brother, I said, was about to marry a local girl but his family was worried that she might be taking advantage of him. I passed over the carrier bag containing the two bottles of whisky, which disappeared under the counter without a word. I gave him another beaming smile and explained that I just wanted to know if the bride-to-be had been married or if she had registered any children.

'No problem,' the man said. 'I'll need her full name and date of birth.'

I had the name written in Thai and English, and her birth date. He frowned. 'No record,' he said.

'Oh,' I said. 'She's definitely from here.'

'The family name is correct?'

'I'm sure it is.' Bill MacKay had given me both the Thai and the English spellings.

'Let me see,' said the man. A few taps on the terminal and the helpful Government official had Joy's details on screen. A smile spread slowly across his face. 'There was a mistake on her birth date,' he said. 'The day and month is okay but the year was wrong. She was born five years earlier than she says.'

I nodded. So Joy wasn't the perfect bride after all. She'd lied about her age. But MacKay was no spring chicken and there'd still be almost two decades between them, so I didn't think he'd mind too much.

The man's smile widened. 'Your brother has married already?' he asked.

'Not yet,' I said. 'Is there a problem?'

'I think so, yes,' said the official.

'She's married already?'

The man shook his had, still grinning. 'No. No husband. No children.'

Now I was confused. Other than shaving off a few years from her age, Joy seemed to have been as true as her word.

He twisted his terminal around and jabbed a finger at the screen. The wording was in Thai but I had no problem in reading what was there. There were details of Joy's date and place of birth, her residential address, and the details of the rest of the family who lived in the home. Mother. Father. Two of her brothers. Three sisters. Then I saw what he was pointing out. The man laughed as I frowned. Two young men came over and the older man explained what was going on. I asked for a print-out of the information on the screen. As I left the building the laughter was spreading around the building.

I could have gone straight back to the airport but I wanted to see for myself so I had the taxi driver park around the corner from the noodle shop. I walked inside and ordered a Sprite and a bowl of noodles with pork. The old man I'd seen earlier had gone but I figured the woman who prepared the noodles was Joy's mother. She was in her fifties with short hair that was still jet black, and wrinkled skin the colour of weathered teak. When she smiled at me she showed two gold teeth at the front of her mouth. She switched on an overhead fan and put a bucket of ice on the table to keep my beer cold.

I spooned chilli powder into my bowl of noodles and added a couple of spoonfuls of fish sauce. Lovely. I must have overdone the chilli because I had tears in my eyes by the third mouthful. I was on my second bottle of Sprite when Joy appeared at the back of the shop. I guess she'd come down from the living quarters above the shop. Tight jeans, a white T-shirt with a teddy bear on the front showing off several inches of a drum-taut stomach, her long hair tied back in a ponytail. She was wearing less make up than she had on in the pictures that MacKay had shown me, and as she went over to the old woman I could see a glittering diamond ring on her wedding finger. Joy was pretty in the pictures, and up close she was still pretty, but the signs were there for anyone to see. Anyone who knew what to look for, of course. Large hands, large feet, broad shoulders, a bump of an Adam's apple. Taller than the average Thai girl. The love of MacKay's life was a katoey. A ladyboy. And while I'd been in Thailand for long enough to be able to spot the difference between a ladyboy and the genuine thing, MacKay was a relative newcomer. The high cheekbones, long hair, long legs and large breasts were probably all he was looking at.

The Government computer had shown that Joy had been born a man. The question I wanted answering was how much of his original equipment remained. The fact that Joy was so tall suggested that she'd been on hormones from an early age, and she'd clearly had breast implants. The fact that Joy wouldn't have full sex with MacKay might have more to do with her still having a penis and less to do with retaining her virginity. It's always a tough call deciding how to refer to ladyboys. 'He' doesn't sound right, not considering the long hair, proud breasts and pouting lips. But 'she' isn't strictly accurate, not if they've got the full block and tackle, if you get my drift. And 'it' just sounds offensive. I was going to settle for 'she'.

More often than not I can tell a ladyboy just by looking at her. The height is a clue, they have deep voices, large feet and hands, and unless they've had it surgically reduced, a large Adam's apple. But if all else fails, I have a foolproof method that has never failed me. You get them into a conversation about Thai boxing and have them show you how they throw a punch. A man's arm will go straight, but a woman's arm will actually bend beyond the 180 degrees at the elbow. Don't ask me why, but that's the way it is, and it's an infallible way of differentiating between a man and woman. But the presence of a penis is a pretty good indicator, too.

Anyway, I took my bowl over to the old woman and asked for more noodles. I smiled at Joy and said '*Sawasdee krup.*'

We started chatting in Thai and I asked her if it was engagement ring on her finger. She beamed and said that yes, she was getting married to a farang, a guy from Scotland called Bill. She took a bottle of water from the fridge and hurried back up stairs.

The old woman handed me my bowl of noodles with another flash of gold teeth.

'She is very beautiful,' I said.

The old woman nodded.

'The farang doesn't mind that she's a katoey?' I asked.

The old woman had the grace to blush. 'He doesn't know,' she said.

'Wow,' I said. 'Isn't he going to find out sometime?'

The old woman shrugged. 'My son is going to have the operation soon,' she said. She made a scissor cutting motion with her fingers. 'As soon as the farang sends the money.' She cackled and stirred her soup with a long metal ladle.

I took my bowl of noodles back to my table. It can be a funny old world at times.

I waited until I was back in Bangkok before faxing my report to the client. I suppose I should have phoned but I couldn't face telling him, even over the phone. I sent him a typewritten report and a copy of the print out I'd got from the Government office and a translation. And I faxed a copy of my bill. Four days later I got a cheque through the post. No note, just a cheque. I figured there was nothing he wanted to say. They way I see it, he had a lucky escape. Sooner or later he would have found out, even with Joy's skill at oral sex, and even with all her family in on the secret. That's what blew me away. He'd met the folks, he'd discussed a dowry with them, all the time thinking that he was getting a beautiful girl, and a virgin to boot. And no one had said a thing. Maybe they were hoping that MacKay would send them enough money to pay for the operation before the wedding. Then I had a thought that made me shudder. If I hadn't found out what was going on, and if Joy had had the final cut, and if she could come up with an excuse for why she wasn't getting pregnant, than MacKay might never have discovered the truth.

THE CASE OF THE
LESBIAN LOVER

Greig Knight was one of the few real success stories among Thailand's expat community. The Thais don't make it easy for foreigners to succeed in business, but Greig had bucked the trend and made a decent-sized fortune building up a chain of American-style restaurants. You know the sort of thing: racks of ribs, barbecued chickens smeared in hickory sauce, burgers covered in cheese and bacon with French fries the size of a labourer's fingers. Not that they were called French fries in Knight's restaurants. Ever since 9/11 they were Freedom fries in all his establishments and there wasn't a bottle of French wine on the menu. Knight had served in the military—he'd been one of the first soldiers into Kuwait—before deciding that he'd rather take his chances in the Land of Smiles. He landed at Don Muang without being able to speak a word of Thai and a cheque from the US Government in his back pocket. He found a decent hotel, decent beer, but couldn't find a decent burger despite looking the length and breadth of the city. He figured the only way he was going to get the sort of food he wanted was to cook it himself, so he set up a small burger joint in a soi close to Patpong. He never looked back and now he owns a huge house in one of the more heavily fortified areas of town and flies himself to Hong Kong to watch his racehorses run.

He didn't tell me who he was when he phoned. He just said that he needed a private detective and asked me to meet him at Starbucks in Soi Thonglor. He said he'd be reading a copy of the Asian Wall Street Journal but his choice of reading material wasn't important because he was the only farang in the place. I recognised him immediately from photographs in the glossy magazines they leave around in my dentist's. Usually he was holding court at the opening of one of his restaurants, or attending a function to honour some visiting American dignitary or other, standing with his arm around a leggy Thai beauty queen or a gay DJ raising a glass of champagne to the camera, grinning with a set of teeth so white that they had to have been capped. He was well over six foot tall, greying at the temples with flint-grey eyes that looked at me inquisitively as I walked over to his table. He unwound himself from his chair. He was thin with a runner's build, and as I knew for a fact that he ate in one of his own restaurants every night, he must have had the metabolism of a humming bird.

'Greig Knight,' he said. He nodded at the muscular Thai man who was sitting in the armchair opposite his. 'This is Gung. My driver.'

Gung stood up and waied me with a cold smile. He didn't look like a driver. He looked more like a bodyguard and from the way he held himself I figured he was former military or police.

Knight wound himself back into his armchair and waved for me to take Gung's place. Gung stood slightly to the left of Knight, his arms crossed. He didn't look like the sort of man you'd want to meet in a dark alley.

'As you've probably guessed, it's a woman,' said Knight.

'It usually is.' I said.

'Do you want a coffee?'

'Black.'

'You don't want a cappuccino or a latte?'

'I'm a traditional sort of guy,' I said.'

'Cappuccino is for wimps?'

'My thoughts exactly.'

Knight grinned and nodded at Gung. 'Mr Olson will have the same as me,' he said. 'Same as we like our heavyweight boxers.'

Gung frowned.

'Strong and black,' said Knight, and he tapped the table in front of him with a large ring on his left hand.

I chuckled but Gung's frown just deepened. He nodded and walked over to the counter.

'He's been with me for ten years,' said Knight. 'Just so you know, I trust him completely.'

'Former army?'

Knight nodded. 'Captain in the Thahan Phran.'

I raised an eyebrow. The Thahan Phran are Thailand's paramilitary border guards. Hard bastards. You wouldn't want to get on the wrong side of one, dark alley or not.

He steepled his fingers under his chin and leaned back in his chair. 'I've got a live-in girlfriend. Ying.' He smiled. 'Beautiful girl. Sexy as hell.'

'You're a very lucky man,' I said.

'If I thought that, I wouldn't be having this conversation,' he said. He sighed. 'I was in a Humvee, a few years back. Had a sergeant who thought he was Michael Schumacher. Took it as an insult to his manhood if he had to put his foot on the brake. We were heading into Kuwait City, full-pelt. I don't know what it was, but I just had a feeling that something was wrong. I told the sergeant to stop. He moaned like hell but he pulled over. I went ahead on foot. Fifty feet in front of where we stopped was a landmine. A biggie.'

'Wow.'

'Wow is right. Humvees are damn big vehicles but the mine would have blown it to kingdom come. But if the hairs on the back of my neck hadn't stood to attention, my army career would have come to an abrupt end there and then.'

'And this Ying is making your hair stand to attention, is that it?'

Knight made a gun out of his right hand and faked shooting me in the face. 'Got it in one. There's nothing I can put my finger on, it's just a feeling.'

He reached into his jacket pocket and took out a couple of photographs and handed them to me. I tried to look at them without drooling. She was beautiful all right. Shampoo commercial hair, toothpaste commercial teeth, moisturiser commercial skin, you get the picture. Drop dead lovely, but as Greig Knight was one of the richest farangs in Thailand, it was only to be expected. The only dogs he'd go near would be at the greyhound track in Macau.

'I've written her Thai name, date of birth and ID card number on the back of one of the pictures,' said Knight. 'Look, I pay all her bills, I've bought her a BMW, a house for her parents in Surin, and I've given her a gold Amex card. She gets an allowance of 200,000 baht a month and I've lost count of the gold jewellery I've bought for her.'

I tried not to turn green with envy but he was giving her twice what I made in a good month. And I didn't have a BMW. Or a gold Amex card. But then I didn't have a body to die for and a face to kill for.

'She's as loving as she ever was,' Knight continued. 'The sex is great, there are no mysterious late-night phone calls, nothing I can put my finger on.'

'Just a feeling?'

Knight nodded. 'That's right.'

I didn't say anything to Knight but in my experience once a guy feels that his wife or girlfriend is up to no good, she probably is.

'I'm flying to Hong Kong this weekend. I asked Ying to go with me but she said she was busy, she's got a conference in Pattaya that she has to go to.'

'A conference?'

'She works for a pharmaceuticals company. Sales director. She doesn't need to, I've told her that, but she wants her independence.'

I wanted to point out that she didn't want her independence enough to turn down 200,000 baht a month or give him back the BMW, but I kept my mouth shut. Discretion being the better part of not pissing off the client and all that.

'Anyway, I'm off to Hong Kong, she'll be in Pattaya, so I want you to follow her. You can do that?'

I smiled confidently. 'No problem. I'll need her car registration number.'

'It's on the back of the photograph,' said Knight. He pulled out a thick wallet and flicked his thumbnail across a stack of 1,000-baht bills, counted out thirty and handed them to me. 'This is on account,' he said. 'But money's no object, I just want to know the truth, one way or another.'

I pocketed the cash and nodded over at the bodyguard. 'Is Gung going with you?'

'No, he's looking after my house.' I'd seen Knight's house in one of the glossy magazines. It was in an expensive area of Sukhumvit, a mix of old Thai teak and white minimalist chic, full of modern Asian art and ancient Buddha figures looted from Burma.

'Get Gung to call me when she leaves the house, and if you can get any details of what hotel she's staying at, so much the better.'

'Whatever you need,' said Knight. He scribbled on the back of an embossed business card and handed it to me. 'My private number is on there. Gung's too.'

I shook his hand and headed out. The money was burning a hole in my pocket, I had several bills that were past their sell-by date and I owed my maid last month's salary.

By Friday afternoon I was all set. Knight was on a three o'clock Cathay Pacific flight to Hong Kong so he left his house at just before midday, sitting in the back of a. large Mercedes. I was in a rental car, an inconspicuous Honda Civic, down the road. He didn't see me. As a rule, guys in the back of big Mercs didn't notice men in small Japanese cars.

Further down the road were three motorcycle taxis that I'd booked for the day. Two thousand baht each. They sat under the shade of an advertising hoarding promoting a shampoo that blackened, thickened and strengthened, all in one. The Thais love black hair and white skin and spend a fortune on products that promise either. The motorcycle riders had short-cropped hair and skin the colour of burnt mahogany, blackened from years ferrying passengers around the city under the unforgiving sun. They were smoking hand-rolled cigarettes and kept looking over towards the Honda, waiting for my signal. I'd lent them mobile phones so that they could stay in touch once we were on the lovely Miss Ying's trail.

Following someone is a difficult business at the best of times, but in Bangkok it can be a nightmare. For a start, there's the congestion. At rush hour many of the city's major intersections hit gridlock. And the traffic lights can sometimes take up to fifteen minutes to change. So you might sit in slow-moving traffic for an hour or so, only to see your quarry skip through a light just as it changes to red. Even if you can keep up with your quarry, following them as they change lanes means taking your life into your hands because Bangkok traffic is the most unforgiving in the world. All pretence of politeness goes out of the window when a Thai gets behind the wheel of a car. That's where the motorcycle taxi drivers come in handy. There are tens of thousands of them around the city, whizzing through the traffic, delivering officer workers to their desks, hookers to the go-go bars and students to their classrooms. They used to wear coloured vests denoting the soi they worked in, but the Government changed the regulations and made them all wear orange vests which makes using them as chasers even easier.

Using bikes doesn't solve all your problems though because the city is crisscrossed with expressways and motorcycles and aren't allowed to use them. Still, if it was easy, everyone would be doing it, right?

At one o'clock Gung called my mobile to say that Ying was packing a bag and that she'd asked him to go down to the carpark to make sure that her car airconditioner was running. It must be nice to have money, I said to Gung. I was going to ask him if he warmed the toilet seat for her as well as cooling her car but the boys in the Thahan Phran aren't renowned for their sense of humour.

I waved over at the three motorcycle riders and they climbed onto their bikes. They were all under 100cc—small bikes that could nip in and out of the traffic. When a farang buys a bike he usually goes for a big Harley or a 1000cc Yamaha and sits there with all that power throbbing between his legs feeling like he's lord of the jungle. But as soon as the traffic locks up the big bikes are locked up too and the farang sits there sweating like a pig and breathing in diesel fumes as the Thais on their little bikes whiz by. Big isn't always best. That's what I tell the girls anyway.

The BMW rolled out of the underground carpark and I let a couple of cars go before following her. Two of the bikes roared past her and then slowed a hundred yards or so ahead of her. If she was going to Pattaya she'd probably use the expressway which meant that I'd be following her most of the way on my own with the bikes making their way along the regular road. But at least once she was on the expressway I'd be able to hang back because I'd know where she was going. The bikes could pick her up at the Pattaya end. Easy peasy.

The BMW took a left turn and that had me frowning because that meant she was heading away from the expressway. The bikes kept her in sight so I dropped back. I lost her ten minutes later but after a phone call to one of the motorcycle riders I was back on track. They saw her park outside a restaurant. One of Knight's restaurants. I left the rental a short walk from the restaurant.

I told the motorcycle boys to hang around while I went inside. On the ground floor there was a large circular bar with half a dozen customers, mainly expats. There were ten circular dining tables but the lunch crowd had gone and it was too early for the evening session. There was no sign of the lovely Ying.

I sat at the bar and ordered a Jack Daniels and waited. One JD became two and two became three and there was still no sign of her. The men's room was upstairs so I grinned at the barman and said that I had to take a leak and headed up. There was a pool table and another dozen tables, but the place was empty. There was a small locked door leading up to the top floor and a note in Thai and English that said 'Staff Only'.

It was getting late, too late to make it to Pattaya in time for a sales conference. I made a call to the company where Ying worked and in my very best Thai explained that my girlfriend was attending a sales conference in Pattaya and that she'd forgotten her make-up bag and that I wanted to get it to her but I didn't know where the conference was being held. The conference was at the Ambassador Jomtien, a very helpful young switchboard girl explained, but that the conference finished at five so there was no need to get the bag to my girlfriend because she'd be back in Bangkok later tonight. I thanked her. So, I'd caught her out in one lie, and in my experience lies are like cockroaches. If you find one, there'll be hundreds of others behind the skirting board. At least in the sort of places that I stay in.

I went back downstairs and paid my bill, then took a walk outside. There were lights up on the top floor so I figured that was where Ying was holed up. Next door to the restaurant was a ten-storey office block. Sitting on a deckchair at the entrance was a dark-skinned security guard in a uniform several sizes too big for him. I wandered over and started chatting to him in Laos. He was a nice guy, his wife was back in Udon Thani taking care of their five kids and he sent back most of his wages each month. Down the road from the office block I'd seen a street vendor selling a variety of fried insects, much loved by the people of Isaan. I asked him how he liked his grasshoppers and then went and bought him a bag of well-salted insects. I shared them with him as we talked. They taste a lot better than they sound, really. A bit like pork scratchings, it's the crunch and the salt you're aware of rather than a definite taste. Fried maggots are okay, too. I've never really had a problem eating insects. There's no difference between a grasshopper and a prawn, really. So we shared the goodies and then I gave him a 500-baht note and asked him if he'd take me up the building stairwell so that I could take a look into the windows of the top floor of the restaurant. I spun him a story about my girlfriend being inside with another farang but he was only interested in the money and he was more than happy to let me go upstairs on my own.

I found a grimy window in the stairwell on the fifth floor which gave me a reasonable view of the restaurant. There were lights on in one of the offices and I could see half a dozen teenage girls sitting on a couple of sofas, laughing and playing with their mobile phones. They were all wearing the traditional Thai students' uniform of white shirt and black skirt. I couldn't see Ying at first but after about fifteen minutes I saw her walk into view and drop down onto one of

57

the sofas. She opened her Chanel bag and took something out. The students started clapping and leaned forward in anticipation.

Ying folded a piece of silver foil into a small crucible and then she flicked a cigarette lighter and I knew exactly what I was seeing. Yah ba being smoked. Amphetamines, the drug of choice for everyone from students at the country's top universities wanting to stay up studying all night to go-go dancers needing the chemical stimulus to ply their trade all night. It used to be called yah ma, or horse drug, because it gave you the strength and stamina of a horse. The cops started calling it yah ba, the literal translation being Crazy Drug. The spin didn't work. By the look of things, Ying was supplying the stuff. I hadn't seen any money change hands so it looked as if she was giving them the stuff free of charge. So in just a few hours I'd caught Knight's live-in lover in an outright lie and found her giving drugs to students. It wasn't looking good, not if Knight figured she was the love of his life.

I went back downstairs, thanked my new-found friend, and went over to brief the motorcycle riders. It looked as if we were in for a long night; if Ying and her friends were fired up on amphetamines it could well be that they might go on somewhere else.

I sat in the rental car, keeping the engine running and the airconditioning going, sipping from a bottle of water that I always take with me on surveillance operations. Ying didn't appear until two o'clock in the morning. There was a teenage boy with her, one of the restaurant workers I figured, with a designer hair cut and baggy jeans. They went to her BMW and a few minutes later I was following them across the city towards Ratchada. There are lots of late-night eating places Ratchada-way so I figured she was taking her friend for a meal. I was wrong. They pulled in front of a dingy apartment block, a far cry from Knight's palatial accommodation.

I watched them go in. The young guy had a keycard to open

the main door so it was probably his place. I waited in the car until four o'clock in the morning by which time it was obvious that they weren't going anywhere. Lies, drugs, and a toy boy. Young miss Ying was a piece of work, all right.

I asked one of the motorcycle riders to stay outside the block with instructions to phone me as soon as they reappeared. If Ying was like every other Thai girl I knew, that would probably be after midday.

As it turned out, it was after two when they reappeared. My guy phoned me while he was following them and I could barely hear him over the noise of the traffic but I met up with him outside a gold shop in Phaholyothin. Ying and her boy were inside, checking out gold necklaces. Ying was clearly being very generous with Greig Knight's money.

'Lucky lad,' I said in Thai.

'Huh?' said the motorcycle taxi driver, frowning.

Thai isn't the easiest language, being tonal and all, so I said it again. 'Lucky lad.'

His frown deepened.

'Pretty girl, buying him presents. Lucky, right?'

He laughed and lit a cigarette. Inside the gold shop, Ying was fastening a gold chain around her friend's wrist.

'Never had a girl buy me anything.'

The motorcycle rider squinted across at me. 'What do you mean?' he asked.

I sighed. He obviously didn't understand what I was getting at. 'A girl, buying gold for a guy. It's not something you see every day.'

'You know that's a girl, right?'

'Of course I know it's a girl. That's why I'm following her. I'm just saying, she's buying gold for the guy.'

'That's not a guy,' he said.

Now I was confused. 'A girl?'

'A tom.'

'A tom?'

'The girl you're following is buying gold for a tom. The one with the short hair is a girl, Khun Warren.'

I stared at the couple in the shop. Ying kissed her friend on the cheek, then they hugged. I groaned. My guy was right. Ying's toy boy was a toy girl. Maybe a bit on the masculine side, but still a girl. I'd been so fixated on the possibility of Ying having a boyfriend that I'd missed the obvious. Lesbianism is fairly common in Thailand, more so than in the West. The problem was, how did I come up with the proof that Greig Knight would obviously want? Same-sex hand-holding is the norm in Thailand, and it's not unusual for girls to share a bed without any sex being involved. In fact, all I had to go on was the kiss and hug and the gold gift. That wouldn't be enough for Knight, he'd want concrete proof. I was going to need a photograph of the two girls in action to convince Knight that Ying had a lover. And I only had two more nights before my client returned from Hong Kong.

First I had to find out which number the girlfriend's apartment was, and that was a job for a Thai. There were few farangs in that part of the city and I stuck out like the proverbial sore thumb. I told one of the motorcycle taxi drivers, Daeng, to lose his orange vest and pick up a carrier bag of food from a supermarket. All he had to do was to stick close to the girls when they left the gold shop and follow them inside the building. If challenged, all he had to do was to claim that he was making a delivery, but I doubted that it would come to that. By the look of it, the building didn't even have a security guard.

I told Daeng to phone me on my mobile when he had the room number, then I drove back to the office to the get the equipment I needed. Nothing spectacular, just a mini video camera hooked up to a transmitter, one of a dozen designs they sell in Pantip Plaza, and a digital camera with a telephoto lens. I picked up a meatball sandwich from my local Subway, a foot-long because I was going to be up late and wasn't sure when I'd get the chance to eat again. I'd just finished the sandwich when my mobile rang. The girls were back in the room. Number 506. I told Daeng to call me if they left the apartment, then I showered and changed. I packed up the equipment in my gym bag, then drove over. It was just after seven when I got there.

Daeng was standing on the pavement and I told him to get into the car with me. We waited with the aircon running and an hour or so later the two girls walked out of the block arm in arm and over to where Ying had parked the BMW. I took a few photographs and waved at the motorcycle guys to follow them.

When they were out of sight Daeng and I walked over to the apartment block. An old lady with snow white hair and skin the colour of polished oak was fumbling with her key card and Daeng helped her, then we slipped inside after her. Room 506 was on the fifth floor and we took the stairs. Daeng stood watch while I went to work on the locks. The door to the apartment had a metal grill across it with a large padlock that took me all of five minutes to pick. The door had an even simpler lock in the handle and I was soon inside the room. Daeng went back downstairs, ready to phone my mobile if the girls came unexpectedly.

The room was about four paces wide and seven paces long with a small bathroom at the far end and a window that had been curtained off. There was a double bed covered with a sheet with a teddy bear pattern and matching pillows and in one corner there was a rice cooker and a sack of Thai rice. On the walls were posters of Thai pop stars and a framed picture of the king of Thailand above the door.

There was a brand new television set and next to it a stereo CD player. Probably gifts from Ying. I used the screwdriver to pry the grill off the left speaker and fitted the camera so that it had a good view of the bed. The battery was good for forty-eight hours and would transmit pictures up to 200 metres. That was fine because I'd be parked across the road. I wouldn't have sound but that wasn't a problem either.

I gave the room a quick once-over on the off chance that there might have been something incriminating, but other than a few snapshots of the girls hugging and kissing, there was nothing to set the pulse racing.

I went back outside and told Daeng to call me when the girls got back, then phoned one of the other motorcycle taxi drivers for an update on her progress. Ying was clearly a creature of habit; she was back at the restaurant where I'd followed her to the first night. I drove over to the restaurant and parked in front of the office building I'd visited the previous night. Another bag of extra-salty grasshoppers and a crisp 500-baht note and I was back in the fifth-floor stairwell clicking away as Ying and her student friends smoked amphetamines and drank Thai whiskey. I did get quite a nice shot of Ying kissing her girlfriend full on the lips which I reckon was clearly more than platonic.

Ying and her girlfriend got back to the apartment at three o'clock in the morning. I paid off Daeng and his buddies and gave them each a 1,000-baht bonus. They were worth every baht because I couldn't have done the job without them.

I sat in the rental car and tuned the receiver to the transmitter in the apartment. I watched the small screen of the video camera, waiting to hit the record button. I didn't have long to wait. The girls went into the bathroom together and emerged a few minutes later wrapped in towels. The towels soon got tossed aside and Ying and her girlfriend hit the bed, kissing and stroking and generally giving me a hard on the size of a baseball bat. I didn't know where to look. Actually, that's a lie. I couldn't take my eyes off the small screen. Ying was a stunner, I'd known that as soon as I saw the photographs that Knight had given me. But the baggy jeans and T-shirt had hidden the girlfriend's figure and as she rolled on the bed with Ying I could see that her body was every bit as curvaceous and supple as her partner's. It would be a tough choice to have to say which one I'd have preferred to have a session with, though from the way the two girls were going at it I was pretty sure I wouldn't be in with half a chance with either of them. The tape ran out and they were still going strong though every so often they'd take a break from the sexual Olympics and smoke yah ba or drink some more whiskey. I kept on watching long after the tape had stopped. I didn't have anything better to do, frankly.

I phoned Greig Knight on Monday afternoon and told him I had the evidence he wanted. I went to see him in his office and gave him a file with my report and the photographs I'd taken of Ying and her student friends. And I gave him a copy of the video.

He had a television and video player already set up and he gave the video cassette to Gung to slot into the player. I didn't want to sit and watch the video with Knight. I'd seen it several times already while drinking a few JDs and Coke back in my apartment. 'I'll be on my mobile if you need me,' I said, getting up.

Knight waved at me to stay where I was. 'I might need you to do more work,' he said.

I looked pained. The tape was as conclusive as you could get. Ying on her back. Ying on top. An especially seductive 69 that made me hard just thinking about it. It wasn't the sort of thing I wanted to watch in company, and I was damn sure that Knight wouldn't want me there either, not once the lovely Ying had dropped her towel on the bed. But Knight ignored my discomfort and stabbed at the remote control.

I looked across at Gung. He had moved to stand at the door, his face impassive, his arms folded.

I sat back in my chair and tried not to look at the screen, just grateful that there was no sound on the tape. Going by Ying's facial contortions, I reckon she had at least two very vocal orgasms during the session.

Knight watched the tape for about twenty minutes before switching off the tape. He looked at me without a trace of embarrassment. 'That's it?' he said.

I could feel my cheeks burning. 'That's it,' I repeated.

'There's no guy?'

'Not that I can see.'

'Just the girl.'

'She was the only one I saw her with. In an intimate setting.' I thought that was a nice touch. Intimate setting. It made it seem a bit less sordid.

Knight nodded slowly. 'It could have been worse, I suppose,' he said.

'If it had been a guy?'

'I'm not exactly the faithful kind,' said Knight. 'I love Ying, but I've been out in Asia too long to ever want to confine myself to one woman. Even in Hong Kong …' He left the sentence unfinished, but I knew what he meant. What's sauce for the goose is sauce for the gander. And while he didn't want the lovely Ying doing the dirty with another guy, having her in bed with another girl every now and again wasn't the end of the earth. Plus, if ever he decided the time had come to part company, the tape would make the split a hell of a lot easier.

'The drugs are a bit of a worry,' I said. If she ever got picked up by the cops while he was with her and they found yah ba, he'd be looking at prison time too.

'I know about the yah ba,' he said. 'Never in the house and never in the car. She promised.'

'That's all right, then,' I said. I wasn't sure that I'd take the word of a girl who clearly had only a passing relationship with the truth, but Greig Knight was the client and the client is always right. Except, of course, when he's wrong.

Knight took out his bulging wallet and took out a handful of 1,000-baht bills. He gave them to me with a rueful smile and then used the remote to rewind the tape.

Gung showed me out, his face still impassive. But as he closed the door, he winked at me.

A few months later I was in my dentist's waiting room and I picked up one of the glossy magazines. There was a photoshoot of the opening of Greig Knight's latest restaurant. At the top of the page was a picture of the man himself, grinning like a man possessed, one arm around the shoulders of the lovely Ying, the other around the waist of Ying's girlfriend. I stopped watching the video after that. The fun had gone out of it.

THE CASE OF THE
WAYWARD WIFE

One of my first jobs as a private eye was to check up on a girl called Fai, a rescued bargirl who was now living a life of luxury on the back of a guy called Arthur. Arthur had met Fai in a Nana Plaza bar and had decided that she was the love of his life. He worked in an oil refinery in Rayong, a couple of hours' drive from Bangkok, and he wasn't short of a bob or two. He paid her family a decent sin sot, or dowry, moved her into his spacious apartment on the outskirts of Rayong, paid her a monthly allowance that was more than I earned in a good month, and kept her on a long rein. Every now and again he had to pop over to his firm's head office in Singapore and while he was away Fai would go to Bangkok to see her family. All was well until one of his friends said that he'd seen Fai on Sukhumvit Road, eating at a street stall close to the Thermae.

Arthur was enough of an old Bangkok hand to hear alarm bells at the mention of the Thermae. It's a Bangkok institution, a late night hang out frequented by freelancers, or Pay For Play girls as I call them, and expats who baulk at paying barfines. There's always a mixed bag at the Thermae: former bargirls who are past their prime; young girls just down from the countryside who don't speak enough English to work in the farang bars; office girls who are struggling to pay their rent. The going rate for a short time with a Thermae Pay For Play girl would be about half what it would cost at Soi Cowboy or Nana Plaza. The expats are a mixed bunch too but generally they are at the scummier end of the market, prowling around like tigers hunting for fresh meat. If Fai was hanging around the Thermae, it wasn't for the bar snacks.

He got in touch with me and asked if I'd keep an eye on her next time he went to Singapore. She normally drove her motorbike to the bus station and took the bus into Bangkok. He paid me a three-day retainer and agreed to put me up in a decent hotel in Rayong for one night and pay for a rental car. I'd stick out too much if I went on the bus with her, so the car was a necessity. I asked him for details of the family members that she went to see in Bangkok, but he didn't know their names or their addresses. He seemed a trusting chap, and in my experience, trusting chaps in Thailand are lambs to the slaughter. I was looking forward to following Miss Fai, especially once he'd given me a photograph of her. She was drop dead gorgeous, long hair, long legs, long eyelashes, perfect natural breasts and flawless skin. I practically got a hard on looking at her photograph.

The night before he was due to fly to Singapore, I booked into the hotel in Rayong and started spending a good chunk of Arthur's retainer in the hotel's nightclub. It got me two bottles of Jack Daniels and a whole lot of new friends, one who was snoring softly next to me when Arthur phoned to tell me that he was leaving the apartment. I knew there was no need to rush as most Thai girls, those that don't have jobs to go to, don't usually surface before noon.

Seeing as how Arthur had woken me up, I figured it was only right that my companion should be awake as well, so I rolled on top of her and had my wicked way with her. By the time I'd showered and shaved, she'd fallen asleep again so I went downstairs for the hotel's eighty-five-baht breakfast. I wasn't particularly interested in the hard strips of bacon and cold scrambled eggs but the half dozen cups of strong coffee were a good way of kick-starting the day. My new-found friend was still asleep when I got back to the bedroom, no doubt dreaming of her life in New Zealand with her new rich farang. I left her a 500-baht tip on top of her neatly folded jeans and went downstairs to check out. I told them that my 'wife' was sleeping but would be up soon.

I picked up a *Bangkok Post* from the lobby, a ten-baht bag of pineapple from a street vendor and a bottle of water from the 7-Eleven and drove the rental car in search of a shady spot outside Arthur's apartment block.

It was one o'clock and I'd polished off the bag of pineapple before Fai appeared, and she looked even better in real life than she did in her picture. She was wearing tight jeans, impossibly high heels and a low-cut top. She got her motorbike from the car park and I followed her to the bus station. I watched from the car as she bought a ticket for the next aircon bus to Bangkok, and waited for fifteen minutes until she boarded. So far, so good.

I got the number of the bus, then drove like crazy back to Bangkok. The bus would take twice as long, with frequent restroom stops along the way, so I had plenty of time to take the rental car back and phone one of my motorcycle-taxi friends to pick me up and run me over to the Ekkamai bus station. We had just finished our chicken satay snack when the bus rolled up.

Fai got off the bus and climbed into a taxi. Following a car when you're on a motorcycle is a breeze in Bangkok and we had no problems tailing them along Sukhumvit Road, down Thonglor and up Petchburi Road to Soi 43/1. She went into Miami Apartments, a notorious block of cheap housing that's home to a good number of Bangkok bargirls. I'd been there a number of times, usually when I was too short of cash to spring for a short-time hotel.

Fai went into the foyer of the rear block, walking by a table where half a dozen girls were tucking into bags of dukadan (grasshoppers) and washing them down with Sangthip whiskey and soda. Two of the girls shouted out to Fai so I figured she was well known there. I waited until Fai had gone before I went over to the table. I recognised two of the girls as Thermae regulars so I gave them a '*Sawasdee krup*' and sat down. As I was offered some grasshoppers, I bought them another bottle of Sangthip, a steal at seventy baht. We had a few glasses before I asked about Fai. The girls knew her, knew that she was married to a farang, and that she often came to stay with her sister who lived in the block. I asked about her sister and the girls told me that she worked in the German bar in Sukhumvit Soi 7. I knew it well. It was a well-known haunt of freelance hookers, most of whom were well past their sell-by date. But with Fai being in town, the girls said, they'd probably be up at the Hard Rock Café in Siam Square, a much more upmarket pick-up joint.

Excellent. I headed home for a few hours' sleep, and by ten o'clock was revitalised and ready to take on whatever the night might hold. I put on my best pair of Chinos and a freshly ironed polo short, splashed on some aftershave and caught a cab. The Hard Rock Café is the haunt of Westerners with money to burn, and hookers looking for a fast buck. The girls don't look like hookers, and they'd probably be really offended if you called them prostitutes, but they are definitely there hoping to hook a wealthy farang. Most of them probably have jobs, working in department stores, beauty parlours, travel agents, or banks, but what they earn in a month wouldn't pay for a night out at the Hard Rock. They turn up, usually in pairs, buy themselves a cheap drink and start the hunt. Play For Pay girls is what I call them. And they can be even more dangerous than the go-go bar hookers. The guys who live in Thailand know the score and treat the place for what it is—a meat market. But tourists who turn up often get the wrong impression. They think that they have suddenly become much more attractive and that the pretty young thing in tight jeans and a sexy top is hanging on their every word because they're God's gift to women. They take her back to their hotel, have a night of great sex, and then get all confused when the new love of their life starts asking for an expensive present, a cash donation, or help with their mother's medical expenses.

I'd been in Thailand long enough to know the score so I ignored all the hot and heavy looks that I was getting from some very attractive women as I walked over to the large square bar in front of the area where the house band was playing some very respectable cover versions.

I slid onto a stool, ordered a Jack Daniels and watched the very sexy lead singer as she belted out some oldies but goldies. Every now and again I'd be accidentally bumped by some lovely hoping to attract my attention but I was working so I ignored them and concentrated on the lead singer and the entrance. It was the normal Hard Rock Café crowd, not particularly attractive middle-aged men drooling over stunning women, with a smattering of American tourist couples who'd come along thinking it was a burger joint as opposed to a pick-up joint. There was a dining area upstairs where farangs with more money than sense were buying expensive steaks for girls who would have been happier with a bowl of noodles.

Fai came in just after midnight. By then the place was packed but I had a prime spot by the bar so I moved over to make a space for her. She was with a girl her own age and a girl who was a few years older who I assumed was the sister. Fai pulled out a 1,000-baht note and bought three bottles of Heineken. They were all buzzing and I figured they'd partaken of some yah ba, the amphetamine-based drug of choice for the city's movers and shakers. I'm old enough to remember when it was called yah ma, or horse drug, because it made you feel as strong as a horse. The cops thought that was too sexy an image for an addictive drug so they managed to get the media to start calling it yah ba, or crazy drug. It didn't make the drug any less popular, though.

Up close I could see just what a stunner Fai was, and if she was looking for a playmate for the night I knew she wouldn't have a problem finding one. She had on tight black trousers, another pair of impossibly-high stiletto heels and a top that showed off a washboard-flat midriff and a diamond pin through her navel. I stopped watching the lead singer and concentrated on the lovely Fai. If I had been Arthur, I'd have taken her to Singapore with me. Or chained her to the bed and locked the door.

I decided to raise my profile and bought a decent bottle of Australian wine and a couple of glasses. Fai and her friends were dancing in front of the band but when she came back to the bar for a gulp of Heineken I gave her my very best Tom Cruise smile and offered her a glass of my wine. Thai girls will rarely refuse a drink and we were soon clinking glasses and looking into each other's eyes. She did have very sexy eyes. And breasts. Don't get me started on her breasts. She told me she was in town for the weekend with her sister and that her name was Fai. Excellent. She was actually telling me the truth. We spoke in Thai and she tested me, speaking quickly and using slang, and I could see that she was impressed. Most farangs, even those who've lived in Thailand for years, rarely get beyond the 'You So Pretty, Me So Horny' stage. I spoke Thai like a Thai, and on the phone most Thais wouldn't even realise that I was a foreigner.

The wine slid down easily, just like my eyes kept doing, but she didn't seem to mind that I kept ogling her body. The occasional hand on my arm and thigh let me know that she was interested, and the baseball-sized hard on in my Chinos was a dead giveaway that I was up for it.

I bought another bottle of wine, making sure that I kept the receipt because Arthur would be covering all expenses. Fai and her friends kept leaving the bar for some energetic dancing, and Fai was attracting a fair amount of male attention. I was worried that some other farang might spirit her away but other than a few snatched conversations she didn't seem to be interested and kept coming back to me and my red wine.

Eventually Hard Rock started to wind down and I found myself outside with Fai and the other two girls. They decided they wanted to continue partying so we all piled into a taxi and went to the King's Disco in Patpong, a popular venue for barfined bargirls to take their customers. By now I was paying for all the drinks, or at least Arthur was. I parked myself at the bar with a Jack Daniels while the three girls danced the night away. Fai was as attentive as she'd been in Hard Rock. She'd dance for a while then come back and give me a squeeze or a peck on the cheek and then she'd be off again. At one point she disappeared for ten minutes and I thought I'd lost her but then she reappeared at my side and slipped something into my hand. It was an ecstasy tablet, worth about 800 baht, and she grinned at me, waiting for me to swallow it. I'm not a big fan of drugs and prefer to get my buzz from booze, so I palmed the tablet and pretended to swallow it. She winked, patted me on the groin, and headed for the dance floor.

Dawn was breaking when we finally left the disco. Fai's sister and the friend flagged down a taxi but Fai didn't complain when I steered her towards another vehicle. I gave the driver my address, and again Fai didn't complain. In fact she slid her nails along my thigh and kissed my neck, which I took as a good sign. The taxi driver wanted to charge me 200 baht and I called him a robbing lizard in his native Isarn language and told him to use the meter.

We got back to my apartment and I went straight to the shower to wash the smoke and grime of a Bangkok night out of my hair.

When I walked into the bedroom with a towel wrapped around my waist, a glorious sight greeted me. The lovely Fai was lying on my bed, her head on my pillow and her shapely legs up on the headboard, wearing nothing but her Chanel Number 7. Arthur would have been impressed. I certainly was. I realised that sleeping with Fai would be unprofessional, but her legs seemed to go on for ever and she made it clear that she wouldn't take no for an answer. What's a private eye to do? There was only one thing I could do. Clients are ten a penny but girls with bodies like Fai are few and far between. I mentally apologised to Arthur and jumped onto the bed.

The girl was an absolute star. She wore me out and I only managed a couple of hours' sleep that night. She was insatiable. Against the door, in the bathroom, on the floor, by the window, every position I knew and a few that I didn't. It was the following afternoon before she finally let me rest. I made her a coffee and we had a little chat. I said that I wanted her phone number so that I could see her again. She was surprisingly honest and told me that she was married and that she had a great husband who loved her and gave her everything that she wanted. She had a great condo in Rayong, but all her friends lived in Bangkok so every now and again she headed to the city to party. 'If I didn't, I'd go crazy,' she said. And the long and the short of it was that she wouldn't give me her phone number. She left an hour later, after another sweat-inducing session where she showed me another position that I didn't believe was possible.

I sat down at my computer and started writing my report to Arthur. I had to battle with my conscience. I liked Fai, a lot. And I could understand why she'd feel trapped in Rayong. What happened with me could well have been a one-off. I'm a good-looking guy so maybe she just fancied me. I just put too much temptation in her way, I guess. But Arthur was my client and paying me a not inconsiderable amount of money. He deserved the truth. But Fai had given me a hell of a time between the sheets. And there was always the chance that I'd bump into her again. I reached a compromise with my conscience. I told Arthur that Fai did go out on the town but that she confined her extra-curricular activities to drinking and dancing with her girlfriends. I didn't mention the night of unbelievable sex I had with his wife, of course. Some secrets are best kept secret.

THE CASE OF THE LYING BARGIRL

The bread and butter work of a private eye in Bangkok is running checks on bargirls. I don't know why but tourists seem to check in their brains on arrival. They go trawling through the red-light districts of Bangkok and Pattaya until they meet a girl they think is 'special'. The love of their life was working as a prostitute, but now she's a good girl. She loves me, only me. Time and time again I hear the same refrain: 'my girl is different.' So different that they want to pay me to check up on the love of their life.

Anyone thinking of starting a long-term relationship with a bargirl has to get one thing straight from the start. Girls work in the sex industry for one reason and one reason only: money. Cold, hard cash. They're not dancing around a chrome pole because they want to be rescued by a White Knight, they're not spreading their legs in short-time hotels because they want to live happily ever after with a guy twice their age. So if a guy wants to settle down with a bargirl, he's going to have to accept the fact that for the rest of his life he's going to be funding her, one way or another. If the guy's prepared to do that, all well and good. But the guys who come a cropper are the ones that leave their new-found girlfriends in situ. After years of running checks on girls working in the bars I'm sure of one thing:

they will not be faithful. It is almost a physical impossibility. A frog and scorpion thing. But like I said, it's my bread and butter so if a guy wants me to check on his bargirl, I'm happy to take his money.

Pete Derbyshire was a teacher from Sydney, Australia. He had met the love of his life dancing in a Soi Cowboy go-go bar. He'd barfined Noi for a week and taken her on holiday. They'd gone to her home town of Buriram and met her family. He'd proposed and offered to buy a plot of land and to build a new home for the two of them. The wedding date had been set, a sin sot, or dowry, of 100,000 baht had been agreed, and Pete had flown back to Australia to give up his job and prepare to make the move to Thailand. His plan was to teach English in Buriram and to live happily ever after with the lovely Noi. But Pete had heard all the horror stories so he emailed me asking if I'd check that Noi was being faithful while he was away.

Pete was in his late thirties and Noi was twenty two, so the age difference wasn't that big. But what sent alarm bells ringing for me was the fact that Noi was continuing to work in the bar while she waited for Pete to return. In my experience, guys who have any chance of making a bargirl relationship work have to get the girl out of the bar scene as quickly as possible. I told Pete to expect the worst but he said that Noi had told him that she wanted to be with her friends, that she'd be bored on her own in Buriram. She wouldn't be working as a dancer, Pete said, and she wouldn't be going with customers. She'd just earn money from the lady drinks that customers bought her. That sounded possible, just about. If Noi had been dancing then alarm bells would really start ringing because the whole payment system for dancers is based around them being barfined. They are paid a basic salary but if they aren't barfined a set number of times in a month, their pay is docked. But if Noi was just working in the bar for drinks, then the bar owner wouldn't be forcing her to go with customers. Pete said that he phoned Noi every night and that she was always there to speak to him. I smiled at that. Anyone who's ever spent any time in a go-go bar would have seen girls sitting quite happily on a customer's knee, then rushing off to the toilet to answer her mobile phone. 'Of course I love you, too much'. There was only one way to find out if Noi was being faithful to Pete. I would have to go in to test her, and that was going to cost Pete a 10,000-baht retainer plus any expenses I incurred.

He emailed me a photograph of Noi. She was a typical bargirl, dyed red hair, low cut black T-shirt, tight blue jeans, too much make up. I was almost ashamed to take his money, but business is business and three days later the funds had come through by bank transfer.

I left it until Friday evening before wandering down to Soi Cowboy with some of Pete's money in my wallet. I went in fairly early to make sure I'd catch her. There was only one other customer when I walked in, a guy in his fifties who was slumped over the bar with half a dozen girls all over him like vultures feeding on a dead buffalo. I sat in a dark corner and ordered a double Jack Daniels.

The waitress was cute and when she came back with my drink I told her to get one for herself. Then I played a game that usually stood me in good stead. I bet her that I could guess what province she was from before she could guess what country I came from. I could normally tell if a girl was from Isaan or not, and most bargirls were from Korat, Udon or Khonkaen, or they'd be Khamen style which meant Buriram, Sisaket or Surin. I got the waitress in three guesses—Surin—by which time she'd guessed Germany, England and America for me. I don't think most Thais even know that New Zealand exists.

Anyway, I bought her another drink and another double Jack Daniels and started talking about provinces and steered the conversation around to Buriram. I nodded at a girl behind the bar and said that she looked as if she was from Buriram but the cute waitress said no, she was from Udon Thani. She pointed at three girls sitting together at the far end of the bar and said that they were all from Buriram. I was playing the slightly drunk farang, so I waved my arm around and said I'd by drinks for all the girls from Buriram. The waitress rushed around the bar and within minutes there were half a dozen girls at my table. At least one was an impostor—she had the pale skin and round face of a northern girl—but I wasn't worried because one of the six was the lovely Noi.

I waved for Noi to sit on my left, and another of the Buriram girls sat on my right. Their drinks arrived and there was much clinking of glasses and laughing and I ordered another round. I asked all their names. The girl on my right was Lek. I laughed at that because Noi and Lek both mean little. 'My two little girls,' I said and everyone laughed uproariously. You have to be careful in bars, you start to believe your own publicity. They weren't laughing because I was a funny guy, they weren't laughing because they liked me, they were laughing because I was buying them drinks and every drink I bought them earned them thirty baht. It was all about money. Everything that happened in a go-go bar was driven by cash. I knew that, the girls knew that, it was only the tourists like Pete who thought there was anything else going on.

Noi and Lek were stroking my thighs and giggling. They'd told me that they were sisters—'Same Mother, Same Father'—but I doubted that they were even related. It was a common ploy among the bargirls, to pretend to be related, because they knew that was a turn-on for farangs.

I asked them if they had boyfriends, and Noi was quite happy to tell me that she had a farang in Sydney who was sending her money and that one day she was going to marry him. 'I love him too much,' she said, as fingers moved gently up my thigh. 'But he far away.'

I bought another round of drinks and Noi and Lek exchanged a look. I was playing the role of drunken farang to the hilt. 'I've always wanted to sleep with sisters,' I said.

'You can,' said Noi. She nodded at Lek. 'Two thousand baht for her, same for me.'

'And you have to pay bar,' said Lek, playing with the zip of my jeans.

I was tempted. Really tempted, but I was a professional so I told them that I was still jet-lagged and that I had to sleep. I promised to return the next night and asked Noi for her mobile phone number so that I could check that she was working.

She happily gave me the number, I bought another round of drinks, and then paid my bill and headed to an Internet café where I emailed Pete with a report of what had happened. I sent him the mobile phone number as proof that I'd spoken to her.

The next day I received a reply from Pete. He'd phoned Noi and asked her what she'd been doing that night. Noi had said she'd been bought drinks by a farang but that she wouldn't let him pay her bar fine. And she'd promised him that she didn't go with customers any more. It was clear from the tone of the email that Pete believed her. That's one thing I could never understand. The client pays for information and then believes the word of a lying bargirl who is taking him for every penny she can rather than trusting the professional he's paying.

I emailed him back, assuring him that Noi would have happily gone with me. Pete phoned me a few hours later. He said he trusted Noi, but to be absolutely sure he wanted me to go back and see her, and this time he wanted me to pay her bar fine and take her to a hotel. Once she was in the room, he wanted me to text him. He'd phone her and that would be that. I agreed, but told him that he'd have to come up with another 10,000 baht, plus the money for the bar fine, plus any other expenses. He promised to send me 12,000 baht by bank transfer. So far as I was concerned he was throwing good money after bad, but the client is always right. Even when he's wrong.

Once the money was safely in the bank I went back to Noi's bar. The staff greeted me like a long-lost friend and the bartender was pouring a double Jack Daniels before I'd even sat down. Noi and Lek appeared within seconds and as the waitress went off to get them two lady drinks their hands were already stroking my thighs.

A couple of drinks later and I paid bar for the two girls and we walked to a nearby short-time hotel. Four hundred baht bought us a room for ninety minutes. I was planning to text Pete while the girls were in the shower, but as soon as the door closed they pushed me on to the bed and ripped off their clothes, and mine. I tried to put up a fight, honest I did, but they were consummate professionals, and besides I figured it was Pete's fault, putting temptation in my way like he did. They were both as cute as hell and had clearly worked together before. Even taught me a few tricks. Twenty minutes later I was flat on my back, drained, while the two girls were giggling in the shower.

I sent a text to Pete, giving him the name of the hotel and the fact that she was there with Lek. I dressed quickly. As I headed out of the door, I heard Noi's mobile phone start to ring. I hurried down the stairs and out onto the street. I didn't want to be around when she tried to explain where she was and what she'd been doing.

I don't know why farangs think that the place to look for a long-term partner is in a go-go bar or massage parlour. I doubt that they'd go looking to marry a prostitute in their own country. Like I said, it's as if they check in their brains when they arrive in Thailand. I often get asked if it's possible to marry a bargirl and actually live happily ever after. I knew of a few cases where it's worked out. Four, in fact. But in all four cases the girls hadn't been working in the bars for more than a few weeks, and the guys they married weren't hardened barflies. But they were the exceptions. Generally marriages to bargirls don't work out. The girls are damaged goods. Many are on drugs, many have a kid upcountry staying with the parents, more often than not there's a Thai boyfriend or even a husband in the background. A girl who's been working the bars for just a couple of years will have slept with hundreds of different guys and is probably supporting her whole family. Any farang who expects to find the love of his life under those circumstances needs his head examined. And the services of a Bangkok private eye.

THE CASE OF THE INTERNET SCAMMER

I was having a dream about two twin go-go dancers doing terrible things to me with whipped cream when my mobile phone started ringing and dragged me back to reality. It was a British voice on the other end of the line. A man.

'What time is it there?' he asked.

'What do you think I am, a speaking clock?' I growled. I squinted at the clock on the bedside table. It was just after three.

'It's nine o'clock here,' he said.

'It's three in Bangkok,' I said.

'That's okay then,' he said.

'In the morning,' I said. 'It's three o'clock in the morning.'

'I'm sorry,' he said. 'I'm in London.'

'Congratulations,' I said.

'Shall I call back later?'

I sat up in bed, rubbing my face. 'That's okay, I'm awake now. Is this business or pleasure?'

'Business,' he said. 'I need help.'

I always keep a notebook and pen by my clock so I took notes as the caller went through his story. His name was Mike Tyson (no relation to the boxer, he said, 'and I'm a fair bit older and whiter') and he was a retired businessmen. He'd built up his own sportswear company and sold out for a decent price once he hit sixty. I got the feeling that he wasn't exactly short of money. He'd sent his Thai girlfriend the money for her ticket to the UK but Mike had waited at Heathrow airport for hours and there'd been no sign of her. He'd tried calling her mobile phone but it was switched off. Mike was sure that something had happened to her and he wanted me to check the local hospitals, go around to her house, to do whatever it took to find out what had happened to her.

It was an easy enough job, so I told him to send me a 10,000-baht retainer through Western Union.

'No problem, that's how I send money to Metta,' he said.

'Have you been sending her a lot of money?' I asked. Alarm bells were already ringing.

'Just a few hundred pounds a month,' he said. 'And some extra money when her father was in hospital. And money for her passport and visa. And for her ticket.'

I asked Mike for as much detail as he could give me. Her name was Metta Khonkaen, he said. I got him to spell it for me twice because Khonkaen is a city in the north east and it seemed a strange surname. It would be like being called Pete Birmingham or Eddie Queenstown. Not impossible, but unlikely. He had her date of birth and I groaned inwardly when I realised that he was almost three times her age. Alarm bells were really ringing now.

'Where did you meet Metta?' I asked. I would have bet money that he'd met the lovely Metta in a go-go bar or massage parlour.

'I haven't actually met her yet,' said Mike. 'Not in person. We met online.'

I was totally awake now. Mike had sent hundreds if not thousands of pounds to a girl he hadn't even met? I was starting to wish I'd asked for a bigger retainer because Mike clearly wasn't a man who kept a tight grip on his money.

I asked Mike to email me any pictures he had of Metta, and to fax copies of any paperwork he had, then I put down the phone and went back to sleep.

The next day I wandered along to Starbucks for a latte and a banana muffin and then took a motorcycle taxi to the Western Union office. Mike had been as good as his word and I collected my 10,000 baht. There was a faxed copy of her passport and copies of the papers that she'd taken to the British Embassy. And he'd emailed me some head and shoulder shots of her. Metta was a stunner, no doubt about it. Pale skin, high cheekbones, long straight hair.

I went through the motions and phoned a couple of dozen hospitals in Bangkok but none had admitted a Metta Khonkaen. I checked my emails and there was a message from Mike. One of life's little coincidences; just a couple of hours after speaking to me, he'd received an email from a friend of Metta's. According to the friend, Metta had been arrested by the immigration police when she was trying to leave the country. There was something wrong with her visa and she didn't have enough funds to cover her time in the UK. The police were holding her in the notorious Bangkok Hilton and the friend said that she needed 50,000 baht to get her released, and another 150,000 baht so that Metta could show she had sufficient funds to travel to the UK. Two hundred thousand baht in all. The helpful friend had included her own name and bank account details so that Mike could send her the money without further ado.

I phoned Mike and the guy was at the end of his tether. It was too late to send the money but the next day he was going to be at the bank first thing to arrange the telegraphic transfer. I told him to wait until I'd made a few enquiries, there were just so many things about this case that didn't ring true. I pressed him for more details about his internet courtship. He told me that he'd first met her in a chatroom, and they'd started talking by email every day. She was working as a waitress in Bangkok but after Mike started sending her money she'd gone back to stay with her parents in Chiang Rai, helping to support her younger sisters while she studied for a degree in accounting. It had always been her dream to live in England, she'd said. They'd traded photographs, and Metta had told Mike that he was the most handsome man she'd ever seen. Like a movie star, she'd said. And she loved the photographs of his large house in central London. His thirty-two-foot yacht. His collection of sports cars. Her email began to become more affectionate. Maybe she could fly to London to see him, she'd suggested. Maybe they'd get on so well together that he would want her to stay with him. Maybe he might one day want to marry her.

By the time Mike had finished telling me the story, he was in tears. I told him not to do anything until he heard from me again.

I picked up a bottle of Johnnie Walker Black Label and went along to the Immigration Department on Soi Suan Phlu. The chief there was an old friend of mine. I went up to the third floor, gave him the whisky and then we spent half an hour talking about golf before I got around to the real reason for my visit. I showed him the fax of Metta passport and he shook his head emphatically. '*Mai chai, mai chai, mai chai,*' he muttered.

He pointed at the passport picture. Metta was smiling happily. The chief explained that smiling wasn't allowed in passport photographs. They were taken in the passport office and the camera operator would make sure that the person didn't smile. Also, the wavy lines that were supposed to run through the photograph were missing, and the surname was in a slightly different typeface to the rest of the wording on the passport. It looked to the chief as if the photograph had been stuck into an existing passport, and the surname had been typed on a piece of paper and stuck into the travel document. The passport was fake.

I asked him what would happen if the girl tried to leave the country with a doctored passport. Would she be arrested?

The chief assured me that the girl would probably have just been turned away. If she had been a known criminal then she might have been held by the immigration police, but she certainly wouldn't have been hauled off to the Bangkok Hilton. To put my mind at rest he tapped the name into his computer terminal. There was no record of any problems with a Metta Khonkaen.

My next call was to the municipal office in Pathumwan. I was a regular visitor and whenever I popped in I took a selection of Thai snacks with me. The head lady saw me coming and came over to relieve me off my tidbits and see what I wanted. I asked her about Metta's surname and she shook her head emphatically. Khonkaen was not a surname that she had ever come across and after a couple of minutes on her computer terminal she was able to tell me that there wasn't a Khonkaen family anywhere in the country.

I waited until late evening before phoning the unlucky Mike and told him what I'd discovered. And I told him of my suspicions—that Metta Khonkaen, or whatever her real name was, was conning him.

Mike was still convinced that there was some sort of misunderstanding. He was still getting frantic emails from Metta's friend, imploring him to help her and he was convinced that she was banged up in a damp, dark cell somewhere.

I told him that I could get proof that he was being taken for a ride and asked him to send me another 10,000 baht. Then I told him to tell Metta's friend that he would send some money to the Western Union office on Sukhumvit Soi 22 the next day.

I was outside the Western Union office with my camera and long lens just before it opened. It was on a busy road but I was able to sit at a duck noodle shop with a perfect view of the shopfront. I didn't have to wait long.

A black Cherokee Jeep pulled up in front of the office and a middle-aged Isaan woman wearing a gold chain around her neck as thick as my thumb climbed out of the passenger seat. She went into the office and spoke to the girl behind the counter. The woman produced a passport and signed a form and was handed a bundle of banknotes. I managed to get a few good shots of her grinning as she counted Mike's money.

As she walked out of the Western Union office and headed towards the Jeep, half a dozen policemen in brown uniforms rushed over to her. At the same time a police car screeched to a halt in front of the Jeep and four police motorcycles pulled up behind it. I took a few more photographs with the long lens, then went over to shake hands with the police colonel who'd planned the arrest. The driver of the Jeep was a farang in his sixties, a bald head and heavy jowls and thick-lensed spectacles. He had a gold chain around his neck as thick as the one the woman was wearing.

The woman was crying and telling anyone who'd listen that the farang had made her do it, that he was the one who prowled around internet chatrooms and sent emails to gullible men around the world.

The farang and the woman were regular visitors to the Western Union office, the colonel told me, and in the last month alone had collected a quarter of a million baht from a dozen or so 'sponsors.' They were handcuffed and taken away. The money that Mike sent was handed over to me and I signed a receipt for it. I went back into the Western Union office and cabled it back to Mike, minus my expenses of course.

I phoned him when I got back to the office. I didn't take any pleasure in telling him that his beloved Metta was a sixty-five-year-old Belgian scam artist, and the photographs that Mike had framed and hung up all around his house were of a well-known Thai soap opera star. He took it quite well, I thought, and thanked me for saving him from making a complete fool of himself.

Mike said that he'd learned his lesson and that he wouldn't be going near internet chatrooms again. In fact, he decided that he'd come to Thailand himself. He asked me if I'd find him a girlfriend, someone who wouldn't rip him off. I put him in touch with a reputable dating agency run by Nung, a good friend of mine. When Mike flew over three months later, Nung fixed him up with a few possibles but none took Mike's fancy. Mike wanted to go travelling around the country and the girls that Nung introduced him to weren't happy about sharing a hotel room with a farang they had only just met. I decided to play Cupid and went to a beer garden in Soi 7 and after a couple of hours stumbled across Riang, a thirty-five-year-old mother of two who looked twenty-five, pretty and with a good sense of humour. I ran the Mike situation by her and she jumped at the chance of a free holiday, especially if Mike would agree to take her back to her home in Phitsanulok for a couple of days so that she could see her kids. To cut a long story short, they got on like a house on fire. A year later and she was his wife and she and her kids were living with Mike in central London. All's well that end's well, that's what I figure.

THE CASE OF THE
MACAU SNATCH

It was a story I'd heard a hundred times over the years in one variation or another. Dang had been born in small village in Khon Kaen, one of six children. Her parents eked out a living on a small rice farm that they leased. Dang was a good student but her options were always going to be limited. She was pretty with a cute smile and she attracted the attention of a good-looking boy who was a few years older. One thing led to another and she fell pregnant just before her seventeenth birthday. Both their families were poor but respectable and the only way for Dang and her boyfriend to save face was for them to elope. They packed a few clothes and caught the bus to Bangkok. The boyfriend had a relative who worked in the Patpong red-light district, and as they had no money and no qualifications Dang had no choice but to start work in a go-go bar. There's no social security safety net in Thailand. If you don't work, you either starve or rely on charity. So Dang started dancing around a silver pole and her boyfriend worked as a tout, standing in the street trying to lure customers inside.

They were earning decent money by Thai standards, helped by the fact that Dang was being barfined three or four times a week. But Bangkok is much more expensive than the countryside, and their hard-earned money went as quickly as they earned it. Dang didn't enjoy going with farangs and she started taking drugs to make herself feel better. She smoked dope for a few months and then a dancer friend persuaded her to start smoking yah ba, the amphetamine that is the drug of choice among the country's go-go dancers. The more she became addicted to drugs, the less she cared about the sort of men she went with. And before long all thoughts of saving were forgotten—any money she made by selling her body went on drugs for herself and her boyfriend.

Dang had left it too late to do anything about her pregnancy, and once the baby started to show she had to give up work. When the baby was born the boyfriend did a runner. He ended working as a dancer in a gay bar and was apparently a natural. Dang had no choice but to go back and beg forgiveness from her parents. They agreed to look after the baby, a girl, but they were short of money and Dang agreed to go back to Bangkok. She started working in a go-go bar in Nana Plaza and was soon in demand. She was sexy and a good dancer and farangs were queuing up to pay bar for her. A girl in the bar introduced Dang to heroin and Dang soon became an addict. Between the money she paid to her dealer and the cash she sent back to Khon Kaen she had barely enough to cover her rent and food.

She decided to cut her costs a bit and buy her heroin in the slums of Klong Toey, buying a week's supply at once, plus a bit more to sell on to her friends. That all went well until she was picked up by a plainclothes cop. He offered her the chance to buy her way out of the problem but he wanted more money than she had so she was charged and sentenced to six months inside. She was eighteen years old.

She went cold turkey while in prison. Not that there weren't drugs—heroin is as easy to get inside prison as it is outside—it was just that she didn't have any money. And when you've no money, a Thai prison is hell on earth. She shared a cell with dozens of other women, many of them hardened criminals and drug addicts, a hole in the ground for a toilet and a bucket to wash in.

Dang survived her ordeal and walked out of the prison drug-free. She swore to herself that she would never take drugs again and so decided not to return to the go-go bars. She still needed money, though, so started working as a freelance prostitute in a well-known expat hangout called the Thermae. The Thermae is a legendary late-night watering hole, where up to 500 girls line the bar on the look out for a customer. Dang was younger than the average Thermae girl, and a lot prettier, so she had no shortage of customers. She started sending money back to her parents again, and began to save.

It was in the Thermae that she met Bob, a wealthy businessman who ran a property company in Bangkok. Bob saw Dang as soon as he walked into the Thermae and made a beeline for her. Most of the girls in the Thermae are well past their sell-by date and Dang was still relatively fresh, despite her six months in prison. Dang for her part could see that Bob was different from the down-at-heel English teachers and sex tourists who normally prowled around the Thermae looking for fresh meat. She jumped at the chance to go back to his penthouse apartment.

By next morning, Bob was smitten. He wanted to keep Dang for himself. He asked her to move in with him, he would pay for her to go to school and a monthly allowance of 40,000 baht a month, about as much as a go-go dancer would earn. Dang asked for the first month's 'salary' in advance and promptly moved in.

All went well for two months, then one day Bob returned home to find that the lovely Dang had packed her bags and gone. Bob frantically rang around the few friends of hers that he knew but all he got was evasive answers or Thai replies that he couldn't understand. He went back to the Thermae but there was no sign of her. That's when he came to talk to me. I listened to his story, and then gave him the benefit of my wisdom and experience: forget about her. She was a bargirl, he'd paid for sex with her, and now she had gone. The best thing he could do would be to forget Dang and find another girl. He could throw a spanner down Sukhumvit Soi 4 and hit a hundred possible candidates.

Bob insisted. He pulled a photograph from his pocket and slid it across the desk. She was a pretty girl, but not a stunner. Blonde streaks in her shoulder-length hair, nice breasts, long legs. I could see the attraction but I was about to tell him he'd be wasting his time when he slapped a fistful of 1,000-baht notes on top of the picture. 'This girl's special,' he said. 'I want you to find her for me.'

I looked at Bob, his eyes burning with a fierce intensity, and I looked at the pile of banknotes.

'I just want to know why she left,' he said. 'If I did something wrong, I want to know what I did. That's all. I want a chance to put it right.'

I knew what was coming next. He was going to tell me that he loved her, and I didn't want to hear that so I just took the money and said that I'd go looking for her.

Unlike most Bangkok expats, my favourite hangout wasn't a trendy nightclub or even a go-go bar. I preferred to spend my late-night drinking hours on a small plastic stool at a table on the corner of Sukhumvit Soi 13, strategically located between Soi Nana and Soi Cowboy. Khun Moi and her family have sold beer and Sangthip whisky on the corner for more than thirty years. Her relatives run the nearby barbecued chicken stall and the corner motorcycle taxi rank where I could always be sure to find temporary assistants when I needed them. Khun Moi's business was a stone's throw from Thermae and is a favourite haunt of streetwalkers. I used to have a stack of twenty-baht notes in my top pocket to help out any down-at-heel girls to buy some spicy somtam or to get the last bus home. So

I already had my network of informants in place; all I had to do was to sit on the corner and show Dang's photograph around. I was only halfway through my second glass of Sangthip by the time I had two of Dang's friends at my table. They helped me work my way through the bottle as they told me Dang's story.

It was yet another story that I'd heard a hundred times before. Much as she appreciated his money, Dang had soon become bored living with Bob. She was stuck in the apartment 24/7. Like most expats, Bob worked hard and long and when he got back to the apartment he was in no mood to go out and party. He wanted to stay in and watch TV, while Dang wanted to go out and hit the city's nightclubs. And by all accounts, Bob had become lax in the sexual area. Dang was bored, pure and simple. But she still needed money. She wanted to build a big house upcountry and one day she wanted to live there with her daughter. Bob was an okay bet short-term, but she felt as if she was in prison. She spoke to a friend—not one of the girls sharing my whisky—who suggested that she go to Macau. Thai girls could make big money in Macau's massage parlours and bars, far more than was on offer in Thailand. The friend recommended an agent who promised to arrange a job for her if she gave him 10,000 baht. She also needed a new passport under a different name because as a convicted drug user she couldn't leave the country. That meant more money. Dang used Bob's second 40,000-baht 'salary' to fund her move to Macau.

I phoned Bob the next day and gave him the bad news. I made it sound as if she'd been 'lured' to Macau because I wanted him to at least retain some of his self-esteem, but I did make it clear that she'd become bored with life as a housewife. I thought Bob would just accept what I'd told him and that he'd move on with his life. The last thing I expected was that he'd want me to continue with the case but that's what he said. He wanted me to go to Macau to talk to Dang.

He wanted me to tell her that he'd marry her, and that he'd take Dang and her daughter to America. I figured he was crazy. Dang had already demonstrated that she didn't love him. She'd turned down an easy life with Bob to work as a prostitute in Macau. Sending me after her would be throwing good money after bad. But before I could say that, he offered me 10,000 baht a day plus expenses. Rule number one of the private-eye business: the client is always right. Even when he was wrong. The following day I was on an Air Macau flight. I explained that I might be on a fool's errand but Bob said he'd be happy enough just to talk to her on the phone. If she told him that it was truly over between them, he'd accept it. Ten thousand baht a day to arrange a phone call. Easy money. Plus I get a free holiday in Macau. If nothing else I'd get a few hours in one of the casinos.

Most of the Thai working girls hang out in the Mandarin Hotel while the Chinese and Russian hookers tended to gather at the more downmarket Lisboa. I checked into the Mandarin, showered and had a meal, then hit the hotel's lounge bar. I recognised a couple of English jockeys talking to a group of pretty Thai girls in evening dresses. Macau has a big racing industry, second only to Hong Kong in the region, and unlike Thailand there are no restrictions on jockeys and horses. I sat at the bar and said hello to a pretty Isaan girl who was wearing a long blue dress that emphasised her large, presumably enhanced, breasts. I spoke to her in her northern dialect and told her that one of the jockeys was renowned for having a small dick and more money than sense. She thanked me and went over to join the jockeys. She was soon by his side, stroking his arm and fluttering her long eyelashes.

I sat and sipped my Jack Daniels. When the jockey with the small dick went to the toilet, the girl in the blue dress came over to me. She bought me a drink and said that the jockey had agreed to pay her HK$5,000 for short-time, twenty times the going rate in Thailand.

She'd be through by midnight and would come to see me in my room, if I wanted. No charge. I thanked her but pulled out the photograph of Dang and said that she was a close friend on my wife's and that I wanted to check that she was okay. I spun the line that Dang had promised to phone once she got to Macau but that she hadn't and my wife was starting to worry about her. The girl looked closely at the picture and then shook her head. She hadn't seen her around, but if she had only recently arrived in Macau then her Chinese employers would probably be watching her quite closely until they could trust her. But most of the off-duty Thai girls went to the UFO nightclub, so she suggested that I try there. We didn't have time to chat further because the jockey returned from the toilet. I knew about UFO. It was in the same building as a number of massage parlours controlled by a well-known Triad boss who went by the name of Broken Tooth. I left it until after two o'clock before heading there, but it didn't start to fill up until after three o'clock. A band crowded onto a small stage and began belting out Thai hits. The audience was mainly Thai, working girls who had finished for the night and young Thai men who worked in the local restaurants or lived off the earnings of their girlfriends. The girls didn't seem as friendly or as approachable as the bargirls I was used to in Thailand. They were mostly in their late twenties or early thirties, eyes dulled by years in the sex industry and associated drug-taking. Usually they came to Macau on three-month contracts to the Triad-owned massage parlours, and providing they were earning good money they were allowed some freedom, and even allowed to do extra freelance hooking in their off-hours. But if they tried to break their contracts they would be deported, often after being beaten or worse. For the fun-loving Thai girls, working in Macau was akin to a prison sentence, and many turned to drugs to get them through it. And the Triads were happy to supply all the drugs that the girls wanted. It wasn't unusual for a Thai girl to return to Bangkok after three months in Macau with no money and a serious drug habit.

I moved to be closer to the band and started joining in at the chorus. I was soon accepted by the Thais and a round of drinks made me even more popular. I showed Dang's photograph around and a couple of the girls said that they knew her but that she had been at home all day with a cold. She worked in one of Broken Tooth's massage parlours.

I was back at UFO the following evening, and after a couple of hours and half a dozen Jack Daniels, one of my new-found friends came over with Dang in tow. She looked tired and drawn, nothing like the happy-go-lucky girl in the picture that Bob had given me. She was a bit wary of me but I told her I was a friend of the girls I'd met in Soi 13 and she began to relax. I waited until her third Heineken before I told her that I knew Bob and that he was worried about her.

She was a bit taken aback but asked how he was. I told her that he missed her and that he wanted to talk to her.

'Why?' she said, genuinely surprised.

'He loves you,' I said. 'He wants you back.' I told her of his offer to marry her and talk her and her daughter to the States.

I wanted to get her out of the nightclub so that we could have a quite chat. The clientele was mainly Thai but there were a few hard-eyed Triad soldiers standing around and I didn't want them getting curious about my conversation with Dang. I asked her if she'd come back to the Mandarin, making it clear that it was only a chat I wanted. She offered to go short-time with me for HK$2,000 and then giggled at the look of horror on my face. 'Just joking,' she said, but I'm sure she was serious. I was sure that Bob was making a big mistake by pursuing this girl, but I remembered rule number one of the private-eye business and took her outside to waiting taxi.

I motioned for Dang to keep quiet in the taxi. You never know who is in the pay of the Triads in Macau. I noticed a motorcycle keeping close tabs on us as we drove to the Mandarin. I figured it was probably a Triad soldier keeping track of their investment. If Dang did decide she wanted to go back to Bangkok, I was going to have to be careful.

We went up to my room and over a few more Heinekens from the minibar I repeated Bob's offer to marry her and take care of her and her daughter. Dang definitely wanted to get out of Macau but she wasn't sure about Bob. 'He so boring,' she said.

I asked her what she wanted for her life.

She beamed. 'I want a house for my mother and father and a house for me and my baby. And a pick-up truck. And someone who loves me too much.'

I got the feeling that Bob wasn't even being considered for the role of 'someone who loves me too much.'

I told her that Bob would take care of all her financial worries. I had no doubt he would build a house for her parents. Up in Isaan, a half-decent house could be built for less than a million baht and Bob clearly had money to burn. I was starting to feel a bit like Bob's pimp.

'I want go back to Bangkok,' she said. 'Macau boring too much. If I stay here long time I take drugs again, I sure.'

That was something, at least. If I could get Dang back to Bangkok at least Bob could talk to her in person. But I had no doubt that Broken Tooth would try to stop me if he found out that I was taking her out of Macau.

I used my mobile phone to book two business-class tickets from Hong Kong to Bangkok. That would allow us to get onto the next flight in Hong Kong, no matter what time we arrived. All I had to do was to get to Hong Kong. I figured that trying to go direct, from

Macau to Bangkok, would just be asking for trouble.

There were two beds in the hotel room so there was no problem with the sleeping arrangements. The next morning I went with Dang to pick up her belongings and passport from her room. Luckily the Triads hadn't taken her passport off her. I had a fall-back position in that I'd brought a passport belonging to a friend who looked a lot like Dang, but that wouldn't have an immigration arrival stamp for Macau so I'd have been chancing my arm. Anyway, we took her things back to the hotel, packed them into my bag, then boarded the hotel courtesy bus to the ferry terminal.

I checked to see if we were being followed. The motorcycle was there. When we got to the ferry terminal, I made a big show of saying goodbye to Dang, lots of hugs and kisses, then she got into a taxi as I walked into the terminal. I saw the motorcycle follow the taxi and knew that I was right. The Triads were watching her.

I ignored the ferry and hovercraft ticket offices and headed for the offices of the local helicopter service. The six-seater helicopter would get us to Hong Kong in fifteen minutes, and there was a designated immigration queue that would have us to the helicopter within minutes. I bought two tickets for the next flight and then went downstairs to wait for Dang.

The plan was for her to go back to her room, wait twenty minutes, then catch a taxi back to the terminal. If she was followed, it wouldn't matter because they wouldn't have time to get us before we were through the fast-track immigration. As soon as her taxi arrived I paid the driver, grabbed her hand and hurried her inside the terminal. I didn't see anyone following her but I didn't take any chances and we hurried through immigration and into the helicopter departure lounge. Half an hour later and we were in a taxi heading for Chek Lap Kok airport in Hong Kong, and four hours later we were safely in Bangkok.

Bob was there to meet us. He thrust a brown envelope full of banknotes into my hand and told me to send him a bill for my expenses. He hugged and kissed Dang and hurried her off to his waiting limousine. Dang was all smiles but I wasn't sure how long it would last. She struck me as a girl who was easily bored. Still, I had my money and I had a satisfied client. A private eye can't ask for much more.

THE CASE OF THE
TWO-TIMING THAI

I normally steer clear of business investigations, especially where Thais are concerned. The thing you have to remember is that Thailand is for the Thais. Even the main political party is called Thais Love Thais. Farangs are outsiders, and the odds are always stacked against us. We can't own land, we need visas to live and work here, we need to own businesses in partnership with Thais. If a farang ever runs up against a Thai in a business dispute, generally the farang comes off worse. And that's if the local is playing fair. If the local is a shady character, he might decide to solve the dispute by hiring a guy on a motorcycle to put a couple of bullets in the farang's head. Don't laugh, it happens. It happens a lot. It's not always a blatant bullet in the brain, either. Pretty much every week a farang will be found dead at the foot of his apartment block or lying on his bed with his head in a plastic bag. More often than not the cops will put it down to suicide but a lot of the deaths are murder, plain and simple. And a lot of the murders are the result of business disputes.

I got a phone call one afternoon from a well-spoken English guy who said that I had come highly recommended and that he had a problem he needed help with. At first I assumed he was just another sex tourist who'd fallen for the charms of a pole-dancer but then he said he'd like to meet me the next morning at 7am for breakfast at a five-star hotel along with his regional manager. I knew then that this wasn't going to be a bargirl investigation—sex tourists tend to stay clear of five-star hotels, they don't get up that early and they don't usually have regional managers.

I spotted them as soon as I walked into the hotel restaurant. Two men in suits drinking coffee and reading the business section of the *Bangkok Post*. They both stood up and shook my hands. The guy who called was Alistair Stewart. He was tall with receding hair, late thirties maybe. His regional manager was Eric Holden, a Norwegian guy with white hair who was a few years older and several kilograms heavier. He was based in Hong Kong and had apparently flown over specifically for the breakfast meeting.

They made me sign a confidentiality agreement before they told me what their problem was. I was already starting to get cold feet but figured that a five-star breakfast was worth hanging around for. Stewart's firm was a major freight forwarder that had been operating in Thailand for five years. They had maintained steady growth and had been in profit since day one. They had a first class finance director and he kept a tight grip on the money side which is why alarm bells had started ringing over the company's cashflow. The company had stopped growing and had actually lost several clients. Turnover was down and profits were starting to fall. Stewart and Holden had put their thinking caps on and had come up with the only possible solution: the company's woes were something to do with the number three man in the local team, a Thai who they had hired the previous years as sales director. They didn't have any evidence, it was a hunch more than anything, but they felt that he was doing something that was taking business away from them.

As sales director, Gung spent a lot of time out of the office and so they wanted me to keep the guy under surveillance for a week. Find out where he went and who he saw.

I ordered another plate of toast and then ran through my concerns. The first problem is that following someone in Bangkok is a nightmare. The traffic is terrible, traffic lights can take up to fifteen minutes to change, parking is problematic at best. I prefer to use motorcyclists but they're not allowed on expressways and intersection flyovers so the only answer was lots of manpower and that was expensive and even then success wasn't guaranteed.

My second concern was a long-standing one. I had an unwritten rule never to investigate Thai men or Thai companies. The breakfast meeting came only a few weeks after an Australian auditor investigating a local firm was shot to death in the back of his minivan. I didn't want to start flinching every time a motorcycle pulled up next to me.

So my advice to the two guys was to hire a local firm to do the surveillance. Stewart and Holden both shook their heads. They didn't trust a Thai firm to do the job. But I came highly recommended. That was nice to hear, but I still wasn't happy about investigating a local. I had no way of knowing how well connected he was. For all I knew his brother could be a high-up police officer or Army general and they're not the sort of people you want to upset.

Stewart asked me to reconsider and said that he'd pay me half up front. I doubled my daily rate and he didn't bat an eyelid. Holden opened a slim leather briefcase and handed me a wad of notes. Unwritten rules aren't worth the paper they're written on, not when you're holding a stack of real money. I agreed to take the case. Holden gave me a manila envelope which contained a photograph of the target, the names and addresses of the company's clients, details of his car and house, his mobile phone number. Holden was clearly efficient, everything I needed was in the envelope.

The two guys shook my hand and left. I had another coffee as I read through the file they'd left. The sales director was thirty-seven, obviously Thai-Chinese, slightly overweight with chubby cheeks and looking full of confidence. He lived in a landed property, which meant there was money in the family. I just hoped there weren't too many relatives carrying firearms.

In the afternoon I wandered down to my outside office, the clump of tables at Soi 13 where I sat and chewed the fat with Big Nong, whose aunt served Thai whiskey and Singha beer throughout the night. Big Nong was one of my most reliable part-time assistants. He was reliable, he didn't drink and he spent most evenings at home with his two children. He used to work the night shift with his aunt, selling alcohol and cigarettes to the local bargirls, but then his wife discovered how much the bargirls who frequented the place earned and she joined their throngs herself, selling her body in a local beer bar and leaving him with the kids. He was a huge guy, and while he was very much a gentle giant he intimidated the hell out of everyone he met. At the nearby motorcycle taxi rank was a butch lesbian motorcycle taxi girl by the name of Nok who agreed to help me on the surveillance job for 500 baht a day.

The next morning I was at a small restaurant at the head of the soi close to the head offices of the shipping company, drinking Cokes with Big Nong. Nok was parked close by on her Honda. I had arranged for Stewart to phone me on my mobile as soon as Gung got ready to leave the office. As no phone call was forthcoming, Big Nong, Nok and I ordered a noodle lunch. My phone rang just as I was sprinkling dried chillies over my bowl of noodles; Gung was on his way out.

Nok got back on her Honda and I put on a helmet and climbed onto the back of Big Nong's bike.

Gung's Toyota drove slowly down the soi and indicated left. We followed him, keeping well back. The traffic was light so we had no trouble keeping him in sight, but five minutes down the main road and he turned onto the Bangna freeway, which meant that we couldn't follow him. A five hour wait and we'd lost him in five minutes.

I remembered that Gung's home was out Bangna way so we headed out there. Sure enough, we saw his car parked outside.

I left Nok to keep an eye on his place and got Big Nong to take me home. According to the information Holden had given me, Gung's mobile phone was from one of the big companies and as luck would have it I had a contact there who, for a few thousand baht, would give me a list of all numbers received and called. I phoned my contact and he promised to drop the information around next day.

The following morning Big Nong and I were at the restaurant near the head office again. Big Nong had been told that a policeman owned the restaurant and I figured it wouldn't be too long before the staff started to wonder what we were up to. I got my defence in first and told one of the waitresses that my wife worked in an office down the road and that I thought she was having an affair with one of her colleagues. I got lots of sympathetic smiles from the waitresses after that.

Gung left the office at ten o'clock and we followed him towards Klong Toey Port. He spent an hour there and then we tailed him to an office block in Chinatown. Then he went home again. I checked the addresses against the customer list that Holden had given me. There were no matches. That could have meant he was drumming up new business for the firm, or that there was something going on that his employers didn't know about. One thing was for sure, he wasn't working hard. A couple of hours in the office in the morning, a couple of business calls, then home. However much Stewart was paying the guy, it was too much.

On the third day Gung visited two more firms that weren't on Holden's list and one that was a major client of the firm, then spent three hours in a short-time hotel in Soi 3 with a very pretty girl who clearly wasn't his wife. I fired off half a dozen long-range pictures with my telephoto lens as they left.

I spent the afternoon at the Company Registrar on Ratchada Road. There's a civil servant there that I've used on several occasions, so I slipped him Gung's full name and date of birth and a 500-baht note. He ran the details through the databases and found that Gung was a director of half a dozen companies, all based in Bangkok. I took the list to the nearest Starbucks and compared the directorships with the addresses that Gung had visited over the past couple of days. There were two that matched: one was the office in Chinatown and the other was in Silom, close to the Patpong red-light district. Both companies were freight forwarders, in direct competition with Stewart's business. Gung had joined the boards of both companies five years before he started working for Stewart. Bingo. It was obvious what was going on. Gung had joined Stewart's company with the sole intention of poaching his clients.

I didn't have proof, of course. But over the course of the week Gung spent more time visiting his own companies and his minor wife than he did attending to Stewart's customers. And one of the firm's that Gung had visited didn't renew its contract with Stewart's company. I made a phone call, posing as a potential customer, and got the name of the freight forwarder they were now using. No surprises there. It was one of Gung's companies.

I gave the information to Stewart and they sacked Gung a few days later. He made noises about suing them for breach of contract, but the photographs of him leaving the short-time hotel with his mistress put paid to that.

There's a Chinese expression about not breaking someone else's rice bowl, and I had definitely broken Gung's. I insisted that Stewart and Holden didn't reveal my involvement in the case, but over the next few days I still found myself ducking when motorcyclists pulled up next to me. Thailand truly is the Land of Smiles but it's also the Land of Hitmen on Motorcycles.

THE CASE OF THE
MILLION-BAHT BARGIRL

I've never understood why so many tourists end up sending money back to their temporary girlfriends when they go home. It makes no sense to me. Paying and playing while you're in Thailand is all well and good, but why pay when you're thousands of miles away? My bread and butter work is checking up on bargirls. And nine times out of ten, the client is a love-struck farang wanting me to check that his beloved isn't doing what she was doing when he met her. There is a theory that sex tourists check in their brains on arrival at the airport, but there's no excuse for long-term residents of the Land of Smiles to be shelling out money to bargirls. Anyone who lives here really should know better. You've only got to sit down at one of the beer bars at the entrance to Nana Plaza to see what goes on. Motorcycles buzz up with a pretty young thing on the back. The girl totters into the plaza to start work, the boyfriend drives off to play pool with his friends. After the bars have closed, the guy drives back and picks up the girl and off they go to spend her hard-earned cash. The girls are hookers hooking and they're not going to stop doing that just because some guy thousands of miles away starts sending her a few thousand baht each month.

Guys who live here know how it works, which is why I was so

surprised when I met Yves. And even more surprised when I heard what the daft sod had done. He phoned me on my mobile and said that he'd heard good things about me from a couple of guys I'd worked for. It's always nice to get a word-of-mouth recommendation rather than a client who has just seen one of the stickers I put on every ATM machine I use. Yves was French, very well spoken and clearly upper class so I put on my best shirt and tie and went around to his office for a chat. Well, not his office, actually. He was a bit wary about being seen with a private eye, so we met in a nearby Starbucks.

I got there twenty minutes early which gave me time for a look around, but he turned up on his own and looked every bit as French as he'd sounded on the phone. He was a small man in his early forties, his hair starting to grey at the temples, fairly good looking and looking dapper in a double-breasted blue blazer, grey slacks and dark brown shoes with tassels on them. He bought a couple of coffees and then told me his story.

He'd been in Thailand for most of his life. His father had been involved in the shipping business at the time of the legendary Jim Thompson, and on occasions they'd done business together. Thompson is just about the most famous farang in Thailand; he pretty much single-handedly set up the country's silk exporting business before disappearing under mysterious circumstances.

Yves had met several members of the Thai Royal Family and had married a Thai woman from a high-class background. She was now on the family estate in Pyrenees raising their three children. Yves travelled back and forth between France and Thailand, though he admitted that the Bangkok office pretty much ran itself. It soon became clear why Yves was spending so much time in the Land of Smiles. He was a frequent visitor to Patpong, one the city's main red-light districts. Being married hadn't stopped him fooling around and, with his wife in France, his sex drive had gone into full throttle.

He usually drank in one of the biggest bars in Soi Cowboy, and was a close friend of the Thai owner. He paid and played and from the 'cat that got the cream' grin on his face, I could see that he enjoyed himself. Yves's life had changed a month earlier when a twenty-year-old girl by the name of Boo walked onto the stage and started dancing around a silver pole.

Boo means crab. It's a common enough name for a Thai girl. Prawn. Chicken. Apple. Orange. For some reasons Thais seem to love to name their daughters after food.

Anyway, according to Yves, Boo was drop-dead gorgeous. Waist-length hair, full breasts, long legs, tight stomach, great arse, hell I was getting turned on by the description alone. And when he took a photograph from his wallet and showed it to me I practically started salivating. She was hot. Hot, hot, hot.

Yves got the owner to send young Boo over to his table and within seconds he was infatuated with her. He offered to let her stay in his penthouse apartment in Silom, and wanted to pay her to stop working. She'd only been dancing for three weeks and the bar owner was none-too-pleased at Yves taking his best-looking dancer away, but a 10,000-baht backhander got everything sorted.

Boo didn't fully move into Yves's apartment, but she did spend a lot of time there. They went out most nights, usually to the bar where she used to work. They'd barfine a few of her friends and visit the city's top nightclubs. Usually at some point he'd slip her some money and she'd return with a few tablets of Ecstasy and then they'd go home where, before too long, he'd crash out. He was twice her age and I figured she was wearing him out. It was funny, Yves didn't look the type to be doing E. Just shows that you can't judge a book by its cover. Anyway, usually when Yves woke up, she was gone.

Then he hit me with the big one, the fact that took my breath away. In order to formalise his relationship with her, he had given her a million baht. One million baht! When I heard that my eyebrows shot skyward and my jaw dropped. A million baht!

Let me put that into perspective. A million baht isn't a million pounds. Or a million dollars. But it is one hell of a lot of cash in Thailand. It would take a Thai schoolteacher the best part of five years to earn a million baht. The sweet little salesgirls in Robinson's Department Store would have to work for a decade, maybe more, to earn a million baht. Even a star pole-dancer in a top Nana Plaza bar who spent every evening on her back with her legs open would be lucky to take home 50,000 baht a month. So a million baht would be almost two years' salary. And Yves had given it to Boo. Given it to her. I shook my head in disbelief but Yves took out a bank statement and showed it to me. Sure enough, there was the bank transfer. One million baht, straight from his account to hers.

I made a mental note to charge him double my usual rate because Yves clearly had money to burn. I tried to work out how many times I could have sex with a million baht, assuming that I was paying the going rate. Six hundred baht for a bar fine, fifteen hundred baht for the girl. Four hundred baht for a short-time hotel. Total outlay, two thousand five hundred baht. Divided into one million was one hell of a lot of sex.

Yves made it clear that he wasn't going to leave his wife. He never actually said that he loved her, but she was the mother of his children plus I figured he knew that a divorce would be bloody expensive in France. He wanted Boo to be his mia noi, his minor wife. A full-time mistress who would be a wife in all but name.

He went to her village in Isaan to meet her mother and Boo had given her 800,000 baht to build a house on some land they owned. That immediately set alarm bells ringing for me because that was three or four times the going rate for building a house there. Labour is dirt cheap in Isaan, and materials are well below Bangkok prices, so I was sure that Yves was being ripped off.

He'd come to the same conclusion shortly after returning to the city from Isaan. But it wasn't the house that made him think twice about his dream girl. A 'sister' appeared, a girl who was a few years older than Boo but with a hundred times more experience by the look of her. Thais are pretty flexible about who they refer to as their 'brother' or 'sister' and the term doesn't necessarily mean that they have the same mother and father. In the case of Boo's 'sister', Yves got the impression that she was just a friend from her village, probably the girl who had enticed Boo into the bar business. The 'sister' started going out with Yves, Boo and her friends on their nightly rounds. She was draped in gold—thick necklaces, rings on most of her fingers and heavy bracelets. The 'sister' suggested that Yves buy Boo some gold and that got Boo all excited so Yves agreed to go along to a gold shop with them.

Now, Yves was no stranger to gold shops, and he knew how they worked. The gold jewellery is pretty much pure metal and is sold by weight, with a few hundred baht thrown in to cover design and workmanship. The daily gold price is usually on a sign in the window, one price for selling and a slightly lower price for buying. In Thailand, gold is as good as money and it's a standard con for a bargirl to take her beloved into a gold shop to buy a token of his love, only to have the girl return alone the next day and exchange it for cash.

Yves went into a gold shop near Soi Cowboy with Boo and the 'sister' and a middle-aged Thai-Chinese woman started the hard-sell. Yves asked the price of a few items, and soon realised that he was being taken for a ride. He figured that the 'sister' had done a deal with the shop and arranged a hefty commission for anything that Yves bought. He refused to buy anything from the shop, and walked out with a tearful Boo.

Now that his suspicions were raised, Yves started taking a closer look at the lovely Miss Boo. He went through his bank statements and discovered that somebody had regularly been withdrawing 20,000 baht from one of his accounts. Yves got most of his spending money from the petty cash float in his office, so it didn't take a Sherlock Holmes to figure out who was hitting the ATM. Yves went to his local police station but the cops told him that they wouldn't act without proof and that they didn't have the enthusiasm to mount an investigation. I smiled when he told me that. The police were hoping he would offer them a reward, in which case they would have immediately swung into action, but instead he had taken them at their word and contacted me. Still, it's an ill wind that blows nobody good and I was as happy as Boo to take Yves's money.

Yves wanted revenge. If it was me I'd have just walked away. Hell, if it had been me I wouldn't have given her a million baht in the first place. Yves wanted her in jail, behind bars, he wanted her punished. It seemed petty to me, she was just a bargirl doing what bargirls do. I don't see why he'd expected anything else. Money to bargirls is like water, it's easy to get and easy to spend. Give a bargirl a hundred baht and she'll spend it. Give her a hundred thousand and she'll spend that. When Yves offered her a million, what else was she supposed to have done other than said 'thank you' and taken it?

Anyway, rule number one of the private-eye game is that the customer is always right, even when he's wrong, so I quoted him a daily rate and he passed me a thick wad of notes in a company envelope.

I got him to fax me a signed authority and a copy of the bank account that had been accessed with the ATM card and I took them along to the branch with a couple of boxes of chocolate almonds. I chose the plainest female cashier, gave her a winning smile and the sweets and five minutes later I had the information I needed and a phone number that I most definitely didn't. All the withdrawals had been from the same ATM, close to Yves's penthouse apartment, and they had all been made between five and seven o'clock in the morning, while Yves was sleeping off the effects of the alcohol, Ecstasy and sex.

I phoned Yves and told him what I'd discovered. We agreed that he'd carry on as usual, and I'd stake out the ATM. He'd text me when he got home and I'd wait with my trusty digital camera. Three days later and I got what I wanted. Yves and Boo got home at just after three after a night on the town. I was sitting outside a 7-Eleven opposite the ATM by four with a motorcycle taxi close by, and at six-thirty a decidedly sexy Miss Boo tottered down the road in skin-tight jeans and high heels and slotted in an ATM card. I fired off half a dozen shots. The last one was a beauty, Boo grinning from ear to ear as she counted a fistful of notes.

She put the money into the back pocket of her jeans and tottered back to Yves's place. True to form she reappeared again at just after seven and hailed a taxi. I was already on the back of the motorcycle taxi and we followed her across town. It was well before rush hour so we had no problem keeping her in sight. The guy I was using was Panu, one of my regulars. He had a disconcerting habit of picking his nose while driving at speed, but he was reliable and knew the city like the back of his hand.

Miss Boo's taxi drove along Rama VII road and eventually stopped outside a six-storey apartment block in a busy side street. I told Panu to follow her inside. No one looked twice at a motorcycle taxi guy whereas farangs attract attention wherever they go.

Panu returned a few minutes later. Miss Boo was holed up in Room 702.

A few days later Yves and I went back to the police station with the photographs and a bank statement showing Miss Boo's latest unofficial withdrawal. And this time I'd primed Yves to offer a 10,000 baht sweetener, just to encourage the boys in brown to do their thing.

The next day at about noon the cops went in. They got Miss Boo and, as it turned out, her husband, who had recently given up his job as a labourer in Isaan and moved to Bangkok to help his wife spend Yves's money. The police also found a dozen yah ba tablets in the room.

Miss Boo and her husband were hauled off to the station where Yves identified the girl and signed forms in triplicate confirming that he wanted to press charges. The cops were prepared to let Boo go with just a 'fine' but Yves insisted that she be charged. The theft charge and the drugs were good enough to put Miss Boo behind bars for a hundred days. And a hundred days in a Thai jail is the equivalent of a year or so in the civilised world. The husband came up with a decent bribe, which coupled with the fact that it was his first offence meant that he walked. He caught the next bus back to Isaan.

Yves was happy with the result. He got his revenge, but he didn't get his million baht back. To be honest, I don't think it was ever about the money. Yves had money enough to burn. It was about being lied to by a girl half his age and about him having to face the fact that the sexy, young, Miss Boo wanted just one thing from him: cold, hard cash. He wasn't the handsome, debonair man-of-the-world that he liked to think he was; he was a punter, and she was a hooker. And they were facts that Yves didn't want to face. C'est la vie, as the French say. Serves him right, is what I say.

THE CASE OF THE
PATTAYA PLAY-AWAYS

By and large, I avoid Pattaya like the proverbial plague. It's a scummy place unless you're a sex tourist and it brings together the worst sort of farangs and the worst sort of Thais. It's a Wild West town with go-go bars where tattooed guys with shaved heads and beer bellies drive around on Harleys with hookers half their age clinging to their backs, where drugs, booze and hookers are on tap twenty-four hours a day, and where there's a murder/suicide pretty much every week. A murder/suicide? Yeah, that's where a guy is found in his room, a plastic bag tied around his neck and his hands tied behind his back. The cops always write it off as a suicide but I've never heard of anyone killing themselves like that outside of the Land of Smiles. The other preferred way of ending it all is for a tourist to throw himself out of his hotel room window. That usually gets classified as a suicide too, even if the tourist's wallet is empty and his watch and mobile phone are missing. You see, murder is bad for business. And Pattaya is all about business. The local press play ball, too, and most of the murder/suicides are never reported.

At any one time there are probably as many as 20,000 hookers in Pattaya, and frankly most of them are well past their sell-by date. That's just my humble opinion. Most of the overage, overweight, overdrinking sex tourists who prowl the beach road at night would probably disagree. A big chunk of the bargirl investigations I get are from guys who've fallen for the charms of a Pattaya hooker. They meet her on a two-week vacation, fall in love, and before they go back to farangland they beg the girl to stop working and promise to send her a monthly salary. After a few weeks they start to wonder if the girl is sticking to her end of the deal and that's when they get in touch with me. Frankly, it's money for old rope. Rule Number One when it comes to bargirls: if their lips are moving, they're lying. Rule Number Two: if their lips aren't moving, they're planning their next lie.

Time after time I hear the same refrain. 'My girl is different.' And 'I know she loves me.' And 'She never really wanted to work in the bar in the first place.' Whatever. I tell them my daily rate and when I've got a few cases lined up I take a run down the coast in a rental car. Over the years I've probably investigated 300 bargirls who've sworn love and devotion to farang boyfriends. And how many have turned out to be loyal, faithful girlfriends, patiently sitting in their rooms waiting for their boyfriend to return? Err, let me think about that for a while. Err, none. Not one. Like I said, money for old rope.

To be honest, I don't enjoy bargirl investigations. They are generally pointless and I'm forever telling clients what they don't want to hear. There's also the risk of violence. Bargirls take no prisoners and they fight mean. I've seen a girl weighing forty kilograms soaking wet take out a guy three times her size by walloping him on the temple with the heel of her shoe. I always try to get in and out without the girl finding out who grassed her up because to a Thai bargirl revenge is a dish best served up cold, hot, spiced with chilli or wrapped up in a pancake with a bowl of sweet sauce on the side.

Anyway, for this trip to Sleaze-By-The-Sea I had two cases and I was feeling good because neither of them involved checking up on bargirls. Case number one involved a Brit by the name of Ronnie who was working for an oil company in Malaysia. Ronnie had married a girl from Pattaya—Gradai, her name was, she used to work in a beauty parlour, he said—and she'd gone back home to supervise the building of a new family home. Building work had slowed and Ronnie got the feeling that his wife was starting to give him the runaround. Case number two was a Singaporean girl called Cindee (she stressed the spelling three times so it obviously meant a lot to her) who was wondering why her husband was spending so much time in Pattaya. As soon as she told me the name of the hotel he was staying at I had a pretty good idea what he was up to. The Penthouse in Pattaya Soi 8 was a well known sex-tourist hangout. If she'd just checked out their website she'd have realised that it wasn't a Hilton or Hyatt. Taking bargirls to rooms wasn't just allowed, it was practically compulsory. Still, if she wanted to pay me to confirm the blindingly obvious, I was happy to take her money.

So with two retainers in the bank, I rented a nondescript Toyota and drove south and booked into the Penthouse. It took me all of five minutes to locate Mr Singapore. The Penthouse has a convenient CCTV system hooked into the hotel's TVs so that punters can check out the girls in the bar downstairs. Mr Singapore and his best buddy—as described to me by Cindee—were sitting there watching the girls dancing. I showered, changed into fresh Chinos and a polo shirt, and headed downstairs. By the time I walked into the bar, Mr Singapore was playing pool with four or five reasonably cute bargirls, all of them drinking heavily, apparently on his bar tab.

I perched myself on a bar stool smiled at a lanky bargirl and before I could say 'I'm fresh off the plane from Auckland' she was by my side with her hand on my thigh, tossing her hair and pointing her surgically-enhanced but nonetheless tempting breasts at me. Her name was Du and she had only been working in the bar for two weeks, she said. The tattoo of a scorpion on her shoulder and the three-baht gold chain on her wrist suggested she'd been at the game a bit longer than that, but I just nodded and smiled, patted her on her very impressive backside and told her to get me a Jack Daniels and herself whatever she wanted. A few rounds later and I had the full story on Mr Singapore. He was a regular who came for a week every few months, she said, which pretty much put paid to her story of only being there for two weeks. That's typical of a Thai bargirl—cunning as a fox, with the mind of a goldfish.

Miss Du kept pestering me to take her for a short-time romp upstairs but I put her off by telling her that my herpes had just flared up and I was probably infectious for a few days. She flounced off which gave me the chance to challenge Mr Singapore to a game of pool. He turned out to be a really nice guy. His name was Alan and he ran a successful business in Singapore, organizing golf trips around the region, and just wanted to have a few days R&R in Thailand at a tenth of the cost of similar shenanigans in the Lion City. After a couple of hours of drinks and pool I had his namecard and an invite for a night out on the town next time I was in Singapore. He made no move to take any of the girls for short-time rumpy-pumpy, so as darkness fell I made my excuses and headed out of the hotel. I found a nearby internet café and sent a carefully worded email to Cindee. The thing was, I liked the guy. And he was just doing what a million guys do, and millions more would do if they could: to blow off a bit of steam with a few good-looking girls in tow. It was natural, it wasn't as if I'd caught him with a mistress or a toy-boy. He was just a guy, having fun. So I told Cindee that I'd seen her husband and his friend playing pool with a few girls, but that I didn't think there was anything serious going on. I still felt like a rat when I hit the 'send' button.

So, off to the other job. Ronnie had been married for almost ten years. He'd moved to Kuala Lumpur as a regional manager with a big oil company with his Thai wife and child. He was on a full expat package—big salary, flights home, nice house, maids, international school for the kid, the works. After a couple of years the wife had said that she was homesick and he'd agreed that she should return to Thailand, which is were he planned to retire to anyway. They bought a large plot of land on the outskirts of Pattaya and he paid an architect to design a ten-room mansion with a pool and a three-car garage. Ronnie spent most of his time in Kuala Lumpur where his son went to one of the top international schools. He had a nanny and a couple of maids and a driver so it wasn't exactly a hardship posting, and every few months he flew back to Pattaya to spend time with his wife. The arrangement worked well for the first year, but then progress on the house slowed to a crawl. And Ronnie's suspicions were raised when his wife started talking about starting up a band and owning a restaurant, two long-term dreams of hers. He got in touch via my website and after a few emails I agreed to go and check her out. He faxed me a map to get me to his dream house and I drove out for a look-see. It was easy enough to find, and easy enough to see that building had stopped some time ago. The house had been half-completed but much of what had been done was now overgrown by weeds. There was bamboo scaffolding around the basic framework of the house, but there was no sign of a roof and there were no windows or doors. There was a large rectangular hole where the pool was going to be, and another hole which I guessed was where the garage foundations would go, but there was no building equipment around, no cement mixers or shovels or pickaxes. According to the schedule that the architect had given Ronnie, the house was due to be finished within eight weeks but there was clearly no chance of the builders meeting the deadline. I took a few snapshots with the trusty digital camera so that Ronnie could see for himself.

I spotted an old man feeding some chickens on the nearby plot and I went over and spun him a line about liking the look of the building and wanting to build one just like it myself. Did he by any chance know who the builders were as they were clearly a most professional firm? The old guy fell for my patter and gave me all the information I needed. According to the old man, the wealthy Thai woman who was paying for the house had told the builders to stop work and to start constructing a restaurant on South Pattaya Road, Soi 2 he thought. He gave me the name of the head builder and his mobile phone number. Apparently the guy gave the old man a few baht every now and then to keep an eye on his scaffolding.

I drove back to the Penthouse Hotel figuring that I'd made a pretty good start on both cases and that I deserved a few tumblers of Jack Daniels as a reward. I showered and headed down to the bar. It went by the name of The Kitten Club and Mr Singapore was in residence and feeling no pain. We started playing pool again and buying rounds of drinks for ourselves and his fan club. We stayed until closing and then we wandered over to the hotel's restaurant which was open twenty-four hours. Alan said that the girls would join us later and that we didn't have to pay barfines. Considering that we'd spent the best part of 10,000 baht on drinks and snacks already, I figured it wasn't much of a saving. Anyway, within an hour we had his fan club sitting with us again and there was lots of leg-stroking and breast-fumbling and tongue-swapping. I popped over to the toilet a couple of times and managed to get a few digital snaps of Alan and his mate and the girls. Eventually the two guys chose a girl each, said good night to me, and staggered over to the elevators leaving me with the remains of the fan club. Alan gave me a leer and a thumbs-up as the doors closed. I waved back feeling like a shit because I was going to have to tell his wife what he was up to.

The four girls left were pulling out all the stops persuading me to take them upstairs and I was starting to think that perhaps I deserved more of a reward than just a few JDs, then Miss Du wandered over and started whispering in their ears. She obviously told them about my herpes flare-up because five minutes later I was sitting on my own and my hard on had faded into a memory.

Before I hit the sack I emailed the pictures to Singapore. I felt bad about dropping Alan in it and did my best to explain to Cindee that her husband appeared to be just blowing off a bit of steam. It wasn't as if he had a mia noy or even a long-term girlfriend, he was just hanging out with bargirls and I figure that ninety-nine per cent of the men in Thailand, single or married, do that at some time. It's only natural, right? As I hit the 'send' button I had a feeling that Cindee wasn't going to see it that way, though.

The next morning I launched into the hotel's breakfast buffet then took a stroll down to South Pattaya Road, Soi 2. It was a rough area, even by Pattaya standards, and most of the residents seemed to be Thai labourers and their families. I sat down at a foodstall area and even though I wasn't hungry I ordered a plate of kow man gai, one of my favourite dishes. It's steamed rice and chicken and a bowl of watery soup. It tastes a lot better than it sounds. I got chatting to the middle-aged couple running the stall. They were from Kalasin but they had moved to Pattaya decades earlier to seek fame and fortune. They had six kids and the foodstall, which wasn't much by Western standards but by Thai standards they were doing okay. I always figure that anyone who isn't up to his knees in water planting rice by hand in the burning sun has got to be ahead of the game. The couple knew about the new Thai cabaret that had just opened further down the soi. They were too old to go out much at night, and they had to be up at first light to go to the market, but they often heard the cabaret's band late at night. 'They're not very good,' chuckled the old man. 'I've heard drowning dogs that were more tuneful.'

I paid for my snack and wandered along the soi to take a look at the cabaret. A pack of mangy soi dogs watched me walk by, wondering what the hell a farang was doing in their neck of the woods. Soi dogs are strange animals. Like Thai people they're good-natured unless riled, and they have a totally laid back approach to life. You'll see them sleeping under cars, in the middle of the road, in gutters, totally oblivious to traffic and pedestrians. The dogs, that is. And the people, too, come to think of it. You never see soi dogs scrounging for food, either, the way you do in the West. They don't go around begging, they just wait to be fed. There's always a dog-loving foodstall owner who'll put out a bowl of rice and meat for them or an old lady throwing out her kitchen scraps. The Lord will provide, seems to be their philosophy. Or Buddha will provide, I guess. I figure the dogs, given the choice, would opt for Buddhism rather than Catholicism or Judaism. The circle of life, and all that. I might only be a humble soi dog but next life I'll be a general or a politician or a massage-parlour owner. Call me a naïve and sentimental old fool, but I always felt that I'd been a soi dog in a previous life. The one question I couldn't answer was whether my karma was improving or not.

There was a large hand-painted banner stretched across the soi proclaiming that the 'Isaan Allstars' were in residence at 'Gradai's Cabaret and Beer Bar.' There was an impressive frontage with a wrought-iron gate that led through to a gravelled area with twenty wooden tables facing a small stage. I figured that didn't open on rainy nights because there was no roof. There were posters advertising Chang Beer, the tipple of choice for workers on the minimum wage, and a big hoarding with a photograph of a middle-aged lady holding a bulbous microphone with a raggedy bunch of Isaan musicians behind. It was obviously Gradai and the Isaan Allstars. There was nobody around so I went back to the Penthouse and had a few Jack Daniels and games of pool with Alan. He was in fine form so Cindee clearly hadn't been in touch. He and his buddy had their fan club in tow though none of them would so much as smile at me.

I went back to Gradai's Cabaret and Beer as the sun was going down. There was a young guy doing some half-hearted tidying up so I spun him a story about wanting to arrange a birthday party for my Thai wife and he gave me Miss Gradai's mobile number. She lived in a posh apartment in nearby Jomtien with her partner, he said. A Thai policeman. It wasn't looking good for Ronnie.

I phoned the number and Miss Gradai answered. I used bad Thai and it soon became apparent that Miss Gradai spoke perfect English so we switched to that. I stuck to my party story. I told her that I was in Jomtien and she agreed to meet me in a hotel lobby. I drove there as quickly as I could and was in the lobby when she arrived. She was in her late thirties and had obviously spent some of her husband's hard-earned money on a nose job and bigger breasts and she was well dressed in a Versace shirt and Gucci jeans with Raybans propped up on her head. She shook my hand with a hand that was festooned with glittering rings. She was chatty and within a few minutes had told me that she was married to an Englishman, but that he was always busy and that he didn't understand her. She was a singer, she said, and had just opened the cabaret and bar. Business was slow, she told me, but she expected it to pick up soon. Her band, the Isaan Allstars, would soon be household names, she said. As we started talking about my fictitious girlfriend's party, her top-of-the-range Nokia mobile rang. She put her hand over the phone but I could hear enough to work out that she was talking to her Thai boyfriend.

'Your husband?' I said, when she'd finished the call.

'My boyfriend,' she said.

'Oh, is he in the band?'

She shook her head. 'No, he's a policeman here in Jomtien. But he likes to sing.'

I made a provisional booking for the Cabaret and gave her a pay-as-you-go mobile number that I was planning to dump in a few days. I promised that I'd drop by the place that night and drove back to the Penthouse. I parked, then popped into an internet cafe and emailed photographs of the Cabaret and the unfinished house to Ronnie, along with an initial report. I didn't like breaking bad news, but that was what I was paid for. And it was better that he learnt the truth sooner rather than later. Gradai was bleeding him dry, with a Thai boyfriend to boot. I knew that Ronnie's options were limited: the Thai legal system isn't farang-friendly and the fact that the guy she was sleeping with was a Pattaya cop meant that Ronnie would have to tread carefully if he didn't want to end up with a plastic bag over his head or at the bottom of a local high-rise.

I showered and shaved and changed into clean clothes, feeling pretty damn pleased with myself. I'd nailed both jobs in record time. I switched on the television and flicked through the channels. Inane game shows, boring chat shows, soap operas with giggling girls and foppish boys, the usual Thai fare. I stopped at the closed circuit view of the Kitten Club. Alan was sitting at the bar, his head in his hands. His mate was standing next to him, patting him on the back. I figured that Cindee had obviously been on him and given him an earful. I suddenly didn't feel so happy about what I'd done. I'd done what I'd been paid to do, no question of that. And I'd been professional. But Alan was just doing what guys the whole world did and I felt bad for him. I just hoped that Cindee would make do with making him feel like shit for a few weeks and that she didn't set Singaporean lawyers on him. I thought about going downstairs and buying him a few beers but there was an outside chance that he might figure out who'd sent the photographs to his wife so I decided that discretion was the better part of valour and I sneaked out for a few JD and Cokes at a bar overlooking the cesspool that passes for a sea. Having my thighs stroked by a long-haired beauty and being told that I'm a 'hansum man' always does wonders for my self-esteem.

At just after ten I wandered down to Gradai's Cabaret. I already had all the information I needed, but Ronnie had paid me for three days so I figured that the least I could do was to see what the Isaan Allstars were like in full swing. The place was half-empty, or half-full depending on your point of view. The clientele seemed to be solely working class Thais drinking Chang beer or cheap whiskey. The cabaret was a couple of old comedians doing a slapstick routine that wasn't funny in any language, and there seemed to be more waitresses and bar staff than there were paying customers. I doubted it would stay in business for more than a few months. It was only Ronnie's money that was keeping it going.

Gradai and the Allstars came on stage just before midnight. She was wearing a too-tight red sequinned dress that showed off her silicon breasts, and far too much make-up. The Allstars were in denim and wore cowboy hats and were actually quite good. Gradai was terrible, though, and any dreams she had of making it to the big time were just that: dreams. At one point she said she'd take requests from the audience. I thought of asking her if she could play 'Over The Hills And Far Away' but figured she wouldn't get the joke. I asked if they'd sing my favourite country tune, 'Hua Jai Kradart' about a man who complains that Thai women treat his heart like paper, screw it up and toss it out when they have used it.

It got a huge round of applause from the staff, but I don't think that Gradai got the significance of the song. That was pretty much how she'd used Ronnie. Taken his money, lied to him, all but abandoned her kid. That's no way for a woman to behave. I understand it when bargirls lie and steal and cheat. That's their job. And their instinct. But Gradai was Ronnie's wife and the mother of their child. There was no need for her to lie and steal. If she'd wanted out of the marriage the honourable thing would have been to have told him, sorted out their financial affairs and left him. I raised my glass to Gradai as the Allstars finished their song and she smiled and waved with her ring-encrusted hand. Rings paid for by Ronnie, I was sure.

I got an en email from Ronnie a few days later. He was divorcing Gradai, and she'd told him he could have sole custody of the boy. She, of course, was keeping sole custody of the cabaret and the half-built house. I got an email from Cindee, too. She was divorcing Alan, and thanked me for my help. I emailed her back, explaining that Alan was only blowing off steam, that the girls meant nothing to him, that she might think about giving him another chance, but I never heard back from her.

I don't know what happened to the cabaret, but I'm still waiting to see Gradai and the Isaan Allstars in the Top Ten. I'm not exactly holding my breath.

THE CASE OF THE
BARGIRL WHO TRIED

Like I said before, the bread and butter work of a Thai private eye is checking up on bargirls. The typical client is a middle-aged guy who's come to Thailand, met the love of his life dancing around a silver pole, and then got back home. Back in the real world he phones his new-found love every day, starts to send her money so that she won't have to sell her body, and starts to dream about bringing her back to his country and living happily ever after. The typical bargirl is from Isarn, dark-skinned and snub nosed, probably has a tattoo or two, a few scars from a motorcycle accident, and stretch marks from the kid she's left in the care of her parents upcountry. Oh yeah, and a Thai boyfriend or husband hidden away and helping her to spend her ill-gotten gains.

Usually what happens is that something starts to nag at the guy. Maybe the girl keeps asking for money, maybe her phone gets switched off late at night, maybe he hears a man's voice in the background. Or maybe he just visits one of the many websites that details all the pitfalls in a bargirl–farang relationship. That's when the guy gets in touch with me. The email or phone call follows a standard pattern. The guy met the girl in a bar, she hated the work and was just waiting for a white knight to rescue her. 'She's not a regular bargirl,' is something I always hear. 'She's different.'

At that point part of me wants to say that they're all the same, that they are all just hookers hooking, and that the best way to see if a bargirl is lying is to check if her lips are moving. Rule number one in the private-eye game: If a bargirl's lips are moving, she's lying. Rule number two: If a bargirl's lips aren't moving, she's preparing her next lie. But I don't tell the client that, of course. I tell them how much I charge and I give them the number of my bank account and then once the money's been transferred I go through the motions.

Do marriages between bargirls and expats ever work? I've known of a few, but success stories are as rare as hen's teeth. I don't understand why anyone thinks they are going to meet the love of their life in what is effectively a brothel. The girls are selling sex, not love. They rarely, if ever, confuse the two, but lots of guys don't seem to understand that there is a difference. Still, if everyone knew the score there'd be a lot less work for the likes of me, so I'm not complaining.

Anyway, when Damien called me from Australia, there was nothing he told me that I hadn't heard before. He'd just got back to Melbourne from yet another holiday in the Land of Smiles and he needed help on two fronts. He had a regular Thai girlfriend, a former pole dancer of course, and he wanted help getting her a visa so that she could visit him in Australia, and he wanted to check that she was on the straight and narrow. In my experience, the only thing straight and narrow about a bargirl is the pole they dance around, but I bit my tongue and had a long chat with him.

First thing I told him was that I couldn't do anything to speed up his visa application. I'm not saying there aren't ways and means of greasing things at the Australian Embassy, but I don't have those sort of contacts and even if I did I'd use them very sparingly because bribing embassy officials is a quick way to end up behind bars.

The Australian Embassy, and the British and United States embassies for that matter, take their time issuing visas, especially to young girls with no steady job, no pay slips, no land or money in the bank. A visa could take as much as six months before it was approved, and that was always good for business because during those six months the boyfriend would be fretting in his country while the girl was sitting in Thailand having to ask him for more and more to support herself, and her family. A lot of bargirls are simply rejected for visas. Hardly surprising when a lot of them turn up for their embassy interview wearing a low cut top, tight jeans, and sporting a tattoo of a scorpion on their shoulder.

Damien didn't try to pull the wool over my eyes. He was in his mid forties and Ann was twenty-two. That always sets alarm bells ringing for me. A twenty-year age gap is huge even when you're dealing with a couple from the same culture. But when the guy is effectively a sex tourist and the girl is a hooker half his age, well, it's hardly a match made in heaven, is it? Anyway, he told me that Ann had been a star dancer at Hollywood Strip but that he had helped set her up with her own business, selling clothes on the street around the corner from Nana Plaza. He'd gone upcountry and met her family in Saraburi and had agreed to pay a small sin sot. Ann had been to the embassy for a preliminary interview but they hadn't been satisfied with the evidence she'd provided. According to Damien she was finding the hours long and the work hard and that she wasn't making much of a return on the business. She'd told Damien that he'd have to start sending her money or she'd go back to the Hollywood Strip. It was the usual scenario for a farang far from Thailand, caught between a rock and a hard place. If he didn't send money, the girl would doubt his intentions. If he did send her cash, he'd start to wonder if she was just after his money.

I told Damien that I could definitely run a check on her, and that would at least put his mind at rest. Plus, if I didn't find anything, that boded well for her visa eventually coming through. He wired me a retainer and emailed me her details and a couple of photographs and I got down to business. Ann was a looker, long hair, long legs, curvy figure, very kissable lips. I was sure she'd have made a small fortune dancing and hooking in Nana Plaza.

I ran the basic checks. She'd never been married and she didn't have any children. She was living alone in a small studio flat in Soi 22, the same place she'd had when she was dancing. Ann's stall was on the corner of Sukhumvit and Soi 7. She only had her pitch from 9pm onwards and had to wait for the daytime vendors to pack up and go before she could set up shop. Thai laws says that you cannot sell on the public footpath, and to make that point Wednesdays are generally declared 'no sell' days but during the rest of the week the day vendors basically pay the local cops for the right to set up shop. Once the day vendor leaves, another vendor can take his place, providing a small fee is paid. That's the arrangement Ann had, and I reckoned she had a good spot with lots of passing traffic. She was selling cheap T-shirts and sundresses and I found myself a seat in an airconditioned bar in Soi 7 from where I could keep an eye on her.

Sales were slow on the three nights I watched her. She worked from 9pm until 3am and I reckoned she was doing well if she took in 1,000 baht a night, which would be less than she'd have been paid for an hour's short-time when she was hooking. The 1,000 baht was turnover, of course. Her profit would be between 300 and 400 baht. Fairly decent money for a Thai, about the same as a schoolteacher or office worker would get, but a fraction of what a pole-dancer would pull in. I saw her chatting to a couple of Thai guys who were selling an assortment of flick knives, samurai swords and knuckle-dusters but there didn't seem to be anything untoward going on and she always went home alone. On the first day I put on a baseball cap and sunglasses and walked by her pitch, bought a T-shirt from her and flirted with her in my very best Thai. I made her laugh but she wouldn't give me her phone number and wouldn't agree to see me for a drink.

I phoned Damien and told him that Ann was being a good girl and that he had nothing to worry about on that score. He asked me to approach her and tell her that I was a friend of his and that I would help her with her visa application. We agreed a fee and the next day I went to see her. I read through all the correspondence from the embassy and it was clear that they weren't convinced that she had gone legit, so I decided to beef up her application. I took her to Bo-Bey market where she bought her stock and I collected some receipts and took photographs of her at work. I went with her to her bank and got copies of her statements showing that Damien was sending her money and that she was putting cash in herself. I got her to give me photographs that had been taken when Damien had met her family. I figured we had a pretty good package, and we sent that in to the embassy. A month later Damien phoned me to say that the embassy had turned her down and that Ann had taken it badly.

I went around to her place in Soi 22 and found her in tears. She'd 'forgotten' to tell Damien that she'd made a previous application for a tourist visa with another Australian guy acting as a sponsor. That's a definite red flag so far as the embassy is concerned. It suggests that the girl isn't particular about who gets her into the country.

Ann wasn't just upset, she was as mad as hell. In true Thai style she said that Australia and everyone in it could go screw themselves. Frankly, as a New Zealander myself, I could sympathise with the sentiment. Anyway, she'd go back to work in Hollywood Strip and find herself a man from a country that would allow her to visit. And that was that. She finished with Damien, sold her business and went back to hooking, and over the next few months I saw her several times leaving Nana Plaza on the arm of one overweight German or another. I gather that Damien flew back to beg her to reconsider but that she refused point blank. He'd had his chance and he'd blown it. He kept calling me asking if I could help, but there was nothing I could do. I felt sorry for him, and for her. I think he loved her, and she was certainly prepared to give up the bar scene and work hard at a real job so that she could be with him. If it hadn't been for the embassy playing hardball, I really think they might have made it work.

Anyway, from then on she wouldn't even look at a guy from Australia, no matter how much money he had. I heard that she hooked a rich German and she now lives with him in Bonn in a huge house and is pregnant with her second child. All's well that ends well, I suppose. Except for Damien, of course. But hey, even a Thai private eye can't win them all.

THE CASE OF THE
BLACKMAILED BEAUTY

Klaus was a German, and I don't get too many German clients. Nothing to do with the war, it's just that for some reason Germans don't seem to have as many problems with bargirls as guys from other countries. I used to ask the girls why Germans never seemed to lose their hearts to the girls who dance around the silver poles. The general consensus seemed to be that Germans think with their heads. The Americans think with their hearts. And the Brits think with their dicks. When a tearful bargirl starts to tell a Brit or a Yank that her father is in hospital or her sister needs a new pair of shoes or the water buffalo has died, he gives her money. The German just shrugs and reaches for his beer. The Germans are more pragmatic, they understand that a bargirl has a history and deals with it. The Brits tend to believe every lie they're told. No, the girl doesn't have a husband. No, she doesn't have kids. No, she doesn't spend hours in an internet café talking to her sponsors around the world. So when Klaus phoned me up and said that he wanted to talk to me about a girl, alarm bells started ringing. I knew it wouldn't be a straightforward bargirl investigation.

He'd worked in Thailand for almost a decade, and that sent up a red flag too because most long-term expats are well aware of the

139

dangers of getting involved with a bargirl. And if they wanted to check out a bargirl's story they usually had plenty of friends who could do the job for them. I'd had a quiet week so I ignored my reservations and arranged to meet him at a Starbucks close to my office.

He was waiting for me at an outside table, smoking a cigarette with an espresso in front of him. He was in his early forties, balding, and looked as if he spent quite a bit of time in the gym. I ordered a white coffee and then joined him at his table. He started by giving me a potted life history. He'd lived in Berlin, married with two children, then divorced and moved to Thailand to start a new life. He'd built up a successful computer company, importing components from Europe, and now had offices in Germany, Hong Kong and Bangkok. He'd married again to a Thai woman, but happily admitted to a series of affairs. Nothing serious, more often than not just a matter of barfining a bargirl and taking her to a short-time hotel.

His life had ticked along perfectly until the time he flew down to Phuket to see about opening an office there. In one of the island's up-market pick-up joints he met Nut, the love of his life. She wasn't a bargirl but a law student, twenty-seven years old and drop dead gorgeous. She was bright, and according to Klaus was able to talk to him about everything. Economics. Politics. Literature. She was on vacation, footloose and fancy free. He had never met such a smart girl before and he was besotted. He started thinking about divorcing Wife Number Two and starting afresh with Nut. He persuaded her to go on holiday with him to Hong Kong, and on their return she said she had to go back to Rhamkamheng University to prepare for her final exams. Klaus was keen to play the white knight. He offered to give her a lump sum to cover all her expenses, and give her a laptop so that she could email him as he travelled around. Nut jumped at his offer of sponsorship. Klaus probably saw it differently, but in my experience young girls aren't attracted to rich middle-aged farangs because of their good looks, witty conversation or sparkling personalities. Nut said she stayed with her sister in Bangkok but that he could visit whenever he wanted. It was a done deal. Klaus gave her 60,000 baht for her first month's 'salary' and a brand new laptop.

After they returned to Bangkok, Klaus gave Nut a couple of days to settle in and then phoned her. There was no reply from her mobile and his emails went unanswered. Klaus was distraught. He was already planning to divorce his wife, he believed he had finally met the love of his life, and now she had disappeared. He'd phoned the apartment block where she stayed with her sister but someone there told him that she had moved out.

'I vant you to find her, Varren,' he said. 'Money no object.'

Ah. The three words that every private eye loves to hear. He was as good as his word and took out an envelope containing 50,000 baht. I spent half an hour with him getting as many details as I could and he gave me a photograph that he'd been carrying in his wallet. She was a pretty girl, all right. High cheekbones, rosebud mouth, long lashes.

My first port of call was the apartment block where Nut was supposed to be living with her sister. I was lucky, it was quite small, just a few floors above the offices of a cleaning company. All residents and visitors had to go in through the offices, which I reckoned was good news because the staff there would almost certainly be able to put names to faces.

Klaus had told me that Nut had spoken of a previous boyfriend, an English guy who'd returned to London a couple of years earlier. I adopted one of my regular personas—an embassy official. Most Thai girls would do anything to get a visa to the West so I walked into the office in a suit and tie and carrying a briefcase. There were two girls sitting at a reception desk and I told them that I was from the British Embassy. I told them that Nut had applied for a tourist visa and that we had some questions for her but we weren't getting a reply from her mobile. I spoke in English and gave them no indication that I spoke or understood Thai. When I finished my prepared speech, the two girls spoke to each other in rapid Thai. I just stood there smiling as one girl said that she thought Nut had moved out two days earlier and that she was now living in an apartment in Rhamkamheng 53.

'Shall we tell the farang?' said the other girl.

'I suppose so. He looks quite handsome doesn't he?'

The two girls looked at me and giggled. I kept what I hoped was an uncomprehending smile on my face.

'She move to Rhamkamheng,' said the girl who knew.

I feigned disappointment. 'That's a pity, I said. Do you know where?'

'Rhamkamheng 53,' said the girl.

'I think I have her mobile number,' said the other girl, in Thai.

I tried to show no reaction. 'Is there any way I could phone her, just to let her know about her application?' I asked.

The two girls exchanged a look, then they nodded together. 'I call her for you,' said the second girl. She took her mobile phone from her handbag, scrolled through her address book and called the number. She handed the phone to me with a smile. I put it to my ear. It was still ringing. I didn't know if it was the number that Klaus had been trying or if Nut had acquired a new SIM card, but a girl answered.

'Is that Khun Nut?' I asked.

'Yes,' said a voice, hesitantly.

I couldn't believe it. I'd barely been on the case for ten minutes and I was talking to the girl that I'd been paid 50,000 baht to track down. I explained that I was with the British Embassy and that I needed to speak to her about her visa application.

'I didn't apply for a visa,' she said.

'Your boyfriend did,' I said.

'He not my boyfriend anymore,' she said. 'I not want to go to England now.'

I could tell she was about to end the call so I started speaking quickly, assuring her that she could still have a visa even if he wasn't her boyfriend anymore and that I just needed to go over a few things with her.

'I busy with exams,' she said. 'I not want to go to England. Thank you.' She cut the connection.

The two girls were watching me so I couldn't show how frustrated I was. I just smiled and fiddled with the locks on my briefcase. I opened it and made a show of fumbling with some papers. What I was really trying to do was steal a look at the last number dialled. The phone was a Siemens and I was used to Nokias but I managed to call up the number and memorized it before handing the phone back to the girl. Outside, I checked the mobile number against the number that Klaus had given me. It was a different, which meant that either Nut had two phones or that she'd dumped the old SIM card.

I caught a taxi to Rhamkamheng 53 and wandered around. Finding Nut was going to be like nailing a needle in a haystack. There were at least fifty large apartment blocks lining the soi, mainly cheap places catering to the 50,000 or so students that attend the nearby Rhamkamheng University. It's rumoured to be the largest university in the world. I stopped off at the motorcycle taxi rank at the head of the soi and spoke to the guys there. They were dark skinned, Isaan boys all of them, so I spoke in Laotian, dropping in an obscenity every few words. I showed Nut's picture around but all I got was shaking heads. I offered a thousand baht to anyone who found her and that got their interest going, but as much as they wanted the money none of them remembered seeing her. I told them the thousand baht was a standing offer and handed out a few business cards, then I strolled over to the university campus.

I went to the registration office and went through my British Embassy speech again, that Miss Nut had applied for a visa to visit England and this age of terrorists and criminals we needed to do thorough background checks on all applicants. I gave the office manager Nut's full name and date of birth but after a few minutes on the computer she returned, shaking her head. There was no one of that name registered at the university.

That was interesting. It was the first lie that I'd caught her telling. And in my experience, where's there's one, there's many.

I went back to the office and phoned Klaus. He was relieved that I'd spoken to Nut. 'At least I know she's okay,' he said. 'I vas starting to think that maybe she had been in an accident.'

He didn't sound quite so cheerful when I pointed out that she'd lied to him about studying law at Rhamkamheng University. I gave him Nut's new mobile number.

Ten minutes later, Klaus called me back. He'd tried phoning the number but after it had rung a few times the phone had been switched off. He figured that she was refusing to take his call. 'I vant you to find her for me, Varren,' he said. 'I need to talk to her face to face.'

I told him that the next step would be to get a list of phone calls made to and from the two mobiles, and to get a friend of mine to crack Nut's email account. And that was going to cost more money. Fifty thousand baht in all. It was up to Klaus to decide if he wanted to pay the extra. I'd already shown that she'd lied about going to university, and she'd got herself a new phone number which suggested that she didn't want to speak to Klaus. My advice, if he'd asked for it, would be for him to cut his losses and either stick with his wife or look for a new love of his life. But he didn't ask, and he promised to send the 50,000 baht around by courier, so I kept my big trap shut. The client is always right. Even when he's wrong.

Once the money arrived, I got in touch with my phone contact. I gave him the two mobile phone numbers and he promised to get back to me with a list of calls and locations where she'd used the phone. Then I phoned my secret weapon, an American by the name of Pete who works for one of those shady American Government organisations that spend their time analysing phone and email traffic listening for words like 'bomb' and 'al-Qaeda' and 'assassination.' He was based in Washington and had access to some very heavy computing power and code crackers and he owes me a favour because a while back I did a check on his Thai girlfriend at the time and uncovered a husband upcountry and two daughters that she hadn't told him about. He had a Harvard degree and a doctorate from MIT and an IQ close to 200 but intelligence and common sense don't always go hand in hand. Anyway, he dumped the lying bargirl and promised me that any time he could help me he would. Not for free of course, but payments to Pete were money well spent. I gave him Nut's email address and Pete said he'd call me as soon as he had anything.

Pete got back to me two days later with the password for Nut's email account and some very interesting information. Somebody else was hacking into her account on a regular basis.

Most of the email traffic was from Klaus, and so I was pretty sure that it was the German who was monitoring her account. But when I told Klaus what was going on he insisted that it wasn't him. I called Pete again and asked him to see if he could find out who was hacking the account.

I started checking Nut's email to see if she was talking to other 'boyfriends' but there was no activity on the account. The emails that Klaus had sent after she disappeared went unanswered.

Pete got back to me with some worrying news. He had the email address and password of the guy who'd been monitoring Nut's email account. He'd had a quick look at the guy's account but backed off immediately when he saw the content of his emails. The guy worked at the American Embassy and from what Pete saw it was clear that he worked in law enforcement, either with the FBI or DEA.

Pete passed on the details and warned me to be careful. The guy's name was Miles Beattie. The account was his personal one but there was some business stuff in it, nothing classified but enough to show that Pete was right to be worried. There were emails from the FBI in Quantico requesting information on two possible drug dealers who were living in Chiang Mai, and responses from the DEA field office in Miami to questions that Beattie had been asking about a Thai family who had extensive property interests there. Among Beattie's personal emails were messages from a friend called Frank, including a promise to get together for a drink at a well-known go-go bar in Soi Cowboy. And there was one email from a guy in Texas which referred to a porno movie.

Like Pete, I was getting a bad feeling about this. American law enforcement officials working in Thailand tend to have high-level police and military connections, the sort of connections that could lead to an inquisitive private eye being locked up and the key thrown away. But I wanted to find out what was going on and that meant I had to go the bar to ask a few questions.

I went in on a midweek night before nine so that it wouldn't be too busy, ordered a Jack Daniel's and then looked around for an older bargirl, one who was past her best and had a chip on her shoulder. Someone who'd spill the beans on what was going on in exchange for a few drinks and the prospect of a bar fine. I found what I was looking for. She was in her early thirties, slightly chunky and with bad skin, the result of too little time in the sun and too long spent in smoky bars. I flashed her a smile and offered to buy her a drink. She looked surprised and pointed at her chest. 'Me?' she said.

'Sure,' I said.

She got herself a cola and then came over to sit next to me. Her name was Um and she was from Surin, so I chatted away in Khamen. I took it slowly, knocking back the JDs and buying her lots of colas. That's how she made her money. The bar paid her a commission on every drink I bought for her. She was a waitress and not a dancer so she didn't have to go with customers, but with so much young flesh on display I doubted that there'd be a rush to pay her bar fine. I gave her the impression that I might take her to a short-time hotel, stroked her leg and planted the occasional kiss on her cheek. She started to beam, probably planning how she was going to spend the thousand baht or so she thought I was going to give her. I persuaded her to start drinking Singha beer instead of the cola lady drinks, and waited until she'd knocked back a few before I raised the subject of Miles Beattie. Um knew him, and wasn't impressed. He was a friend of the owner, another American, and he tended to take young girls and mistreat them. Several had returned with bruises after going short-term with him. I asked her why the girls didn't just refuse to go with him. She smiled tightly and told me that Beattie had a lot of 'mafia' friends. That was the last thing I needed to hear. It was bad enough that Beattie was involved in law enforcement. Now I was being told that he was involved with criminals, too. If I crossed him, I could end up being caught between a rock and a hard place.

A few more drinks under her belt, and Um became even more talkative. She grabbed my arm and whispered conspiratorially, 'we no use short-time room, here, okay?'

I asked her why. She looked around as if worried that someone might be listening, then told me that the owners of the bar had rigged up a camera in the short-time room. 'They make DVDs, sell overseas.'

That came as a shock, all right. I'd heard rumours of short-time hotels having video cameras behind the mirrors, but this was a first. Most girls barfined from go-go bars take their customers to nearby hotels, but this bar had its own room upstairs where for a modest 200 baht the customer could get down and dirty with his temporary girlfriend. It was good news for the girls because they could be back dancing a few minutes after taking care of the customer, but clearly it was bad news for the customer if his nocturnal activities were going to be on sale for all and sundry to gawp at.

'We go hotel, okay?' pleaded Um. 'I give you good time.'

I bought her another beer and asked her to get me a Jack Daniel's. I was starting to get the picture. Beattie liked to be rough with his girls, and he was friends with a guy who was secretly recording sex sessions of his customers. And he was monitoring Nut's emails, which suggested that he had an interest in her. Either she was a girlfriend, former or otherwise, or he wanted something from her. Beattie would have seen the emails from Klaus and realised that the German wanted to marry Nut. Maybe he'd threatened her, with violence or blackmail.

Um brought me a fresh Jack Daniel's and I sipped it. I knew Nut was alive and well, but she was obviously hiding. But now it was starting to look as if it was Beattie she was hiding from, not Klaus.

I paid the bill and gave Um 1,000 baht as a tip. 'I still go with you,' she said. 'Free.'

I told her that I had a wife at home and that if I fooled around she'd cut off my private parts and throw them to the ducks. She laughed at that, told me that I was a good man with a good heart and kissed me on the cheek. I felt sorry for her. She was the sort of woman that Klaus should have fallen for. She was closer to his age and I was sure she'd be so grateful to any man who took her away from the bar scene that she'd be a loyal and faithful partner. But Klaus had fallen for a girl almost half his age and he was paying the price.

The lie about being a student at Rhamkamheng was still worrying me. I wanted to make absolutely sure that she wasn't there. One of

148

the problems with tracing people in Thailand is the language. The Thai alphabet has forty-four consonants and twenty-six vowels, so translating a name from Thai into English is fraught with problems. If I was just one letter out, a computer check might well show a negative. Nut was her nickname, the name that everyone knew her by, but her official name was much longer, six syllables in all. To be absolutely sure that I had Nut's official full name correct I'd have to go back to the municipal office in her home town. That was going to cost money, so I had to go and see Klaus to see if he wanted me to continue with the investigation or call it quits. I warned him that an American law enforcement official was checking Nut's emails so that he should refrain from emailing her or checking her account. He wanted to know who the guy was and I gave him the name but it didn't mean anything to him. I didn't say anything about the porno DVDs or the fact that Beattie liked to abuse his girls.

I explained that I'd have to go to municipal office in Surat Thani and gave me a further retainer and an advance on expenses. I flew down to Surat Thani. The officials in the municipal office were very helpful. They usually are when a farang turns up wearing a suit. The story I was using this time was that I was a lawyer representing a foreigner who had died leaving a considerable sum of money to Nut. I explained that I was having trouble finding the girl in Bangkok and showed them the name and address that I had been given. The young woman who was helping me tapped away on her computer terminal, then gave me a beaming smile. She told me that the reason I was having such a hard time locating Khun Nut was that she had recently changed her name by the Thai equivalent of a deed poll. Name-changing is common practice in Thailand, and it's relatively easy to obtain a new ID card and passport in a new name.

The girl wrote down the new name for me, and also a list of Nut's family members, including Nong, a young sister who had moved to Bangkok.

I was feeling pretty pleased with myself on the flight back to Bangkok. It wouldn't take me too long to track her down now that I had her new name.

My contact in the phone company had come through and there was a printout waiting for me in the fax machine when I reached home. I opened a bottle of Jack Daniels, flopped down onto the sofa and went through the printout. I knew most of the dialling codes by heart and I could see that the majority of the calls to Nut's mobile had come from Rhamkamheng, with a few from the Sathorn Road area. The printout also showed me the nearest transmitter to Nut's mobile at the time of each call.

Nut had only made a couple of dozen calls over the past month. Most were to a landline in Rhamkamheng. I phoned up my contact and asked him to get me an address for that number. He called me back within the hour. It was an apartment on Rhamkamheng Soi 53. I promised to send him another 5,000 baht.

The next day I went around to the apartment block with a bag full of Thai food for the office staff. That got them on my side right away, and they were more than happy to check if Nut was living there. Nut wasn't, but the younger sister was. The room wasn't rented in her name but as far as the staff were aware she lived there alone. Nong was in her early twenties so I assumed that she was a kept woman, possibly a minor wife, or mia noi. I didn't want to raise suspicions by pressing them for the name of whoever was paying her bills. Besides, it was Nut I was interested in, not Nong.

The staff hadn't asked what my interest was, but I could sense they were becoming increasingly nervous at my questioning. I decided that the best way was to go in hard. I told them that I was a policeman from Interpol investigating a serious crime involving pornography, and that while Nong probably wasn't involved, her sister almost certainly was. The staff phoned up to Nong's room and asked her to come down as there was a farang policeman who wanted to speak with her.

As soon as Nong stepped out the elevator I waved her over to a couple of sofas by the window. She was a pretty little thing, short hair and large, soulful eyes, and looked a good five years younger than her true age. I had no doubt that someone was paying her bills in exchange for sexual services. I kept a stern look on my face as I explained that I was a policeman with Interpol investigating pornographic material that was being sent to Europe. I told her that I believed that her sister Nut was involved, along with an American called Miles Beattie. I spoke to her in Thai and was quite aggressive because if at any time she demanded to see my ID it would be all over. By speaking quickly and forcefully I was able to keep her off balance. I told her that Nut had changed her name and address and I needed to know where to find her.

She kept shaking her head and said she knew nothing. I told her that I knew Nut had phoned her at home, and that she often phoned Nut. Then I told her that if she didn't talk to me I'd take her to Rhamkamheng Police Station for further questioning. I was really pushing my luck because she could see that I was there on my own and any moment she was going to start wondering why I wasn't accompanied by the local boys in brown. But like most Thais she feared authority and feared even more being held in police custody.

Close to tears, she admitted that her sister knew Charles Beattie but that's he didn't see him any more.

'He was a boyfriend?'

Nong nodded tearfully.

I asked her about Klaus. 'He help my sister. He bought her a laptop and gave her money. But she doesn't see him any more.'

'Why?' I asked.

151

'He very jealous. Ask my sister about other men all the time. Now she just want to be on her own so she can study.'

I asked her where Nut was living but she said that she didn't know. I didn't think she was lying. 'But she comes to see you, right?'

Nong nodded. She wiped her nose with the back of her hand. 'You real policeman?' she asked.

'Real enough to put you in prison,' I said harshly. I could see that she was starting to realise that it was unusual for a farang policeman to be operating in Thailand, and even more unusual for him to be working alone. I told her that I'd be back with more questions and left.

I figured that it wouldn't be long before Nong was on the phone to Nut. If I was lucky, Nut might phone Klaus to see if he knew what was going on. And even if she didn't, tracking Nong's phone records might give me Nut's new home number.

I phoned Klaus and arranged to meet him at Starbucks again. This time I got there first and I had an espresso waiting for him. He lit a cigarette and blew smoke as I ran through everything that I'd discovered. He looked hurt when I told him that Nut had changed her name, and I could see the anger burning in his eyes when I ran through what I'd found out about Miles Beattie. I told him what Nong had said about Klaus being jealous and he nodded with tight lips. 'Ve argued sometimes,' he said. 'There vere phone calls on her mobile in the middle of the night, times ven she disappeared for a few days. Said she was with her family and I guess I suspected the worse.'

'Even though you were supporting her? I guess you were annoyed.'

Klaus shrugged. 'I know the way these girls are. But I had hoped that Nut vas different.'

'What about the mobile? Did you call again?'

'I call her every day. Most times it's switched off. When it's on, she doesn't answer.'

'So what do you want me to do now?'

'I vont you to find her. I vont to talk to her.'

I sipped my latte. If I had a baht for every time I've heard that, I'd have enough money to barfine every hooker in Patpong. I don't know what it is about farangs and Thai girls. I've no doubt that if Klaus had met a German girl and she'd given him the runaround the way that Nut had, he'd have walked away without a moment's hesitation. He'd paid her a monthly salary, given her a place to live, promised to marry her, and in return she ran away and changed her name. If it was me, I'd have just cut my losses. But then I wouldn't have got into that situation in the first place. I've never seen the point in paying a woman to stay with you. If you're paying them, they're hookers. And why would any man want a hooker with him full-time. I know that Klaus wouldn't want to hear that his beloved Nut was a prostitute, but she was taking money to live with him and if the cap fits, wear it, as my old grandmother used to say.

Then I had a brainwave. 'How did you pay her?' I asked.

He frowned. 'Vot do you mean?'

'You were giving her a lot of money. Did you give it to her by bank transfer or did you give her cash?'

'Bank,' he said.

'Which bank?'

'Bangkok Bank. In Silom.'

I grinned. I had a very good Thai friend who had contacts in most of the local banks who would happily give me all the information I wanted. For the right price, of course. I explained to Klaus that I could probably come up with Nut's home address but it would mean 5,000 baht for my contact and another day's retainer for me. He had his wallet out before I'd even finished the sentence. Klaus had it bad.

Klaus gave me the bank account details and on the way back to the office I phoned my friend. I gave him the information and stopped off at an ATM to transfer five thousand baht into his account. I hadn't been back in the office for ten minutes when my mobile rang. Nut was living in the City Court apartment block on New Petchburi Road.

Game, set and match. Just as I was about to call Klaus with the good news, my phone rang. It was Klaus, and he was frantic. He'd just received a phone call from an American. The Yank didn't say who he was but told Klaus that if he didn't get out of Thailand he was a dead man. It could only have been Miles Beattie, and that opened up a whole can of worms. How had he found out about Klaus? And more importantly, did he know about yours truly?

I tried to calm him down. There was a good chance that he'd just found Klaus's number by checking Nut's phone records. It isn't difficult, providing you know the right person to pay tea money to. And as Beattie was in law enforcement, he'd know the right people. Klaus told me that his phone was on a contract which was bad news because Beattie would also have Klaus's address. I always use Pay-As-You-Go mobiles. And I change the SIM card every few months.

'Vot's going on, Varren?' he asked.

I told him that I now had an address for Nut.

'I must talk to her,' said Klaus. 'And I vont you to come with me.'

'Why?' I said.

'Protection,' he said.

I didn't like the sound of that. If Beattie's bite was as bad as his bark, who was going to protect me?

'I vill pay you twenty thousand baht,' he said. 'Just to go with me while I talk to her.' I said I'd see what I could do and that I'd call him back. I went back out to Petchburi Road and cased the

154

apartment block. It was ten floors high and looked like a typical low-rent building, probably all studio flats, room for a bed and a sofa and a tiny bathroom with a toilet and shower. I was pretty sure by now that if Klaus and I turned up and rang her bell Nut would refuse to see us. And I didn't think Klaus would want to be shouting through a locked door. And Klaus had already tried phoning.

I bought a carrier bag full of Chang Beer and walked over to the nearest group of motorcycle taxi drivers. There were half a dozen Isaan teenagers wearing orange vests playing checkers under a tattered beach umbrella and smoking Falling Rain cigarettes. I gave them the bag and showed them a photograph of Nut.

A couple of the guys recognized her and said that she usually left the building at eight o'clock in the morning and headed to a nearby bus station. As she wore a white shirt and black skirt band carrying a large shoulder bag, she was obviously on her way to university.

The next day, Klaus and I were outside the apartment block bright and early. I had an envelope containing 20,000 baht in my jacket pocket and a small can of mace in my trouser pocket, along with a brass knuckleduster that I usually had on my desk as a paperweight.

She walked out just after eight. Without make up and with her hair tied back, she didn't look especially pretty, but the white shirt was tight and showed of her firm, full breasts and the skirt was a good six inches above her knees and it was clear she had one hell of a figure. Even so, Thailand is full of beautiful women and if I were Klaus I would have cut my losses long ago.

She froze when she saw Klaus and for a moment I thought she was going to turn and bolt back into the apartment block but then her shoulders sagged and the fight went out of her. Klaus put a hand on her shoulder and told her earnestly that he loved her and wanted to take care of her and that he couldn't understand why she'd run away.

Nut listened, then shook her head. 'I'm sorry,' she said. 'I'm a bad girl.'

Her English was okay, good enough to talk to Klaus. He told her that he didn't care what she'd done in the past, that he could take her to Hong Kong or Germany, he didn't care if she had a boyfriend before. 'Ich liebe dich,' he said. 'I love you.'

She started to cry. Passers-by started to pay attention, wondering why two big farangs were bullying a poor little Thai student. If we weren't careful someone might call the police. Or decide to take matters into their own hands. I suggested that we adjourn to a nearby coffee shop.

While Klaus went to order our coffees, I spoke hurriedly to Nut in Thai. I told her that we knew that she was involved with Beattie and that he was involved in the production of pornographic DVDs. And I took a chance by saying that I knew he was blackmailing her.

She buried her head in her hands, sobbing. I was right.

'You have to tell us what happened,' I said. 'If you tell us, we can help you.'

'You can't help me,' she sobbed. 'He's a policeman. He works in the American Embassy.'

'He took you to the bar? To the upstairs room?'

She nodded and wiped her eyes. 'I said I wanted to see the bar and he took me. I didn't like it, but he gave me something to drink. I felt dizzy and the next thing I knew I was in bed with him.'

'And he filmed the two of you together?'

More nods. 'I didn't know what was happening at the time. But when I tried to stop seeing him, he sent me an email with some video. You couldn't see his face but you could see mine. He said if I didn't keep seeing him he'd send it to everyone I knew. And he said he'd send it to the university.' She looked at me fearfully. 'How could I ever be a lawyer, with people seeing something like that? If my father saw it, he'd kill me.'

'So what happened then?'

'I moved apartments. I changed my name. But he found me again. I had to see him. I had to do whatever he wanted.' She shivered, and stared down at the table. 'I have to do whatever he wants. Until he is tired of me.'

'And what about Klaus?'

She looked over at Klaus who was putting the coffees onto a tray. 'He is a good man. He wanted to take care of me.'

'Do you love him?'

Nut shook her head sadly. 'I just need someone to take care of me.'

'This American, he gives you money?'

Nut nodded. 'Some.'

'And does he make you do the videos?'

She nodded again. 'Sometimes. I have to go to the room with men. Sometimes two or three men at the same time. Afterwards, he pays me. He says they are only for sale in America and that no one else will ever see them.'

Klaus came over with the coffees. He put them down on the table and then went back to the counter.

'You have to tell him,' I said.

'I can't,' she said. 'Will you? I don't want him to keep bothering me.'

Klaus returned and sat down next to Nut. He put a hand on her arm but she flinched and sat with her arms crossed.

'Vot is the problem, theerak?' he asked.

'I have to go to university,' she said. 'I am late.'

'Ve need to talk,' said Klaus.

'Okay,' she said. 'I will phone you.'

Klaus gave her his business card. 'Phone me when your classes are finished this afternoon,' he said.

She nodded.

'Maybe we could have dinner tonight,' said Klaus.

'Okay,' she said.

'Whatever the problem, I can help you,' he said. 'I vont to take care of you.'

She forced a smile. 'You are a good man, Klaus. You have a good heart.'

'I love you, Nut,' he said.

'I love you, too,' she said. I could tell that she didn't mean it. But Klaus beamed, accepting what she'd said at face value.

'Everything's going to be all right,' he said. I knew that what he said was every bit as false as her declaration of love. The difference was that Klaus meant what he said. Which was a bit sad, really.

Nut stood up and walked away, clutching her bag. Klaus was smiling as he watched her go. He turned to grin at me. 'See, Varren,' he said. 'She does love me. This will work out.'

She never phoned, of course. The next day, Klaus went to the apartment block but she'd moved out of her room without leaving a forwarding address. Her mobile phone was switched off. He asked me to find out where she'd gone, but I told him there was no point in throwing good money after bad. I didn't tell him what Nut had said. There was no point. There was nothing Klaus could have done to help her.

Being a private eye in the real world isn't like it is in the movies: there aren't always happy endings. Sometimes you find out the truth but realise that knowing the truth doesn't help you one bit. Sometimes you just have to accept that the world can be a shitty place and get on with it.

THE CASE OF THE
VANISHING BEER BAR

L ike most private eyes, I get more than my fair share of missing person cases. Thailand is a big country with a population of sixty million or thereabouts, and there are about ten million in Bangkok alone. But finding farangs who have gone missing is usually a fairly easy proposition because they represent a small percentage of the population. And they stick out. Often I'd be contacted by worried parents who hadn't heard from their backpacking offspring for a few weeks. And more often than not said offspring would turn up on a beach somewhere stoned out of his or her mind living their own version of *The Beach*.

Finding missing Thais isn't quite as easy. And what Peter from New Zealand asked me to do sounded next to impossible. He'd been in Thailand on holiday and had spent a few days bar-hopping in Bangkok. He'd visited the usual haunts—Nana Plaza, Patpong, Soi Cowboy—and one night he'd visited a complex of beer bars at Sukhumvit Soi 10. He'd strolled from bar to bar and then found a girl that he really liked. Her name was Apple and she worked as a cashier in one of the bars. He'd offered to pay her bar fine but Apple had told him that she wasn't interested in 'short-times'. Peter had spent the rest of the night in the bar, talking to her as she worked and buying her colas, then when she knocked off for the night she went with him to his hotel. Peter didn't go into too much detail other than to say that it was the best night of sex that he'd ever had and that he realised there and then that Apple was the girl that he wanted to spend the rest of his life with.

He opened his heart to Apple, but she was sceptical. She saw hundreds of farangs pass through her beer bar, and knew that more often than not they were butterflies, flitting from girl to girl. She wasn't working in the bar because she wanted a boyfriend, or because she enjoyed the job. She worked because she had to support her family upcountry. Peter was determined to show Apple that he was serious about her so he arranged to see her the next evening. She agreed to speak to her boss so that she could finish work early, and they could go and have dinner and talk.

Peter was over the moon. He went to a jewellery shop and bought an engagement ring which he planned to give her that night. He booked a table at a good restaurant, went for a haircut, and withdrew a stack of cash on his credit cards. The wind went out of his sails when he turned up at Sukhumvit Soi 10 that evening. The entire complex of bar beers had gone. It had been razed to the ground. A wire fence had been erected around the whole area warning people to keep out. At first Peter thought he'd gone to the wrong place. He looked around, scratching his head, but gradually realised that he was where he should be. The Ambassador Hotel was opposite, the Sky Train roared by overhead. But the bars had gone. Every one of them. Peter was distraught. All he knew of Apple was her name. She didn't have a mobile phone, and when he'd asked her where she lived the name of her road seemed to have a dozen syllables.

He spent the night on his own in his hotel hoping that Apple would contact him, but his phone never rang. He went to the airport the next day, flew back to New Zealand and emailed me. I knew what had happened to the beer bars. The owner of the land—who also happened to own a big chunk of the city's massage parlours—had decided that he could make more money by developing the site than renting it out to bar owners. Rather than waste his valuable time negotiating with the dozens of tenants, the landlord decided to send in bulldozers at dawn instead.

I told Peter that I might be looking for a needle in a haystack. If he'd had her full Thai name it would have been easier, but her one syllable nickname was all he had. Thais often have several nicknames, one for their family, one for their friends and another for work. There was every chance that Apple was only known as Apple at the bar. Peter was adamant that he wanted me to try so he wired over a retainer and I got to work.

Peter was able to tell me the approximate location of Apple's bar, so my first stop was at Lumpini Police Station, which had responsibility for the Sukhumvit Soi 10 complex. I got there just after nine o'clock in the morning and found fifty irate Thai businessmen and women, all of them owners of various businesses in the flattened complex. One of them had a plan of the area and from Peter's description I was able to figure out that Apple worked in the Mai Pen Rai Bar. The It Doesn't Matter Bar, in English.

I chatted to the tenants, all of whom were livid at the way their livelihoods had been taken away from them. Sadly, that's the way it is in Thailand. The rich assume that they have the Buddha-given right to ride roughshod over the poor. And the quality of justice you get in the courts often has as much to do with your wealth as it does with the quality of your case. They were talking about mounting a media campaign, and hiring a top legal firm to represent them. But it was clear that they had an uphill struggle ahead of them. And even if they were successful in the courts, their businesses were still gone for ever. A fair number of the beer bars had been owned by farangs and I asked why there were no farangs at the police station. The consensus seemed to be that the farangs didn't get up before noon. I figured that the farang tenants had realised that their chances of getting their money back was close to zero and they had simply given up.

I managed to find one chap who told me that the Mai Pen Rai Bar had been owned by a Taiwanese guy and that his Thai girlfriend had run the bar. No one seemed to know his name, or hers.

The investigating officer was having a hard time. The tenants were hounding him, and newspaper and television journalists were yelling questions at him whenever he appeared from his office. I hung around until midday by which time most of the tenants and journalists had drifted away to eat. I used my very best Thai and a bag of freshly cut pineapple to persuade his assistant to allow me a few minutes of her boss's time. He was an affable fifty-year-old, and became even more affable after I slipped him a 1,000-baht note (for the widows and orphans fund, naturally) and asked him if he could get me a phone number for the Taiwanese owner of the Mai Pen Rai Bar. I told him that I'd left a bag in the guy's care, figuring that would get me more sympathy than a lovelorn farang on the hunt for a bargirl. He pocketed the banknote (on behalf of the widows and orphans, naturally) and told me to call him back the next day.

He was as good as his word, and the following afternoon I was on the phone to Lek, the Taiwanese guy's girlfriend. Lek was fairly sure that she knew who Apple was but told me that all the girls were casual labour, pretty much free to come and go as they pleased. The bar kept no records, and all the staff were paid in cash. Lek only had phone numbers for a few of the girls and Apple wasn't one of them. According to Lek, a lot of the Soi 10 girls had gone to work at Soi Zero and Soi Asoke.

I did the rounds of Soi Zero. It was never one of my favourite places, it has to be said. Despite the attempts of various bar owners to put some life into the place, it remained a dingy, dirty unattractive area under a busy freeway and the only people who made any money out of the area were the Thai middlemen who bought and sold the bars, usually to farang tourists who had been talked into buying a lease for their bargirl friend in an attempt to get her to go straight. Anyway, after half a dozen JDs I'd only managed to find two girls who'd worked in Soi 10, but neither had worked at the Mai Pen Rai Bar and neither remembered a girl called Apple.

The following night I headed for Soi Asoke, a rough and ready collection of beer bars that was itself demolished a year or so after Soi 10 bit the dust. Soi Asoke was as soulless a place as Soi Zero. I quite enjoy the buzz of Soi Cowboy and Nana Plaza, with their go-go bars and shows and endless supply of beautiful dancers. The beer bars at Soi Asoke were short on pretty girls, and most of them were freelancers. The bars didn't pay them a wage, they sometimes earned a small commission on drinks that farangs bought for them but the bulk of their money was earned on their backs. As a result the girls were pushier and every girl I spoke to did her utmost to persuade me to take them short time, long time, any time.

Eventually I found a bar where two former Mai Pen Rai girls worked. That was the good news. The bad news was that neither were there that night. One had just gone off with a customer, the other hadn't been seen for a couple of days. I came back the next day, but the girls were still AWOL. The next day I struck gold and found Top, who remembered Apple and who had the mobile phone number for a friend of Apple's. I phoned the friend who told me that Apple had left Bangkok and gone back to stay with her parents in Udon. The friend didn't know the address, or Apple's full name, and trying to track down a girl called Apple in a city as big as Udon really would be needle in a haystack time. I offered the friend 1,000 baht if she could get me Apple's full Thai name and she said she'd ask around. She phoned me back the next day and told me that she had the name but that she wanted the 1,000 baht first. Clever girl. She lived in Soi 101 so we arranged to meet at Onut Skytrain station. I waited on the train side of the barrier so that I didn't have to pay for the journey until Apple's friend appeared. It was like handing over a ransom demand. She had the name written on a piece of paper and she wouldn't pass it over the barrier until I'd given her the money. She grinned once she had the cash, gave me a pretty wai and handed me the piece of paper. Apple's full name was Miss Areerat Phromcharoen. And Apple's friend had also come up with her date of birth as an added bonus. Tracking down Apple had moved from being an outside chance to a dead cert.

I emailed Peter and told him that I was on the case, but that if I was going to find Apple I'd have to go up to Udon. Absence had truly made the heart grow fonder and Peter promised to wire me another three-day retainer and enough money to pay for a plane ticket to Udon and a night in a reasonable hotel.

I caught a motorcycle taxi to the Pathumwan District office and found my friendly computer worker. I gave her the piece of paper and a 500-baht note and my winning smile. Fortunately, much of Ubon Ratchathani's data was linked to the main network so she could call up all Apple's info on her computer screen. Within seconds I had Apple's place of birth and the sub district where the family home was. It was a big step forward, but to get the exact address I'd have to pay a visit to the district office.

I bought a ticket to Udon and hired a taxi driver from the airport to the district office. Another 500 baht and the taxi driver and I were on our way to Apple's house. It was in a tiny, dusty village in the middle of nowhere, just a couple of handfuls of wooden shacks. Apple was at home, and amazed to have a strange farang turn up on her doorstep.

Her mum was there and so was a younger brother so to save her any embarrassment I said that I was a reporter for the *Bangkok Post* writing a story about people who had lost their jobs as a result of the trashing of the Soi 10 complex.

While her mum went off to fetch me some food, I gave the young lad 100 baht and asked him to go and buy a Coke. While we were alone I quickly explained the real reason for my visit; that Peter wanted to see her again. Apple sighed and said that yes she remembered Peter but that she had a big problem.

I said that Peter really liked her and hat I was sure that he'd be able to help her.

Apple started to get a bit tearful then. Her father had a gambling problem and had run up debts of almost 50,000 baht, a small fortune for a rural Thai. That was why she'd gone to Bangkok in the first place, to earn enough to pay off her father's debts. The man who her father owed the money to had an obnoxious and overweight son who fancied Apple and if the debt wasn't paid off quickly the man wanted Apple to marry the boy with the 50,000-baht written off as the sin sot, or dowry. Apple's father was happy enough to accept the deal, but Apple herself was horrified at the idea. I could practically see the wheels turning behind her eyes as she realised that Peter was a much better option.

I checked my cell phone and was pleasantly surprised to find that I was actually getting a weak signal. I wouldn't normally call overseas on a cell phone but the expense would be down to Peter so I rang him and explained that I had found the elusive Miss Apple. I ran the situation by him and gave the phone to Apple.

To be honest, if it was down to me you wouldn't have seen me for dust. Gambling is an addiction and even if Peter paid off the father's debts, there'd be more down the line. Apple was a nice enough girl and I wouldn't have kicked her out of bed, but she was a poorly educated farm girl and I couldn't see that she'd have much in common with Peter. They'd spent only a few hours together and while I was sure the sex had been good, there's a world of difference between a night of steamy sex and a lifetime of companionship.

Tears were welling up in Apple's eyes and she started telling Peter how much she loved him and missed him. 'I have you, only one,' she said. 'I want you help me and my family.'

They spoke for a while and then Apple handed the phone back to me. Peter said that he'd agreed to give her 50,000 baht to pay off the debt and that he'd send her another 20,000 baht a month until he came back to Thailand. He was hooked. I figured he was throwing his money away. Thailand is full of pretty girls, girls with university degrees and good jobs and respectable parents who don't run up gambling debts with local shylocks. He thought he was helping Apple, riding to her rescue like a white knight. But I thought that he was buying her affection and that he'd only have her so long as he continued to hand over cash. But Peter was old enough to make his own decisions and who was I to rain on his parade?

THE CASE OF THE
CHINESE CLIENT

I get a lot of business through the internet, so it isn't unusual for work to come my way through emails. More often than not it's a tourist who has gone home and is having second thoughts about the fidelity of his new girlfriend. But the email that arrived from 'Charles' was different from the average internet inquiry.

For a start, the client didn't give his full name, or supply an address or telephone number where I could contact him. I ran a check on the ISP address and found that he was in Shanghai, so I figured that he was an expat up in China. Anyway, Charles wanted me to keep tags on two rotund Englishmen who would shortly be arriving in Bangkok. They would be staying at the Landmark and were conducting banking seminars during the day. They were both fans of Playskool Bar at Nana Plaza, which was just around the corner from the hotel. Playskool was always one of my favourites, what with the staff dressing up in sexy school uniforms and having some of the prettiest girls in the plaza. Charles wanted to know how much it would cost for me to keep an eye on the two guys and I told him. Two days later and the money had been transferred into my bank account so I stopped worrying too much about who my client was. Charles also emailed me head-and-shoulder photographs of the two men and promised me a big bonus if I could get a photograph of the bigger of the two guys leaving with a lady of the night.

On the day the two men arrived in Bangkok, I went around to the hotel. I did a quick walk through of the bars and restaurants but there was no sign of the two men. I waited until reception was busy then wandered over and asked to speak to Andrew, the one that Charles was particularly interested in. The harried girl behind the reception desk looked at her computer screen, tapped out a number and handed me the phone. Andrew had a typical upper class plum-in-his-mouth English accent and sounded like he'd been asleep. I switched into my very best Antipodean accent. 'Howyagoing Cobber, ready to go sink a few tinnies then are ya?'

I got a very polite 'I beg your pardon' from Andrew before I apologised and put the phone down. Now that I knew he was in his room, all I had to do was sit in the lobby and watch the lifts. Turned out to be a wasted evening. By midnight he hadn't appeared so I figured he'd decided to have a night in. He might well have phoned an escort agency for a takeaway but even if that was the case I wouldn't be able to get a picture, and without a picture there wouldn't be a bonus.

The next night, I checked the hotel again at 7pm and this time Andrew wasn't in his room. I checked the bars and restaurants in the hotel and drew a blank, so it seemed fair to assume that the boys were out on the prowl.

I hit Playskool at 8pm, parked myself in a seat at the back and ordered a Jack Daniels. A pretty little thing from Sisaket was soon sitting by my side, massaging my thigh and telling me how handsome I was. After another couple of JDs I was starting to believe her. I'd bought her half a dozen lady drinks by the time a fat, balding man waddled in. It was Andrew. He was greeted like a long-lost friend by the elderly mamasan and ushered to a front-row seat where he could get an eyeful of the girls on offer. It wasn't long before he had a girl either side and he was buying ladies drinks like there was no tomorrow. I kept buying drinks for myself and my new best friend from Sisaket until Andrew called for his bill. I did the same. I gave Miss Sisaket a big tip and got her phone number, then followed Andrew outside. I had my digital camera with me and was hoping to get a few shots to send to Charles.

I overtook him on the way out and got myself a vantage point in the Nana Hotel car park when he came out. He'd paid barfine for the two girls which got me thinking that perhaps I'd be able to talk Charles into giving me a double bonus. My luck was in. There was an elephant at the Nana Plaza exit and its mahouts were trying to extract cash from the drunken tourists in return for the opportunity to feed a few green bananas to the beast. The authorities don't like elephants wandering around the city streets. Every now and then one puts a foot through a drain and the traffic gets backed up for miles. Part of the problem is that the old work that the elephants used to do upcountry had now been replaced by machines, so the mahouts don't have any choice other than to beg.

I made it look as if I was snapping away at the elephant but in fact managed to get several good shots of Andrew and his two hookers. He waddled over to the Nana Disco with the two girls.

I went home, satisfied that I'd earned my fee and bonus. Early next morning I went back to the hotel, hoping to catch Andrew and his two bargirls having breakfast. The two chubby bankers were sitting at a table, devouring plates piled high with a food. As I watched them my heart sank. Sitting in Playskool I'd been sure that it was Andrew who'd walked in. But now that I saw the two Poms together, I realised that I'd had the wrong man. The guy I'd followed and photographed was Andrew's colleague. Andrew was bigger and balder and about five years older. The whole surveillance operation had been a waste of time. Other than the fact that I'd got Miss Sisaket's phone number, of course.

I sent the pictures off to Charles, along with a brief report and a note that Andrew had stayed in the hotel. Not strictly true, of course, but I didn't want to admit that I'd been tailing the wrong guy. Charles took it better than I expected and said that he'd be in touch next time Andrew was back in Bangkok.

I thought that would be the end of it, but three months later I got another email from Charles. Andrew was heading back to Bangkok for a couple of days and would be staying at the Landmark again. The bonus was still on offer—all I needed was a photograph of Andrew with a bargirl. I accepted the job and Charles put the money in my bank account, and emailed me with Andrew's flight details.

According to Charles, Andrew had an afternoon meeting so I left it until early evening before I went to the hotel. I spotted him in the Huntsman studying a menu, and figured that he'd be there for a while. It looked as if he was eating alone and I started to have visions of my bonus slipping away again, so I decided that maybe I could short-circuit the process by supplying my own temptation.

I took the footbridge over Sukhumvit, ignoring the family of Cambodian beggars who had set up there, and headed for one of my favourite watering holes, the German bar in Soi 7. It's a well-known pick-up joint, packed with freelancers on the make. There are a lot of over-the-hill hookers and go-go girls who've failed their medical, but there are pearls among the dross and one of the pearls was Gay. I worked my way through the growing evening crowd and spotted Gay sitting between two large Australian tourists. I caught her eye and signalled for her to meet me outside.

Gay was in her early twenties with shampoo commercial hair and great breasts courtesy of one of Bangkok's best plastic surgeons. She had at least two sponsors that I was aware of who both sent her a fair whack every month, and one was trying to get her a visa to visit the UK. She had no plans to visit the UK, though, the guy was going to be disappointed. She had a young son upcountry and was saving to build her own house. She spoke good English. She told the punters that she'd learned English at university, but the truth was that she'd been hooking for more than seven years and had picked it up from the hundreds of guys she'd slept with. I'd used Gay on a few jobs, and I knew she'd be perfect for Andrew. I told her what I wanted, and promised her 1,000 baht plus whatever Andrew gave her. Ten minutes later we were walking into the Huntsman. I made sure we were seated at the table next to Andrew and that he could get a clear view of Gay and her very impressive breasts. I ordered a JD for me and her usual Black Label and soda, and chatted away in Thai for fifteen minutes or so, pretending not to notice the occasional smile that passed between Gay and the Englishman behind me. After I'd finished my drink I said goodbye to Gay and promised to phone her, then left her to it.

While Gay went to work on Andrew, I adjourned to a nearby Pizza Hut. I'd told Gay to get Andrew to buy her dinner and then suggest that they retire to his hotel room. When they were on their way, she was to send me a text, so I was able to relax, order a medium pepperoni pizza and flirt with one of the cute waitresses. By the time Gay sent me the text I had polished off the pizza and had the waitress's phone number. I was back in the lobby by the time Gay and Andrew were heading for the lifts. I got several good pictures with the zoom lens of them walking arm in arm, which I figured would make Charles a very happy bunny.

I went back to the Pizza Hut for dessert and bit more flirting, and an hour later I got another text from Gay saying that the dirty deed had been done. I met her in the hotel lobby. Andrew had given her 3,000 baht so she was well pleased, especially because he'd wanted nothing more than a blowjob. It had been easy money and there was plenty of time to get back to the German bar to reel in another punter.

I asked her what sort of guy he was and she said he was a gentleman. He loved Thailand and would love to live here, but he had a good job in Shanghai. He'd told her that he didn't enjoy working with Chinese people and that some of his colleagues were always trying to get him sacked. There was one woman, Char-lee, who really hated him and who made his life a misery. 'He said he was very happy to meet me because I helped him to forget about her,' said Gay.

Alarm bells started to ring. Char-lee? Charlie? Charles? I started to wonder if my mysterious client was Andrew's colleague. Suddenly it started to make sense. If the Chinese colleague got hold of a photograph of Andrew in a compromising position, she could do him a lot of damage. She could have sent it anonymously to the board and it wouldn't be long before Andrew was told that his services were no longer required. Or maybe she'd decide that a little blackmail would be more profitable. I wasn't happy about being part of whatever her devious plan was, but on the other hand I didn't want to lose the bonus that I'd be promised. What's a private eye to do?

Now, not all investigators have the same high moral standards as yours truly. It's not unknown for a less-than-professional private eye in Thailand to approach the subject of his investigation and, for a higher fee, agree to file a false report. It wasn't something that I was in the habit of doing, but I didn't like the way that Charles had been using me. He (or she) had been less than honest, so I didn't think that he (or she) deserved any less from me. Andrew was just being one of the lads and I wasn't happy about being the architect of his downfall. So, the next morning I went over to the hotel in time for breakfast. I saw Andrew attacking the buffet and I waited until he'd sat down before I headed over to his table with a cup of coffee. He didn't look happy as I sat down at his table, but I went quickly into my speech. I explained that I'd been paid to follow him, and that I had compromising photographs of him. I told him about my mysterious client in Shanghai, and that I had become uneasy about what I was being asked to do. For all I knew the girl he'd taken to his room the previous night could have been a client, I said, even though we both knew exactly what he'd been doing. I said that I didn't want to lose the bonus I'd been promised if I emailed the pictures to my client, but perhaps there was another option. A small token of Andrew's appreciation, perhaps, and I could tell the client that Andrew had been whiter than white. I smiled and waited for his reaction. To be honest, I had nothing to lose. If he told me to go and screw myself, I'd just send the pictures and report to Shanghai and pocket my bonus. He stared at me for a while, then nodded and pulled out his wallet. He took out a wad of American dollars, peeled off a few 100-dollar notes and handed them to me.

'Cash,' I said. 'That'll do nicely.'

I pocketed my retainer, wished him a safe trip home, and left him to his breakfast, picking up a sausage from the buffet on my way out.

Later that day I sent an email to Shanghai Charles. I said that Andrew did little more than eat in the hotel restaurants and visit the Huntsman Bar in the basement. He never even had a sniff of a bargirl. I had no misgivings about telling a little white lie. Andrew was a decent enough guy and I had double the bonus that had been promised, so I reckoned justice had been done. Justice à la Thai private eye.

THE CASE OF THE
HUA HIN HUSBANDS

They say that all good things come in threes: the Three Degrees, the Three Stooges, the three very attractive young women that spent ninety minutes making my every sexual fantasy come true in one of the upstairs rooms at the Eden Club in Soi 7. I love things that come in threes, especially three cases in the same place because then I can swing three sets of expenses for a single trip. I figure it's a perfectly reasonable arrangement. If I have to go and do an overnighter then it's only fair that the client pays for the hotel, my meals and my transport. The client would be paying the same no matter how many cases I was working on. It's not like I'm being dishonest by billing them all for the same expenses, it's more that I'm taking advantage of an advantageous situation, and hand on heart I don't think there's anything wrong with that.

Anyway, I was on my way to Hua Hin with a song in my heart and three sets of retainers in the bank, all from women as it happens. When I first got into the private-eye game it was almost always girls I was checking up on, and bargirls at that. But as my fame spread, I started to get a fair number of female clients, usually farang women who wanted me to prove that their husbands or boyfriends were straying. Generally it was money for old rope. There are two

175

golden rules about relationships in Thailand: bargirls always lie, and farang men sleep around. They just do. It's instinct. The scorpion thing. And generally it's easier to do a check on a farang man than it is to follow a Thai bargirl. The guy will almost certainly stick to one of the farang areas—Sukhumvit Road, Silom Road, Pattaya or Phuket. He'll probably be staying in a hotel full of tourists or in a condominium building used by farangs so if I'm tailing him, I'm not going to stick out like the proverbial thumb. But bargirls tend to live in predominantly Thai areas where farangs are few and far between and a hell of a lot more visible.

I like Hua Hin. It's a seaside resort, but it's a lot less scummy than Pattaya. The sea's cleaner, for a start, and there's a better class of tourist. Families go there, mainly, and retired couples. It's where the Thai Royal Family likes to holiday so the police in Hua Hin keep a tight grip on the nightlife side and there are no go-go bars or soapy massage parlours. There are plenty of beer bars, and more hookers than you can shake a stick at, but it's nowhere as in your face as Pattaya or Phuket's Patong beach.

I drove down in a rented Toyota and booked into a room with a sea view at the Hilton. Lovely.

My first case was Bob from Seattle, a frequent visitor to the Land of Smiles. Too frequent, according to his wife, who had decided to divorce him and felt that there would be a certain irony in having the divorce papers served on him while he was in Thailand. I had a quick shower, downed a couple of JDs from the minibar, then wandered down to the hotel where Bob was staying. The wife had emailed me a picture of her husband so I knew who I was looking for. I got myself a corner booth in the hotel coffee shop and settled down with a copy of the *Bangkok Post*.

I was lucky and I had only started on my second cup of coffee when in walked the man himself, with an obvious bargirl in tow.

By obvious I mean that she was wearing tight blue jeans, a low-cut black T-shirt, and had a tattoo of a scorpion on her right shoulder. Elementary, my dear Watson!

Bob looked bored and the girl had the sultry pout that bargirls adopt when things aren't going their way. They sat down in the booth next to mine and I flashed her one of my winning smiles. '*Falang kee-neo chai mai?*' I said.

'*Nan-non loei*,' she sighed, confirming that old Bob was indeed a Cheap Charlie.

Bob was so impressed to hear a foreigner speak Thai that he introduced himself and asked if they could join me. He was keen to chat and I guessed he'd been stuck with the sour-faced hooker for a while. The girl started to play footsie with me under the table, which was nice. She slipped off her high heels and massaged the back of my legs with her toes, all the time keeping a butter-wouldn't-melt look on her face. It seemed that they were both bored stiff with each other.

Bob told me his life story, pretty much, most of which I'd already got second-hand from the wife. He liked Thailand, he said, and was thinking about moving permanently to the Land of Smiles. The problem was, he didn't know what sort of work he'd be able to do, as work permits are as rare as hen's teeth in Thailand. Any job that can be done by a Thai, no matter how badly the Thai does it, can't be given to a foreigner. So other than running a bar or teaching English, there aren't too many career opportunities.

Bob asked me what I did for a living. 'Well, Bob,' I said, 'I'm a private investigator.'

'Must be an exciting line of work,' he said.

I shrugged and took the envelope of legal papers from my jacket pocket. 'Actually, Bob, it's pretty boring most of the time,' I said. 'Just mundane tasks, like serving summons.' I dropped the envelope on the table in front of him. 'By the way, this is yours.'

He said thanks, not realising that I was serious.

As I stood up he shook my hand, and again I don't think it had quite sunk in. I clapped him on the back. 'The wife says the next time you'll see her, it'll be in court,' I said. His jaw dropped and I could see that the message had got home. I heard the envelope being ripped open as I walked away and a low groan as he started to read the contents.

I headed back to the hotel, feeling pretty good with myself. I'd only been in town for an hour and I'd already earned a day's money and covered the cost of my room, the car, two JDs and two coffees.

The second case was a missing person, sort of. A New Yorker called Ann phoned me to ask if I'd track down her husband, Joe, who'd gone missing in Thailand. He'd been at a body-building competition in Australia and had broken his flight in the Land of Smiles with a couple of buddies. The last phone call she'd had from Joe was two weeks earlier and he had said that he was in Hua Hin and that he was drinking in a bar owned by a guy called Kim, and wasn't sure when he'd be back in the States. If I could find Kim, she said, she was sure I'd be able to find Joe. Now, there's a pretty big farang population in Hua Hin. Not as many as in Pattaya, but still enough to make it a needle-in-a-haystack job without more definite information. She emailed me photographs of Joe. He was an amateur bodybuilder, a stocky, balding guy in his late twenties who couldn't have been much more than five foot tall.

I did a quick trip around the bars that were open for the afternoon trade but no one knew of an owner called Kim. I figured I'd have more joy later at night but then I had a brainwave and phoned Ann. It was about one o'clock in the morning in New York and I'd obviously woken her up and the fact that it was a collect call did seem to annoy her somewhat, but she was able to answer my question—which flight did Joe travel to Thailand on? It was Japan Airlines. Flight JAL 006, two weeks ago on Tuesday.

I phoned the airline and told the girl who answered that I was
the boss of a tour company based in Bangkok and that I'd lost track
of a client that I'd taken to Hua Hin. Had my client by any chance
phoned in to reconfirm his ticket? I gave her Joe's full name and the
details of his flight to Bangkok.

Indeed the ticked had been reconfirmed. By a travel agency in
Hua Hin. And Joe had also changed his ticket to an open booking,
with no flight home. The travel agency wasn't far from the Hilton
so I had a plate of fried noodles and an ice cold Heineken at a street
stall and wandered over. The agency was a tiny shop wedged between
two bars, both of which had a quartet of fairly attractive girls who all
declared that I was a 'handsum man' and that I should spend some
of my time—and money—with them. I resisted the calls of the sultry
sirens and went inside the travel agency.

There was only one girl working in the office, so I played the
stupid farang and said that I was a friend of Joe's and that we were
driving back to Bangkok together but that I'd forgotten what hotel
he was staying at. She checked her computer and gave me the name
and address of his hotel. It was called Kim's Hotel, which I figured
was a good sign.

Kim's Hotel wasn't as prestigious as the Hilton and it didn't have
a sea view but it did have a decent-sized pool and I guessed that was
where a diminutive body builder might spend his afternoons. I was
right. Standing by the diving board was the man himself, wearing
nothing but a black thong, flexing his muscles in front of two teenage
girls. I watched his show as he went through a full work out, his
oiled muscles glistening under the afternoon sun. The two girls
were giggling and kept offering him a two-for-one special, staring at
2,000 baht but dropping to half that pretty quickly. Joe just laughed
and said that he wasn't up for an afternooner but that he'd catch

up with them later.

After about half an hour, Joe finished his workout and showered at the poolside shower. In view of the nature of the case, I didn't think there would be any harm in being up front with the New Yorker. I waited until he had towelled himself dry before going over and introducing myself. I told him that I was a private eye and that his wife had paid me to track him down and to find out why he hadn't gone home.

Joe grinned and nodded at the two sexy girls. 'That's why,' he said.

We went over to a table and sat under a large umbrella and drank beers as Joe gave me his side of the story. I had a Heineken, Joe had a Charng Beer. Another sign of the newbie, that, drinking the local beer. He might as well have had a neon sign over his head flashing 'I've just got off the plane'. Pretty much the only Thais who drank Charng were construction workers. Anyway, Joe told me that he didn't love Ann. He wasn't even sure why he'd married her. In New York, his lack of height and hair meant that he didn't have much luck with women. Ann was pretty much the only woman who'd expressed any interest in him, and it had been her idea to get married. She wasn't pretty and she wasn't especially bright, but Joe had said yes because being married to her was better than being on his own. Then he'd come to Thailand and suddenly short, balding Joe was a 'handsum man'. Within the space of his first week in Thailand he'd had more sex than he'd had in his whole life in the States. And he wasn't sleeping with dogs either. Every girl he'd bedded had been drop-dead gorgeous, he boasted. And the supply of beautiful girls waiting to have sex with him seemed to be never-ending. Joe was like a kid in a sweetshop, a pig in shit, and all those other clichés. And the way he told it, he was NEVER going back to the United States. He'd already met a couple of body-builders who ran a gym in Bangkok and they had offered him a job. Joe had never really wanted to be an accountant, he'd never loved Ann, and had never enjoyed living in New York. He was taking control of his life, Joe told me. He was starting again in Thailand.

He was, in my humble opinion, making a huge mistake. Like a lot of newbies, he was starting to believe his own publicity. Joe wasn't a 'handsum man', he was just a short, balding, thick-necked Yank with more money than sense. The girls weren't flocking to him because of his muscles or his personality, it was because he had money and they wanted it. They were bargirls, their job was to make punters feel good so that they would hand over their money. The smiles, the kisses, the sex, were all part of the act. But newbies like Joe sometimes forgot that it was all about money and started to believe that they were somehow more attractive and desirable than they were back home. And providing that he continued to shell out the bucks, they'd continue to live out their fantasy. But as soon as they stopped paying, the girls would stop playing, and reality would hit home. If often hit hard, too, and there are probably hundreds of farang suicides every year in the Land of Smiles, as guys like Joe realised that their fantasy lives were just that—fantasies. And once a guy has got used to being surrounded by attentive, beautiful women who behave like submissive pornstars between the sheets, it was hard, maybe impossible, to go back to the real world.

I always say that when a newbie first starts to hang out with Thai bargirls, the newbie has the money and the bargirls have the experience. At the end of it, the bargirls have the money and the newbie has had the experience.

Anyway, Ann wasn't paying me to burst Joe's bubble. She just wanted to know where he was and what he was doing. Now I could tell her, it was up to her what she did next. I got Joe to promise me that he'd phone or email his wife. It seemed the least he could do, under the circumstances.

Case number three was an American woman living in Japan, whose husband Gary was a marine who seemed to be spending more than his fair share of shore leave in Hua Hin. After a little do-it-yourself snooping Carol had discovered a couple of email addresses, one of them belonging to a girl called Mem, Thai phone numbers and a photograph of a pretty young thing working in an opticians store. Carol had also found a bank account number in Hua Hin with details of a 5,000-dollar transfer and had jumped to the obvious conclusion. She told me that she was a reasonable woman and wanted to make absolutely certain that her husband was fooling around. What she didn't say, of course, was that any evidence I got that incriminated Gary would be useful when it came to thrashing out the divorce settlement. If I could show that Gary was supporting a Thai mistress, an American divorce court would skin him alive.

The name and the number of the bank account was a big help. It would have been a fairly simple matter to get a home address but it would require a large 'donation' to a friendly bank clerk so I thought I'd try a cheaper alternative first. The name of the opticians shop was in the photograph and there were only two branches in Hua Hin. I walked by both outlets several times during the day but didn't see anyone who looked like the girl in the photograph.

Mem was in her mid-twenties and looked fit, not bargirl material but I wouldn't have kicked her out of bed. I decided to use the old 'I'm from the embassy and I'm here about Mem's visa application' scam. I got my clipboard and a US Immigration application form from my rental car, put on my serious face and marched into the store nearest the Hilton. I gave them my standard speech about Miss Kongyou (Mem's Thai name) applying for a US visa. The shop girls knew Mem but said that she had quit her job a few months earlier. I put on my worried face and said that there were a couple of things I had to clear up about her visa application and did they know where she was living.

I spoke in English. One of the girls asked the other '*Mem you kup Ning chai mai?*' which let me know that she was staying with someone called Ning.

I put on my helpful face and suggested that Mem had mentioned that she might be staying with her good friend Miss Ning but that I didn't have her address. Two minutes later I had the name of the apartment block Mem was staying at, in Thai and English, with a hand-drawn map thrown in for good measure.

According to the shop girls, Mem was staying with her friend Ning, who'd just had a baby. The apartment building was a fifteen-minute walk from the opticians. It was a tidy, middle-class type of block and I figured a small apartment there would probably cost 4,000 baht or so a month, about what Miss Mem would earn as a salesgirl.

I found the office and asked the middle-aged Thai Chinese manageress if Ning or Mem were in. She wanted to know what room so I played the idiot tourist and said that my friend Gary had left Thailand suddenly with some money to give Mem. Mentioning money to landlords is a sure-fire way of getting their help. If their tenants have got money, the rent is going to be paid, and the one thing that keeps a landlord sweet is rent money paid on time. She picked up a phone, buzzed a room, then handed me the receiver. It was Ning, and I heard a baby crying in the background. The manageress was out of earshot so I switched back into embassy official mode and told Ning that I had some papers for Mem to sign. Ning said that Mem had gone back to her home in Khon Kaen for a week but that she would come down and see me.

She was a plain girl and looked worn out, and the baby she had cradled in her arm wouldn't stop crying. I asked Ning if she knew whether or not Mem still wanted to go to the US and Ning shrugged and said that she didn't think she did. I decided to change my story and said that I didn't actually work for the embassy, but for a visa service that handled visa applications for various countries.

'Like Switzerland?' asked Ning. 'I want to go to Switzerland.'

It turned out that the father of Ning's baby was Swiss and he had told her it was next to impossible to get a visa for Switzerland. That's not true, which made me think that perhaps Mr Swiss had a wife back in the land of cuckoo clocks and chocolate, but I put on my happy face and promised her that I'd send around the necessary Swiss forms. Ning said that Mem would probably want the Swiss forms too, as she was seeing a friend of Mr Swiss and that he was paying for her to go to school and was planning to marry her. 'Mem finish Mr Gary,' said Ning. 'He butterfly too much.'

'So she won't want to see Mr Gary again?'

Ning shook her head. 'She happy now,' she said. 'Her boyfriend good guy. Good heart.' Good heart generally means generous with money. Over-generous.

I wondered if Gary knew that he'd been kicked into touch in favour of a more reliable sponsor. I guessed that he didn't, but that his wife would take great pleasure in telling him, probably at the exact moment she served him with divorce papers.

So that was that. I went to an Internet café and sent off three emails. Mission accomplished. Three cases, three fees, three sets of expenses, all in one day. A private eye can't ask for much more. And I had the rest of the evening to enjoy myself at the expense of my clients. All three of them.

THE CASE OF THE
MAGIC FINGERS

The Thais, it has to be said, are not great inventors. There are no Thai-designed cars or planes, or electronics, or computer programs. They are famous for two things, really. A spicy soup called tom yam gung, and the body massage. And, truth be told, they didn't actually invent either. Until the Chinese moved into Thailand, all Thai cuisine was dry. Meat, seafood, vegetables, rice, all of the above, but no soup. And massage, well that came from India. But the Thais are great at taking someone else's invention and putting a Thai spin on it. There's no soup in Chinese cuisine that comes close to tom yam gung. And the Thai body massage is the closest thing you can get to sexual nirvana.

There are massage parlours all over Thailand. Most of them cater to a Thai clientele, but there are many, especially in Bangkok and Pattaya, that are geared for Westerners. I've never understood why any self-respecting man would fall for a massage parlour girl. They're really only one step up from the girls who work in the blowjob bars. A go-go dancer can choose who she sleeps with. She always has the option of saying no. And I've known two go-go dancers who never went with customers. They were both married and had kids, and earned enough money from dancing and lady drinks, to support themselves and their families. They didn't go with customers, period. But massage parlour girls don't get to choose their customers. They sit in ranks with numbered badges and customers look at them through a window. Literally, a goldfish bowl. The guys decide who they want, their numbers are called, and the girls take them along to a room for a soapy massage and sex. The girls don't have a choice. And they have sex at least once a day, often as many as three or four times, whereas go-go dancers might only go with a customer a few times a week.

I've always understood the attraction of go-go dancers. Over the years I've probably sampled the delights of several hundred pole-dancers, and every now and again I'd even think about settling down with one. But I've never even entertained the idea of settling down with a massage parlour girl. A massage girl who's been in the business for a year has probably had sex with more than a thousand guys. A thousand random guys. Fat guys. Thin guys. Good-looking guys. Ugly guys. Black guys. White guys. Healthy guys. Sick guys. I wouldn't be able to look at her in the morning without thinking of all the guys who'd been there before me.

Not all massage girls are prostitutes, of course. All over Thailand there are places offering therapeutic massage, and the girls who work there wouldn't dream of doing anything in the least bit naughty. Derek, an Australian based in Dubai, who had built up an import–export company and was a frequent visitor to the Land of Smiles, had fallen for the charms of a foot massage girl. He'd met Wanna at a 'Reflex' massage outlet, a fairly reputable chain around Thailand, where the girls are all well trained, and as far as I know, stick to the basic straight massage. And at Wanna's salon, foot massages took place on the ground floor by the window so there was no chance of anything naughty going on.

Wanna hadn't been an easy conquest. He'd courted her for six months before she agreed to go back with him to his hotel, and even then she didn't have sex with him. They'd since become lovers, and now he was preparing to take the next step—marriage. When he was back in Dubai she sent him text messages every day and he was sure that she was a 'good' girl, he just wanted me to make sure. He emailed me a photograph and she seemed like a good sort. Mid-twenties, long hair, cute button nose, sexy smile. I could see the attraction. Derek had asked her to stop work but she said that she preferred to support herself, which was a good sign. But he sent her a monthly allowance and showered her with expensive gifts, which was a bad sign.

I told him I'd need a three-day retainer. For that I'd check that she went straight home after work and that she didn't have a boyfriend or husband waiting for her, I'd check that she arrived at work on her own, and then I'd get a massage from her and check that 'extras' weren't on the menu. Derek sent the money through to my bank and I was on the case. Early indications were that Derek had got a decent girl. She left work at ten o'clock each night, ate some Thai food on the street with her workmates, then caught a bus to her studio flat in Sukhumvit 71. She lived there alone, and every morning caught the bus to her place of work. After three days of following her to and from work, I went in and asked for a massage from Miss Wanna. I told the cashier that Wanna had been recommended by a friend, and that I wanted a full body massage. I was shown upstairs to a small cubicle where I swapped my T-shirt and jeans for white wraparound baggy pants and jacket. Miss Wanna came in, looking professional in black trousers and a green polo shirt with the name of the company on the pocket. Up close she didn't look as attractive as her photo. That's par for the course in Thailand. Most photographic studios run their portraits through Photoshop, lightening skin, wiping out wrinkles and reducing fat, and they had certainly done the business with Wanna's photograph. She was a bit better looking than the average therapeutic massage girl, though, and had a fair enough figure.

I lay down on the massage table while she went to work on me. She had strong fingers and knew what she was doing. In between grunts and groans I chatted away in Thai. I started by telling her that I had a sore back because I'd been driving my wife and daughter to Nong Khai and back, and it was easy to go from there to asking her about her family.

She told me that she had a four-year-old son—something that Derek wasn't aware of—and that he was being cared for by her parents in Sisaket. Her Thai husband had run off when the baby was born and hadn't been heard of since. She had to work to support her son and her parents and she made a reasonably good living doing massage. The boss of the shop gave her half of the fee, plus she got to keep all the tips. Most of the customers were farangs, and generally farangs are better tippers than Thais, she said.

It was easy to start chatting about farangs, and I suggested that she wouldn't have a problem finding a Westerner to take care of her. She laughed. I asked her if she had any special farang friends and she said that there was an American that she liked but there was no mention of an Australian and certainly no mention of Derek. As we got towards the end of the massage I asked her if there were any extras on the menu and she just laughed and suggested I try one of the soapy massage parlours. 'They have girls there that can take care of you,' she said, 'I am sorry but I cannot.' Fair enough, I thought.

After an hour of pinching and pummelling I tipped her handsomely and went home. I emailed a report to Derek, saying that she wasn't going with customers, and was doing nothing more than regular therapeutic massages. I pointed out that she had a son, and that she hadn't mentioned him.

He emailed me back within minutes so he must have been

online. He asked me if I was sure. He phoned her every day and she always said that she loved him. She sent him several texts a day proclaiming her love. Derek suggested that perhaps I'd got the wrong girl so he wanted me to go back and get another massage and for me to tape the conversation. He offered to pay me another day's retainer. I figured he was throwing good money after bad, and I was aching so much after the first massage that I was tempted to pass, but my rent was due so I told him to transfer the money and I'd go back the following day.

A good night's sleep had actually made my muscles ache even more but a promise was a promise so that afternoon I turned up at the massage place and asked for another rub down from Miss Wanna. She was surprised to see me lying on the table in my baggy jacket and pants, but I told her that she'd done such a good job on my back that I'd come back for round two. What she didn't know was that I'd put a tape recorder in the pocket of my jeans that were hanging on a peg by the end of the table.

I had arranged with Derek to send her a text while she was working on me. I chatted away, wincing as her fingers bit into my aching muscles. After twenty minutes of torture, her mobile phone beeped. She seemed happy enough to ignore it, but I said that she should see who it was as it might be a 'special' farang. She laughed and checked her phone.

She read the text and I asked her again if it was from her 'special' farang. She shook her head and said that she was still waiting to meet someone special.

'So who was that from?' I asked.

'An Australian guy,' she said. 'He texts me all the time.'

'What does he say?' I asked. 'Does he say he loves you?'

'Sure,' she said.

'And what about you?' I asked. 'Do you say you love him?'

'Of course,' she said. 'He is a nice man. I don't want to make him sad and he bought me this gold bracelet.' She held up her right arm and showed me an expensive bracelet on her wrist. 'He gives me money, too. All the time. I say "I love you" very loudly, but then I add very quietly "the same as I love my father". Which is the truth.'

I felt a bit sorry for Derek then, because no guy wants to hear the love of his life saying that she loves him the same as a father. He hadn't told me how old he was but I figured he was probably in his fifties. To be honest, that's one of the major reasons that Thai–farang relationships end in tears. The guys are generally much older than the girls they fall for, and in a way it serves them right. Does any fifty year old guy really believe that a twenty-five-year old is going to think that he is God's gift to women? It's about money and security, which is what ninety per cent of Thai women want. They want someone to take care of them and their families. And if they have to tell the odd white lie to get that money and security, then they will.

Anyway, I had what I wanted on tape. Wanna went back to kneading my back and by the end of the hour I was in agony. I showered and dressed and limped home. I sent the cassette tape to Derek in Dubai and never heard from him again.

Wanna was a nice enough girl, and genuine in her way. She wanted enough money to build a house for herself and her boy in Sisaket, and maybe one day she would find a man that she would love. But Derek wasn't that man, and he'd just have to accept that. The beauty of Thailand is that there are plenty more fish in the sea. The drawback, of course, is that there are a fair amount of sharks, too.

The next day, I got another email from a guy in Canada who'd also fallen for the charms of a massage girl. Rick had met Vee in a traditional Thai massage place of Sukhumvit Road while he was on holiday six months earlier. He'd fallen for her hard and had been back twice since. Miss Vee was twenty-nine and had never been married and from the picture he sent me she had the most amazing pair of breasts. I could see the attraction. On his last trip he'd offered to support Vee and told her that she could stop work. He'd started to send her money, but wanted me to check that she was keeping to her end of the deal. I thought he was crazy. In fact, I think anyone who offers to support a girl that he's met on holiday needs his head examining. I reckon there must be something in the water in Thailand that makes farangs act irrationally. Would a Canadian go to America on holiday and pay a waitress to stop work? Would he hell. Anyway, I wasn't being paid to tell Rick that he was crazy. He wanted to pay me to check up on the lovely Miss Vee and I was more than happy to take his money. Normally I'd be right on the case, but the problem was that the last two massages courtesy of Miss Wanna had left me aching all over and I really couldn't face another.

I phoned the parlour where Miss Vee worked and confirmed that they did hotel visits, which is usually a sign that there's more than just regular massages going on. I asked if Miss Vee was available and was told she was. I said I'd call back to confirm a booking. I headed for Gulliver's in Soi 5, one of my regular watering holes. The barmaid pulled my bottle of Jack Daniels off the shelf as soon as she saw me walk in. It was early afternoon but I needed something to kill the pain. I looked around and smiled when I saw that my timing was perfect. Sitting on the far side of the bar was 'Aussie' Andy, a former helicopter pilot from Brisbane. I asked him if he had a couple of hours to kill which was a pointless question because he was retired and did little more than hang around bars and pick up attractive women. I said I'd pay for the hotel room and the massage. He wanted the Oriental but I told him he'd have to settle for the Miami Hotel in Soi 13 which would only cost 500 baht and which was just around the corner from Miss Vee's place of work.

I took Aussie Andy around to the hotel, booked him in, then called the parlour and arranged for Miss Vee. The fee would be 300 baht for a one-hour massage, I was told, payable in advance. Then I headed back to Gulliver's. I wished I was as sure of the next Grand National winner as I was of Miss Vee asking for more money for 'extras'.

I'd had four JDs and my aches and pains were starting to go when Aussie Andy came back, smelling of soap and looking like the cat that had got the cream. Miss Vee wasn't a bad sort, he said, considering she was thirty-eight. He'd checked her ID while she was in the toilet, which I thought was using his initiative. It showed that she'd been lying about her age and from my experience if a girl lies about one thing then you can't believe a word she says. Anyway, Miss Vee hadn't been in the room for two minutes before she was offering him a 'special' massage for an extra 2,000 baht.

Andy played it straight and handed over the 300 baht that he said was the agreed fee. She phoned the agency and said that she'd been paid, then she started giving him the massage. A lot of baby oil was used, and she spent most of her time concentrating on his nether regions before telling him that he could have a 'special' massage for 1,500 baht.

Andy gritted his teeth and said that he was happy with a regular massage. She poured on more oil, then asked him to roll onto his back. The price of a 'special' massage dropped to 1,000 baht. Andy declined, but then her top came off and more oil got poured and Andy said he'd be willing to go an extra 500. They agreed to split the difference and settled for 800 baht. I handed him the money and he bought me a drink. Miss Vee had performed admirably, he said, and her magnificent breasts were most definitely the real thing.

As soon as I got home I sent Rick an email telling him that not only was Vee working, she was also more than happy to have sex with clients. He must have been straight on the phone to her because the next day I got a reply from him. Rick wanted to know if I was sure that she was having sex because she's told him that she was just helping out with the hotel visits because the parlour was short-staffed. She'd assured him that she only did straight massages.

I've never understood why clients will always take the word of their girlfriend over the evidence that I've given them. Time and time again I'd present my report only to have the client phone or email asking me if I was sure. Was I sure? Of course I was sure! What did they think they were paying me for? And of course the girlfriend is going to lie. She's hardly likely to admit that she was screwing around, not when there's money at stake, is she? I didn't argue with Rick, I just phoned Andy and asked if there were any details he could give me that would convince Rick that he'd had sex with his nearest and dearest. Andy told me about the tattoo of a butterfly that she had on the small of her back, the three moles on the inside of her right thigh, and the fact that she whimpered like an injured kitten when she came. I passed on the information to Rick and I never heard from him again. It was probably more detail than he wanted. I felt a bit bad about bursting Rick's balloon, but I figure I was saving him money and heartache down the line.

THE CASE OF THE
SUSPICIOUS SPOUSES

A big chunk of my work in the early days came from sex tourists who'd fallen in love with bargirls and wanted me to check up on whether or not they were being faithful. Ninety-nine times out of a hundred the answer was no, she was still sleeping with paying customers. It was money for the proverbial old rope. Initially I got work through word of mouth, but after a year or so I figured I should go out looking for business, and the best way to do that was through the internet. I set up a website advertising my services, *www.thaiprivateeye.com*, and before long I was getting assignments from around the world.

One of the first emails I got through the website was from a woman named Barbara who lived in Glasgow in bonnie Scotland. Any country that makes Johnnie Walker Black Label has got my vote of thanks, so I was more than happy to help Barbara. Plus she sent my retainer by bank transfer within forty-eight hours of me taking the case, which in my mind at least put paid to the theory that the Scots are tight with money. Barbara's husband had been in Thailand for a couple of months, and while she had no evidence that her husband was fooling around, she had a feeling that something was wrong. Women's intuition. And she wanted me to find out if he was having an affair with a Thai girl.

Her husband, William, was an artist and he'd been travelling around the Chiang Mai area, painting. For a lot of the time he'd been staying with a friend, but she didn't have an address for him. All she knew was that it was a penthouse apartment with a stunning view. Not much help, really. He was going to stay in Bangkok for a week or so before returning to Scotland, but she didn't know which hotel he'd be staying at. I explained that Bangkok was a city of more than ten million people, so without an address I had no hope of finding him. She did know the date of his return flight, and that he was flying British Airways. He'd bought a cheap economy ticket and he was locked into his return date so he'd have to be on that flight. I asked her to email me a photograph of him and I'd put him under surveillance at the airport. In my experience, if a guy has a Thai girlfriend she will see him off at the airport, for no other reason than he'd probably give her all his unwanted baht before heading for the plane.

The money, and the photograph, arrived within forty-eight hours. William was a good-looking guy with blonde hair tied back in a ponytail, in his early thirties. If he'd wanted to fool around in Thailand, I didn't think he'd have had any problems.

I got to the airport a good three hours before the flight was due to leave and wandered around with a paper cup of coffee. He appeared ninety minutes before the flight was due to close, pushing a trolley loaded with two suitcases and a dozen or two cardboard tubes that I assumed contained his artwork. And hanging on his arm was an absolute stunner. The girl was in her early twenties, waist-length glossy black hair, smooth white skin, great figure and a mouth that just begged to be kissed. I took a few pictures with my digital camera. She kept planting kisses on his cheek, and I got a belting photograph of him with both hands on her bum, kissing her full on the mouth. A lot of times on surveillance operations I'm always amazed at how plain the girls are. Maybe it's because I've been in Thailand so long but I've become very selective whereas a lot of tourists seem to jump on the first girl they see. I get paid to check up on some of the ugliest girls in the country, and the guys get really upset when I tell them that the love of their life is still sleeping with customers. But William's girl was faultless, and I had half a mind to 'accidentally' bump into her and get her phone number after he'd flown off. But I'm nothing if not professional so I carried on taking a few long-range photographs.

They went and sat in a pub on the first floor while they waited for his flight, and I managed to get a couple more shots of them getting close and personal, then followed them to the departure gate where true to form he took out his wallet and gave her all his Thai money. She put up quite a performance, shaking her head and wiping tears from her eyes, but she took the money. After he'd kissed her and waved and gone through to immigration, I followed the girl to the taxi rank. Lots of heads turned to watch her as she walked. She got into a taxi and it headed down the expressway.

I caught a cab home and emailed the pictures to the wife, along with a report of what I'd seen. Easy money. I could imagine the scene in Glasgow when William arrived home. Thai girls tend to cut off the dicks of unfaithful husbands. Upcountry they toss the bloody remains to the ducks, and in the cities they put it in a food blender. I doubted that Barbara would be as cruel as that, but I reckoned William was still in for a shock when he got home.

A couple of days later, I got an email from the husband. I opened it, expecting a torrent of abuse, but to my surprise it was quite a chatty epistle, complimenting me on my professional approach to the job. And he thanked me for bringing an unhappy situation to an end. According to William, the love had gone from his marriage years ago and he had been trying to find a way of ending it. My investigation had been the spark for him and his wife to start talking about divorce, and now they had decided to consult lawyers and end the marriage. There were no kids and his wife had a well-paid job, so all they had to do was to decide on a fair split of the marital assets. Once that was out of the way, William planned to fly back to Thailand and start a new life with Som, the girl who'd been at the airport. And the main reason for the email was that William wanted to pay me to run a check on the lovely Som! I couldn't believe it at first and thought it was a wind-up, but William was serious. Som had been a go-go dancer in the Long Gun Bar in Soi Cowboy, and while he'd paid her to stop work he was worried that she might go back to her old ways while he was in Scotland. I gave him my bank details and told him to send over a retainer. I told him I didn't need a photograph of the lovely Som, but I'd need her date of birth, full Thai name and any other details he had.

A couple of days later he emailed me all the information. Som was twenty-two and lived in a cheap hotel in Soi 15, not far from Soi Cowboy. I knew the place. It was a well-known bargirl haunt. She went to school in Siam Square most mornings. Her mother lived in Pattaya with an elderly German.

William said that he'd agreed to transfer 15,000 baht a month into Som's bank account. That set alarm bells ringing right away. A halfway decent bargirl can easily earn four times that dancing around a silver pole and sleeping with customers. A real pro with high-spending Japanese customers can earn six figures. Som was a stunner and I found it difficult to believe that she was staying at home for just 15,000 baht. Her hotel bill would be almost 10,000 baht a month, even on a long-term lease, then there would be her mobile phone bills, clothes, cosmetics, food. And as a bargirl, even a former one, there would be a good chance of a drugs problem and a very good chance that there was a family to support.

William said that she emailed him pretty much every day, and that she always answered her mobile.

I started to follow her. It wasn't difficult. She didn't own a car or a motorcycle and used taxis, motorcycle taxis and the Skytrain. Over a few days I kept a close eye on her. She went to school during the week, spent most of her time in her room, probably watching TV, and went out to eat at night with girlfriends. More often than not, Som would pick up the bill. I saw her using several different mobile phones, but I couldn't get close enough to hear what she was saying. Multiple phones is always a bad sign. It suggests multiple boyfriends or sponsors. She never went to a nightclub or to the city's red-light districts. She went to Pattaya one weekend but stayed with her mother and didn't go near the bars.

I didn't see her with another guy, Thai or farang, but it was clear that her lifestyle was costing well over 15,000 baht a month and as she wasn't working the money had to be coming from somewhere.

I reported back to William. Som wasn't seeing anyone, but she was living well beyond her means. I said that if he wanted to be sure that she didn't have any other sponsors I'd have to check her bank account. At best that would mean a visit to a branch to sneak a look at a computer terminal, at worst it would mean a bribe of tens of thousands of baht. William said he'd pay me for another day to visit the bank and sent through the extra money to my account along with the details of her account.

I went along to a branch of Som's bank in a tourist area, found a sweet young cashier, flashed her my most charming smile and told her that I'd sent money to my girlfriend but that she'd told me that it hadn't arrived yet. I asked the cashier if she could check that the money had actually gone through. The girl told me what I already knew, that I'd have to go to Som's branch to confirm the transfer, all she could do on her terminal was to check the balance. She called it up on screen and as she did I leaned over and took a quick look. There was close to two million baht in the account. I flashed the cashier a thumbs up. 'Great,' I said. 'The money must have gone through,' I said. 'We're building a house.' I thanked her and hurried out.

I phoned William and told him that Som had a stack of money in her account, far more than she could have saved, even as a go-go dancer. The only way she could have amassed that amount of cash was from a generous sponsor, and probably more than one. She certainly didn't need William's 15,000 baht a month.

'But you've never seen her with another guy?' he said. I could hear the hope in his voice. I've heard it hundreds of times over the years. It was the sound of a man who wanted to believe that he wasn't being lied to, even when all the evidence suggested the contrary. I don't know what it is with these guys. They really do check their brains in at the airport. I don't understand it. I understand bargirls. They work for money. Period. They don't dance in go-go bars and sleep with men twice their age for fun. They do it for money. But the guys who fall in love with them, just what goes through their minds? The guys who cling to the hope that their bargirls are special, that their bargirls don't lie and cheat, they're the ones that I really don't understand.

'No, I've never seen her with a guy,' I said. But just because I hadn't seen her walking arm in arm with another farang didn't mean that she didn't have a string of overseas sponsors, men who would send her a monthly 'salary' in the hope that Som would be faithful to them. It was laughable. The best they could hope for was a form of timeshare: regular payments would entitle them to her company on their occasional visits to the Land of Smiles. She was providing a fantasy, and getting well paid for it, too.

'There you go, then,' said William. 'That's all I need to know. I'm going to give her the benefit of the doubt.'

I wished him well and cut the connection. I'd done my job. I'd told him what I thought, but he preferred to cling to the fantasy.

I opened a bottle of Jack Daniels. I'm sure Som would make William welcome when he came back to Thailand. She'd probably move in with him for a while, but as soon as a wealthier sponsor came to town she'd be off, spinning William a line about a relative being sick or her mother needing company. The only way to keep a girl like Som would be to keep upping the ante, to keep paying, until he had nothing left to give. And once she'd bled him dry she'd be off for ever. I raised the bottle in salute to the man on the other side of the world, a man who didn't know what was about to hit him. Another lamb to the slaughter.

THE CASE OF THE
WORRIED HEIR

Robyn was a well-spoken guy and sounded like he had his head screwed on right when he phoned me from the UK. He lived in Oxford and the way he told it he was one of the few guys who'd married a Thai girl and made a success of it. Sorry if I sound cynical, but in the Western world marriages have about a fifty-fifty chance of actually ending up as till death do we part. In the States most marriages fail, and the UK has the worst marriage failure rate in Europe. Throw in the fact that the wife was a hooker prior to tying the knot and that she is from a totally different culture and I'm always amazed to hear that a Thai–farang marriage has lasted longer than five minutes.

Anyway, when Robyn was in his forties he'd been in Thailand working for an NGO when he'd met the love of his life. He didn't say that he'd met her in a bar and I didn't ask. They'd married and he'd taken her back to Oxford where so far they'd lived happily ever after and raised a couple of kids. They were getting on fine, he said. He wasn't a rich man, far from it. He worked in a bookshop in the city centre and didn't seem to be particularly ambitious. But he wasn't worried about his long-term prospects because his elderly father was very wealthy. Robyn's dad, Jack, owned a huge farm on the outskirts of the city which he leased out while he lived in a bungalow. Robyn's mother had passed away a few years earlier, and as Jack was now in his late seventies it wouldn't be too long before the estate passed to Robyn. Don't get me wrong, I didn't get the feeling that Robyn was waiting vulture-like for his old man to pass on, but death comes to all of us and when the Grim Reaper called for Jack, Robyn would get his inheritance.

Anyway, Robyn kept telling his dad what a great place Thailand was and suggested that he head out to the Land of Smiles for an extended holiday. The warm climate and the hospitable people would be a tonic for the old man, and a welcome change for the grey clouds and gloomy faces of a typical English winter. Eventually Jack agreed. Robyn was all too well aware of the dangers of Thai bargirls so he made sure that Jack steered clear of Bangkok, Pattaya and Phuket and suggested that he rent a serviced apartment in Cha-am. Robyn's wife had friends and relatives in the beach resort, which is a couple of hours drive from Bangkok, so Robyn knew that Jack would be well looked after if he ran into any problems.

Robyn figured that his dad would have three months in the sun before returning to Oxford revitalised. What he didn't plan on was the Thai gossip network, which went into overdrive almost as soon as Jack walked into his serviced apartment. A rich, elderly farang, staying alone. It was like a wounded tuna thrashing around in a shark-infested sea. Within days a beautiful young girl by the name of Ying was offering to show him around. Ying lived in the block and worked part-time as a real-estate agent. The way Robyn told it, she'd started cooking and cleaning for Jack, telling him that she had a Thai boyfriend in the past but that now she was footloose and fancy free and much preferred farang men to Thais

Jack and Robyn spoke every few days on the phone and at first Robyn was happy enough that his father had someone to cook and clean for him and to show him around. But Robyn's happiness was short-lived when Jack dropped the bombshell that he and Ying had become more than just good friends. They were in love, Jack was going to marry her and as soon as the winter was over, he planned to bring her back to the UK. Jack was especially pleased that Ying was only a few years younger than Robyn's wife so she wouldn't be lonely.

That's when Robyn got in touch with me. He realised that if the marriage went ahead, the family estate would quite probably end up in the hands of a twenty-something Thai girl.

Like Robyn, I was hearing alarm bells ringing. A ten-year age gap is perfectly acceptable in a relationship. I've known marriages work where the husband is twenty years older than the wife. But Jack was half a century older than Ying, and I doubted that it was his wrinkles or shrunken gums that she fancied. You didn't have to be a private eye to realise that Jack had been hooked by a gold-digger, but the old man was clearly thinking with his dick rather than his brain, so the son wanted me on the case. He'd found my firm on the internet and called me straight away. Robyn had already done a bit of detective work himself. His wife had recommended the apartment block to Robyn's father and she'd telephoned the staff there to get the low down on Ying. The staff didn't think much of Ying, apparently, and were fairly sure that she had a Thai boyfriend. I assured Robyn that I'd be able to help and gave him my bank details.

As soon as the retainer had been transferred I phoned my contact at the British Embassy. Generally the embassy officials are not too helpful to guys like me but over the years my contact Clive had been less obstructive than most. I ran Jack's situation by Clive and asked him what the chances would be of Miss Ying getting a visa to the UK. 'About the same as a snowball in hell,' said Clive. In cases like that—which were not unusual in Thailand—the embassy would keep on stalling, hoping that the husband-to-be would come to his senses. I passed that information on to Robyn so that at least he could stop worrying about anything happening in the short term.

The next step was to have chat with Jack. I caught a VIP bus to Cha Am, then paid ten baht for a motorcycle taxi to take me to the apartment block. I asked the girls at the reception desk to phone Jack's room and five minutes later we were sitting at a beachside bar enjoying a couple of beers. I told him that I was from the British Embassy and that I had a few questions about his application for a visa for Ying. He didn't question the fact that I had a New Zealand accent, and he was eager to chat. I figured that during the weeks he'd been in Thailand he'd been starved of intelligent conversation. We chatted about his life in Cha Am, his family back in Oxford, rugby, football, and then eventually we got around to the subject at hand. Miss Ying.

It was Jack's first trip to Thailand, so I explained the basics to him. There are no pensions, unemployment benefits or sickness payments, so Thai girls would do whatever they had to do to survive and to support their families. And attaching herself to a wealthy older man was a much better option than planting rice by hand.

Jack shook his head, refusing to accept that I might be telling the truth. At his age he deserved a little pampering, he said. And he was sure that while Ying might not yet be in love with him, she would make a perfect wife.

According to Jack, she phoned him every morning, then came around in the early afternoon. Most days she went downstairs to the local hair salon to make herself look good for him. They would eat together most evenings, and then at ten o'clock she'd head off to her own room. They had become lovers he admitted coyly, but she didn't want to move in with him until after they were married. That set more alarm bells ringing in my cynical head. Ten o'clock was the perfect time for a young lady to head off to a nightclub with her Thai beau.

I had a couple of more beers with Jack and I told him a few horror stories of farang men who'd lost everything to their Thai wives or girlfriends, but he just laughed and said that Ying was different. If I'd had a dollar for every guy who's told me that his girl was different, I'd be a hell of a lot richer than I am. I didn't tell Jack that, though. I wished him well, told him that his application was working its way through the system, and I went off to phone Robyn.

I told Robyn that his father was still determined to marry Ying and that the next stage would be to start checking her background. He was keen for me to proceed and agreed to wire over further funds. I already had a game plan. In my experience, girls having their hair done tended to chat away merrily. In the past I'd tried using my wife to glean information from various hairdressers but she tended to march in and tell all and sundry that her husband was a private eye and ask her questions point blank. Her elder sister Boo was a bit more devious, though, and in recent years she'd had many a free cut and blow dry courtesy of my investigations. I left it until Friday afternoon, figuring that was a dead cert for a day that Miss Ying would get her hair done. I took the VIP bus down to Cha Am with Boo. I showed her a photograph of Ying and made sure that she was in the salon by three o'clock.

Half an hour after Boo had sat down, Ying walked in. She was obviously well known and as luck would have it she sat down next to my sister-in-law. I love it when a plan comes together!

As it happened, Boo didn't have to do any fishing. It turned out that Ying loved the sound of her own voice and she wanted to tell all and sundry about her good fortune. She had a hooked a rich old farang, there was a huge dowry on the horizon and she was going to be moving to the UK before long.

I'd briefed Boo to see what the hairdressing girls knew, so she used delaying tactics and asked for a dye job. They were still working on her hair when Ying dropped a big tip and headed into the apartment block for her rendezvous with Jack.

It was easy enough then for Boo to get the full scoop on Miss Ying. Later, as we sank a couple of congratulatory Jack Daniels, Boo told me what she'd learned. According to the girls, who were getting a bit fed up with Ying's boasting, she was the long time mia noi, minor wife, of a local car dealer and that he was also planning to move to the UK to set up a business exporting cars back to Thailand. The farang was old and according to Ying wouldn't be alive much longer and that she and her boyfriend would have the lot. I gave Boo a 1,000-baht bonus and complemented her on her red hair.

I put Boo on the bus back to Bangkok and staked out the apartment block in a rental car. If I had Miss Ying right, she'd be hanging out with Jack until ten o'clock and then she'd be out on the town with Mr Car Dealer. I couldn't stop myself grinning when at ten thirty an older model BMW arrived in front of the block, and a few minutes later Ying hurried out and climbed in to give the driver a peck on the cheek. Bingo.

I followed them to a trendy bar-restaurant where a local band belted out pretty good cover versions of Eighties songs to a packed house of middle-class Thais. I got a seat by the bar and munched on my favourite snacks—gung shar nam pla, or raw prawns marinated in fish sauce and chilli, with lashings of raw garlic. Lovely.

Miss Ying and Mr Car Dealer sat at a table and sipped champagne as they listened to the band. There was a large group at the neighbouring table that were celebrating a birthday and at midnight a big cake was taken to their table and everyone began singing 'happy birthday'. I took the opportunity to pop over with my digital camera and join the other revellers who were taking photographs. I managed to fire off a few shots that clearly showed Miss Ying and Mr Car Dealer together.

I booked into a hotel at Robyn's expense and the following day headed back to Bangkok. I emailed Robyn a full report and copies of the photographs I'd taken. I figured that would be the end of the case. As it happened, I was wrong. I hadn't taken into account how attached Jack was to young Miss Ying. When Robyn had told his father about Ying's boyfriend, Jack point blank refused to believe him. Ying had told him that the man was her brother, and that Jack was the only man she loved. Jack believed her, which just goes to show that there's no fool like an old fool. It's a standard lie for Thai girls to pass off their boyfriends, or even husbands, as their brothers. 'Oh, I share my room with my brother' they'll tell their farang sponsor. Bullshit. I've been at airports on surveillance jobs when I've seen a bargirl tearfully wave off her farang lover, accompanied by her 'brother'. As soon as the farang has passed through Immigration, the 'brother' and the bargirl are at it like dogs in heat.

Anyway, Robyn was starting to panic as he realised that he was faced with the loss of his inheritance. He wanted to know what I thought he should do. I said that if he sent me another 10,000 baht I'd head back to Cha Am and speak to the girl. I might have given Robyn the impression that I was going to get heavy with Miss Ying, but in fact I was just going to play a mind game on her. It was clear from what Boo had told me that Ying wasn't the sharpest knife in the drawer so I figured she'd be gullible to fall for any line I gave her.

I waited until the money had come through before catching the VIP bus back to Cha Am. I'd put on a suit and carried a briefcase and added a pair of spectacles to give me added authority. I knocked on Miss Ying's door, gave her the 'I'm from the British Embassy and I'm here to talk about your visa application' speech. I had a fistful of leaflets that I'd picked up last time I'd been at the embassy, and I gave them to her.

Part of me felt sorry for the girl. She was only doing what she had to do to survive. If she'd been born in the West I doubt that she'd have thrown herself at an old fart like Jack or a married man like Mr Car Salesman. But Thailand wasn't the West and she would soon be thirty and in Thailand a thirty-year-old woman is well over the hill. But Miss Ying wasn't paying my wages and Robyn was so I hardened my heart and lied to her. I told her that she wasn't going to get a visa to the UK because the embassy was unhappy at the huge age gap between Jack and herself. I also told her that Jack had very little money, and that he lived off a small allowance. If he'd told her that he was wealthy, he was lying, I said. And I told her that any assets he had in England would, under English law, go to his children on his death. Even if they did go ahead with the marriage, all she would be entitled to would be half of any money that Jack had in Thailand. And there wouldn't be much of that.

She took it quite well, under the circumstances. She nodded and smiled, fluttered her eyelashes and asked me if I was married. A real trooper.

Jack returned to the UK a few weeks later. I got an email from Robyn saying that I'd killed the romance stone-dead and that his father was busy sending off angry letters to the British Embassy complaining about no-good interfering busybodies and threatening to sue them. It would be water off a duck's back and I doubted that he'd ever get a reply. I figured Jack had had a lucky escape. He seemed healthy for his age and I got the feeling that Ying might well have been tempted to hurry things along, death-wise. It wouldn't be the first time that an old farang had been found dead at the bottom of the stairs by a tearful Thai wife. Divorce Thai-style, they call it.

THE CASE OF THE
BAD GOOD GIRLS

I've lost count of the number of times over the years that guys have said to me that they were ninety-nine per cent sure that their Thai girlfriends weren't fooling around 'because she's a good girl.' They're not making a moral judgment, of course. What they mean is that she wasn't dancing around a silver pole when they met. She wasn't a bargirl. And, their logic goes, if she wasn't a bargirl, then she must be a good girl. The problem with that argument is not all bargirls are bad girls. And not all bad girls work in the bars. There are plenty of girls in regular jobs, or going to college, who are every bit as dangerous as the most hardcore go-go dancer.

There's a pattern to my 'good girl' investigations. I'm usually hired by guys who've made several visits to Thailand and who have got bored with the bar scene. Bored with watching beautiful semi-naked girls dance around silver poles, I hear you cry. Never! Nah, it's true. After a while they get bored of hanging out with hookers, and they dream of having a true 'girlfriend experience'. They start to look elsewhere for female companionship. They pick up a smattering of Thai and start to strike up conversations with shop girls in the local Robinsons department store, or the girl who cuts their hair, or the receptionist in their hotel. One thing leads to another and before long the love-struck tourist is taking the 'good' girl to the movies, to dinner, and eventually, to bed. He can't believe his luck. He's going out with a regular girl. A girl who hasn't slept with thousands of other farangs, who doesn't have a tattoo of a scorpion on her shoulder or stretch marks across her stomach. A girl who says that she loves him, who doesn't demand a bar fine before going out with him or 2,000 baht every time they have sex.

Stop right there.

What's wrong with this picture?

I'll tell you what's wrong. Despite what most tourists believe, Thai girls are not easy. They do not fall into bed with handsome strangers. They do not fall head over heels in love with men twice their age, five times their weight or one tenth as attractive. Good Thai girls from good families are choosy about who they date. And they generally have higher moral standards than their Western counterparts. Good Thai girls do not hold a man's hand in the street, they would not go out with a man, Thai or Westerner, without a couple of chaperones in tow, and they would not have sex until they are married, or at the very least, engaged. Good Thai girls do not fall into bed with farangs. But bad girls do. Hundreds of them, every year. Thousands.

Usually the tourist has gone home and is staying in contact by phone or via email. More often than not there are requests for money. Sometimes the girl switches off her mobile phone at night. Or in the evenings. Sometimes a man answers her phone and claims to be her brother. Suspicions are raised, but the tourist consoles himself be thinking that his girlfriend is a 'good' girl. But the suspicions festers like an open wound, and that's when they call me. They always start the conversation the same way. 'I know I'm worrying about nothing, because she's a good girl. She isn't a bargirl.'

Rule number one of the private-eye game: if you think that your girlfriend is being unfaithful, she almost certainly is. I don't tell them that, of course. I don't want to burst their bubble. Besides, if I did tell them the cold, hard truth there'd be no point in them wiring me a retainer, would they?

Anyway, one day I was sitting at my desk wondering whether two o'clock in the afternoon was too early to open a bottle of Jack Daniels when my mobile rang. It was a Danish guy who said he was heading back home the following day and would appreciate a few minutes of my time. He had a Thai girlfriend, 'a real girl, not a bargirl,' he stressed. He planned to marry her and take her back to live in Denmark, and in the meantime had agreed to support her. His name was Lars and he said he wasn't far from my office having coffee at a Delifrance outlet. I said I'd be there within half an hour, figuring that if nothing else I'd get a free coffee and a croissant.

I was across the road from the Delifrance within five minutes and spent a quarter of an hour watching the place. I'd done several bargirl investigations the previous week and the last time I visited Soi Cowboy I had the distinct impression that a few of the girls were talking about me behind my back. Nothing concrete, just a prickling of the hairs on the back of my neck, but I had been looking over my shoulder a lot over the past few days. I didn't know Lars and for all I knew a girl might be using him to set me up. I spotted him straight away—he was the only farang in the place, and by the look of it he was on his own. No Thai heavies nearby, nothing out of the ordinary. When I was absolutely sure he was alone I wandered over and introduced myself. He asked me what I wanted and I said I'd have a white coffee and a chocolate croissant.

He was in his mid-forties, losing his hair and gaining weight, with a receding chin and ears that stuck out like teapot handles. I'm no oil painting, but I reckoned that fate hadn't been kind to Lars in the looks department. After eight years of being told that I was a 'handsum man' maybe I was starting to believe my own publicity.

I could understand why a man like Lars would come to Thailand looking for love. I doubted he'd have much chance of pulling anything better than a three-bag girl back in Denmark.

I munched on my pastry as he told me his story. He was on his fifth trip to the Land of Smiles, and on his third visit he'd been drinking in a pool bar in Sukhumvit Soi 4, a regular place with no go-go dancers, short-time rooms or barfines. Just pool tables and waitresses, with maybe a few freelancers playing pool who wouldn't say no to a short-time with a punter but who wouldn't be too upset if they went home alone.

Lars was with a Danish friend who had started going out with a bartender, another 'good' girl who wouldn't dream of trading sex for money. Lars had told her that he was fed up with bargirls and wanted to meet a 'real' Thai girl, a 'good' girl. A girl he could love and who would love him. Miss Bartender, as it transpired, had the perfect candidate. She knew of an attractive young student who was all alone and who would very much like to meet a handsome farang such as Lars. An introduction was arranged, and Lars fell in love. Her name was Pim, she was a twenty-three year old student at Rhamkamheng University, and she had never been anywhere near a go-go bar. Lars took her on holiday to Hua Hin, then they went up to Chiang Mai for a week, and before long he had agreed to pay her 20,000 baht a month. My eyebrows headed skyward when he told me that. If she was a 'good' girl, why was he paying her twice the national average wage to attend university? Was that how courtship worked in Denmark? Of course it wasn't. I didn't say anything, though. I wasn't in a bubble-bursting mood, and I'd yet to receive a retainer, so I just nodded and smiled and ate my Danish.

Lars said that he had visited the girl's small apartment, and she'd taken him to her university once, dressed in the traditional uniform of black skirt and white blouse. Miss Pim was set to graduate the following year but Lars had decided not to wait and that he was set to marry her within the next few weeks and take her back to Denmark. Pim had done nothing to arouse his suspicions, but Lars had been visiting a few websites devoted to Thailand and Thai ways, including a site that was full of horror stories of the 'farang boy meets Thai girl, farang boy falls in love with Thai girl, Thai girl steals everything the farang boy has and runs off with her Thai husband' type. Lars was sure that Pim was a good girl, and that she loved him, and that she would make the perfect wife, but he wanted me to run a few basic checks, just to make absolutely sure. The next night he was due to go back to Denmark for a month and that seemed the perfect opportunity to put me on the case. If the mouse did play she was more likely to do it while the cat was 6,000 miles away. He paid me a three-day retainer in cash and gave me her address and her landline phone number. She had a mobile but Lars always called her on the landline at night so he always knew where she was. That made good sense. A common sight in the city's red-light districts is a bargirl huddled in a corner, a hand cupped around their mobile phones, assuring their sponsor that they were at home, tucked up in bed, already sleep.

Lars showed me a photograph of Miss Pim but it was a small passport type and I doubted that I'd be able to recognize her from it. Lars was staying at the Amari Boulevard and she was coming around to see him the following afternoon so we agreed that I'd wait in the lobby and see her in the flesh. I was there, reading the *Bangkok Post*, when Miss Pim arrived in her university uniform. She looked like any of the other thousands of students you can see in Bangkok any day of the week. Tidy, a little over five foot, slim, hair tied back in a ponytail. Not too pretty, but I wouldn't have kicked her out of bed. The only thing out of the ordinary was the confident way she walked across the lobby to the elevators. Most young Thai girls would have been too shy to walk into a major tourist hotel and go up to a man's room, but Miss Pim clearly had no reservations.

I sent Lars a text saying mission accomplished and that I'd keep in touch by email.

According to Lars, Miss Pim went to university every day, taking the bus from her apartment on Sukhumvit Soi 77 at about eight o'clock and getting home just after four. So Monday morning at seven I took the Skytrain to On Nut and a motorcycle down Soi 77 to where she lived. There were four massive apartment blocks, creatively named A, B, C and D. It was a working-class Thai area and I was the only farang for miles. I sat down at one of the many pavement foodstalls and ordered my staple kow man gai and a Coke. With breakfast at thirty-five baht I was keeping expenses down, which would make Lars happy. Hundreds of students in black skirts and white blouses walked by, others whizzed by sitting side-saddle on the back of motorcycles. Eight o'clock came and went with no sign of Miss Pim, and by the time my watch read 9am I realised that she was either still at home or I'd missed her.

Pim's apartment was number 305C, which I figured was Block C, third floor, apartment five. I waited around the entrance to the block until a group of students came out, and I hurried inside before the door closed. There were no elevators and the temperature was heading towards the predicted low-forties so I took off my jacket and headed for the stairs. There was a metal grille across the door to apartment five on the third floor. On the door itself were the numbers 305 so I figured I had the right place. The grille was padlocked on the outside, so there was obviously no one inside which meant that I'd missed her. Or that she hadn't gone home that night.

I left it until four o'clock in the afternoon before returning to the roadside foodstall. The mid-forties forecast had been breached, and it was hellishly humid, and the boiled chicken had been sitting in the sun all day so I gave the kow man gai a miss and just ordered a Coke and a ten-baht bag of fresh pineapple. I ate my pineapple and sipped my Coke and scrutinised the faces of the passing students for any sign of Miss Pim. Five o'clock came and went and there was no sign of her, but as the majority were whizzing by on the back of motorcycles at five baht a time, I figured I could easily have missed her.

I got a motorcycle back to the Skytrain, then went home for a shower and a nap. I had a bargirl investigation that I'd been meaning to do for a while so after dark I caught a taxi to Soi Cowboy and parked myself in a dark corner of the After School Bar with a JD and Coke. The girl I was looking for was the fiancé of a Swiss guy currently in receipt of a 30,000-baht-a-month retainer until her visa came through. Her name was Ann and there was no sign of her on the stage or sitting next to the half dozen or so customers scattered around the bar.

I started chatting in Khamen to one of the prettier girls. Yu-ee her name was, and she was determined to get me over to the Naughty Boys' Corner but the only oral I was interested in was the sort that produced answers to my questions. I offered to buy her a cola but she said she'd prefer a Heineken beer and a tequila chaser. She told me she was eighteen but I figured she was a few years older than that. But even if she was in her early twenties that was still a pretty impressive drinks order for eight o'clock in the evening.

She slipped her hand on my knee and than ran it slowly along my thigh and asked me again to visit the Naughty Boys' Corner with me. Five hundred baht and I was guaranteed a smile on my face. I told her that I was actually there to see a girl called Anne because a friend of mine had barfined her last month and he wanted her mobile phone number so that he could call her from Australia. I was pleasantly surprised when Yu-ee told me that Anne had stopped work, that she had a rich farang taking care of her, and that she was planning to start a new life in Zurich. She pronounced Zurich to rhyme with rich, which was cute.

I bought her another beer and chaser and spent another ten minutes having my thigh rubbed before I figured that the Naughty Boys' Corner wasn't that bad an idea after all. I left the bar at midnight with a smile on my face, and not just because I'd finally found a bargirl who was doing the right thing by her sponsor.

I went over to the motorcycle taxi boys and was about to tell them to take me home, when I remembered Lars. I decided to pay a night-time visit to Miss Pim's apartment. I negotiated a round-trip fare with a guy with a 100cc Honda and got him to wait for me outside Block C. It was cooler than during the day, but it was still a hot evening and many rooms had their doors open, TVs on full blast, radios playing. The door to Miss Pim's room was shut. The grille was unlocked, though, so someone was obviously inside. I bent down, pretending to tie my shoelace, but I couldn't hear anything inside. But I did see two pairs of cheap flip-flops in the corridor outside the door, and one of the pairs was way too big for a girl. It's the Thai way to leave their shoes outside the front door, and I've cracked more than a few cases by checking footwear outside an apartment at night. There were a number of reasons that could explain away the man-size pair of flip-flops outside her door. Her father might be visiting. She might have called a repairman out to fix her fridge. Or she might be on the other side of the door having torrid sex with her boyfriend or husband. If I was a betting man, which I am, I'd be betting the farm on the latter.

I got my motorcycle taxi guy to run me home. On the way I stopped off at a late-night internet café and fired off an email to Lars laying out the shoe situation for him.

He phoned me three hours later, forgetting about the time difference in his haste to hear about the shoes from the horse's mouth. I gave him a run down on what I'd seen, and suddenly he didn't sound so sure of himself. Once when he'd phoned Pim on her landline a man had answered. Pim had hurriedly taken the phone and explained that it was her brother visiting. Lars said it was probably her brother again, but I could hear the uncertainty in his voice. I said I could easily check if she had a brother, though it would mean a trip to her home town.

Lars asked if I'd keep her under surveillance and promised to send me more money. I spent a couple of hours at the kow man gai stall the following morning, but I still couldn't spot Miss Pim. There were just too many students on the move. I was starting to think about knocking on her door and giving her the old 'I'm from the Danish Embassy' speech and taking it from there. The temperature was heading towards the mid-forties again so I moved into a small shop where a dozen motorcycle taxi guys were watching a football match on a big screen TV. There was a small fan mounted on the wall and I positioned myself so that I could watch the game, keep an eye on the entrance to Block C, and enjoy a cool breeze. A couple of the guys were munching on fried grasshoppers and chatting away in a Laotian dialect so I nodded at the bag of insects and said '*sapp-e-lee?*', the Laos phrase for delicious. They roared with laughter and asked me if I'd like to try. I've eaten bugs before so in the interests of a bit of male bonding I took one. I'd like to say it tasted like chicken, but I'd be lying. It tasted like a fried insect. A bit like a slightly bitter cashew nut, with legs. I ordered a bottle of Sangsom whiskey and some soda for my new-found friends and they found me a plastic chair. I figured I'd missed Miss Pim for the day so I might as well enjoy the football.

It turned out that one of the guys came from my wife's village, so we did plenty of glass-clinking and shouting '*chon-gel*' which sort of means 'cheers'. A few hours later and I figured I'd better head home to freshen up and dig out a suit to catch Miss Pim in my embassy guise later that evening.

My new best friend said that he was knocking off for the day and that he'd give me a lift to the Skytrain station at On Nut. It was one hell of a ride due to the combination of the whisky I'd bought him and the amphetamines he'd been popping. We zig-zagged through the traffic, me with white knuckles and clenched teeth, him with a manic look in his eyes and a tendency to scratch his groin with his gear-changing hand whenever we overtook a smoke-belching bus. By the time he pulled up in front of the Skytrain station I was feeling fairly light-headed.

The guy wouldn't take any money from me. I was just about to head up the stairs to the platform when I thought I'd try a long shot. I pulled out Miss Pim's picture and showed it to him. It was probably all the whiskey I'd drunk but I didn't bother with a cover story, I just told him the truth, that Miss Pim's boyfriend was worried that she might be being unfaithful and that I hadn't been able to find out whether or not she was fooling around. The motorcycle taxi guy grinned the moment he looked at the photograph, then he beamed, then he burst out laughing. 'I know her,' he said.

'Are you sure?'

He nodded. 'If I tell you something, you mustn't say it was me that told you, okay?'

'Big okay,' I said. And I promised him 500 baht to seal the deal. He asked me if I remembered a big guy who was sitting right in front of the television, drinking beer from an ice bucket through a straw. I remembered. He was an ugly brute with a huge mole on his top lip that looked as if it was about to turn cancerous. He'd glared at me when I spoke Laotian as if I had no right to be using his language, and he'd jumped to his feet every time a goal looked likely.

I nodded. The guy laughed again and jabbed a dirty fingernail at the photograph. 'That's his wife,' said the guy gleefully.

'No.'

'Yes.

'Are you sure?'

The guy nodded emphatically. He told me that the guy with the mole was the boss of the local motorcycle taxi rank, that he was a nasty piece of work and that nobody liked him. Like most ranks they operated on a rota system but the boss had a habit of grabbing the best jobs for himself, best meaning young, pretty and female. But what had really got up his men's noses was that the boss had started boasting that he was able to get drunk every night on a farang's money and that he was about to buy a new high-powered motorcycle as his wife was due to receive a stack of money from Denmark and an airfare. Pim was most definitely his wife, my guy had seen them together, and he lived with her in Block C. They had a two-year-old son who was being cared for by her mother back in Chonburi.

I gave the guy 500 baht and stumbled up the stairs to the platform, marvelling at my luck. The Chinese have a saying that pretty much covers it: even a blind cat can stumble over a dead mouse sometimes.

The next day I emailed Lars with the details of Miss Pim's web of lies. I never enjoy breaking bad news, but at least I'd be saving him a lot of heartbreak down the line. I just hoped that he didn't ask for proof, which a lot of my clients did. 'Just a photograph,' they say. 'So I can see for myself.'

I've never understood that. They pay me to get the information they want, then when I get it they want more. It's as if they want to torture themselves. Or maybe they don't believe me. Or don't want to believe me.

Often they start firing questions at me, as if somehow I know all there is to know about all things Thai. How could she lie to me? How could she sleep with me when she has a husband? How could a husband allow his wife to sleep with another man? All good questions. And to be honest, I don't have the answers. I'm a private eye, not a psychiatrist. I have my opinions though, not that they're much use to Lars and the thousands of other farangs who get ripped off by Thai girls every year.

How can they lie so easily? For money. Most of the girls that farangs meet are from the countryside, or are one generation removed from working the land. Rice farming is back-breaking, sweaty, unpleasant work. So is factory work, twelve-hour shifts and one day's holiday a month. Is it surprising that a girl would be prepared to tell a few lies if it means an easier life? And once she's started lying, wouldn't the lies get easier and easier? Especially if she's gone into the relationship solely as a way of earning money.

How can they sleep with farangs when they already have a Thai husband or boyfriend? Because by doing so she gets a better life for herself and for her man. It's work, pure and simple. And in comparison with local wages, it pays well. A half-decent go-go girl can earn over 100,000 baht a month, about six times what a nurse or a teacher would get. As a student, Miss Pim's earnings would be zero. Her husband, even as the boss of the motorcycle rank, would be lucky to pull in 10,000 baht a month. Then out of the blue appears Lars, flashing his Euros and offering her 20,000 baht a month just to go to university and have sex with him on his occasional trips to Thailand. Lie back and think of the money. I've heard that refrain from countless bargirls. Farangs like Lars assume that girls would be ashamed to take money for sex, that there is something morally wrong with trading sex for money. The Thais don't see it that way. They see it as commerce, and more fool the farang if he mistakes commerce for love.

How can the husband tolerate his wife sleeping with another

man? Because he understands that it's work. She doesn't love the farang, she probably doesn't even like him. She is the mother of his child. She is his wife. The farang is just a customer. A fool with more money than sense.

I hoped that Lars would just do the sensible thing and cut off all contact with Pim. But I knew from experience that often the girl would be able to persuade the farang to give her a second chance. Or a third. Or a fourth. Thai girls can be very persuasive. And farangs can be very stupid. A perfect match, really.

I can never remember if it's good things that come in threes, or bad things, but that week I got two more 'good' girls that guys wanted me to check up on. Like Miss Pim, they were both girls who had never been within a hundred yards of a naughty bar or a short-time hotel. Both ladies were in their early twenties.

A guy called Terry who lived in the UK had lost his heart to Nam, who worked as a private secretary in a Thai oil company.

A South African by the name of Mark who worked for an estate agency in Bangkok had hooked up with Suming, a hi-so girl who seemed to do nothing other than shop, take care of her daughter from a previous marriage, and socialize. She had a maid to clean the ten million-baht penthouse that she shared with Mark. Hi-so girls, in my experience, should come with a Government health warning. Hi-so stands for 'high society' and you'll see them in all the trendy bars and restaurants, hanging out in the expensive shopping malls, or parking their BMWs or SUVs while talking nineteen-to-the-dozen into mobile phones. The hi-so girls are generally high maintenance, they rarely pay their own way and expect to be courted with expensive gifts, holidays and sometimes cold, hard cash. They also, from what I've seen, tend to have the moral standards of alley cats that have snacked on Viagra. A pal of mine who is a good deal more cynical than me once said that if a hi-so girl is at the wheel of an expensive car then she's either having sex with a rich guy, or is the daughter of someone who had sex with a rich guy. Mind you, he's the same guy who swears blind that bargirls who wear high heels only ever adopt the starfish position when they're in bed and I know for a fact that he's wrong on that one.

Anyway, Terry and Mark got in touch with me shortly after I'd burst Lars' bubble. Of the two cases, Suming was the more interesting because according to Mark she spent most of her evenings at Rivas nightclub in the Sheraton Hotel. Usually she was with Mark, but when he was out of town she went alone or with friends and it was on one of these nights that he wanted me to check on her. That meant sitting in a top bar eyeing up hard bodies and drinking JD and Coke at 200 baht a throw. Mark had okayed all expenses and sent me a decent retainer to kick off the case.

Nam's routine was much more mundane. She worked in the company's head office in Yannawa, a huge building more than thirty storeys tall, and I had to hang around in the midday heat trying to spot her among the thousands of office workers pouring out for a noodle or fried rice lunch or at five o'clock when they headed to the bus stops.

Terry had sent me several good photographs of Nam plus a copy of her ID card and passport so it didn't take me too long to spot her. He didn't expect me to find out anything untoward. He loved her, she was from a good family in Chonburi and was a university graduate. They were engaged and had already set a date for a wedding in Thailand in six months time and were already talking about starting a family. Everything had been going along swimmingly until Terry had started visiting several websites devoted to Thailand and Thai ways, especially the Stickman website at *www.stickmanbangkok. com*. Stick's an old mate and his site is packed with first-person accounts of farangs who have lost their hearts, and their cash, to lying bargirls. There are some success stories too, written by guys who have settled down with former bargirls and never regretted it, but I'd say that the horror stories outnumber the success stories by about fifty to one. Terry realised that the odds were stacked against him, and while he had no reason to doubt that Nam was anything other than the perfect fiancé he figured it would be prudent for me to run a few basic checks. Smart boy.

As always, I ran through a list of questions with him, partly to get a feel for the girl but also because there are often telltale signs that something is wrong that only a long-time resident of Thailand would spot. Women with kids asking for a sin sot, or dowry, for instance. Payment of a sin sot is common enough in Thailand, but the amount paid depends on the girl's social status and frankly, her condition. A hi-so virgin would set a suitor back several million baht. A bargirl who has been around a bit and has a couple of kids wouldn't merit anything. So when clients tell me that their bargirl's parents are insisting on a big dowry, I usually tell them to run a mile.

Nam's parents ran a small supermarket in her home town and they had asked for a sin sot of 100,000 baht. She wasn't a virgin when she'd met Terry, but she had only had a couple of boyfriends and no kids so I figured that sounded reasonable. He'd met her in a cinema, she'd been with a girlfriend, he'd been there alone. They'd started chatting, he'd asked her out and she'd accepted. That sounded okay, though it was slightly unusual in that she'd turned up alone on the date. Usually a 'good' Thai girl would bring along a friend or two as chaperones.

But what really set alarm bells ringing was that he had never been to her apartment. Not once in all the months he'd known her. She'd told him that as much as she wanted him to see it, the block was for women only. It was close to her office, walking distance. Now, there are woman-only apartment blocks in Bangkok, but they are few and far between, but in my experience it's always a red flag when a girl doesn't let a guy see where she lives. They'll pull out a whole host of excuses: it's a mess, it's in a dangerous area, she lives with a friend and the friend has the key. But the bottom line is that she's probably living with a boyfriend or husband, or the place is full of his pictures and his toothbrush is in the bathroom.

Terry had given me Nam's office address but he didn't know the name of the apartment block. That was another red flag raised. Anyway, I went out to Yannawa one afternoon and took a few bags of fried insects over to the nearest motorcycle taxi stand and started chatting to the guys there. The motorcycle taxi guys pretty much know everything that goes on in their locality and they're always my first port of call in an investigation.

I got chatting away in Khmer and asked them if they knew of any women-only blocks within walking distance. There was lots of frowning and head-shaking but when I said I'd pay a hundred baht to anyone who could come up with a name one of the guys said he thought there was a hostel for women fairly close by so I had him run me over. Another hundred baht for the security guard on duty and I learned that no one who looked like Nam lived there. It was a small place, probably only two dozen studio flats, so I was pretty confident that the guy knew what he was talking about.

My motorcycle guy saw that my wallet was well-packed with 100-baht bills so he came up with another women-only block in Silom. That was well outside walking distance from the office where she worked but I figured it was worth a try so we took a run out there. Another hundred baht later and I had confirmation that Nam didn't live there either.

By four o'clock I was back at the office block, sweating in the heat and waiting for Nam to finish work. I was pretty sure that she was lying about living in a women-only block close to her office and having caught her out in one lie I was sure there'd be others.

Nam appeared just after five by which time I had large damp patches under both armpits and I could feel puddles of sweat in my shoes. She waved goodbye to a group of her co-workers and walked across the road to a bus stop. A bus came and went and Nam made no move to board it. She looked at her watch, then made a call on her mobile phone. Another bus came and went.

I went inside a coffee shop, bought a Coke and settled down to wait. I figured she was waiting for a bus and that once she'd boarded one I'd get one of the motorcycle taxi guys to follow her. Following busses is a piece of cake because the motorcycle taxi guys all know the bus routes. I was sipping my Coke when a new model Toyota Corolla pulled up at the bus stop. Nam got in and the car roared off. I managed to get a look at the number plate before it vanished around a corner. I rushed over to the motorcycle taxi rank but by the time I'd explained what I wanted the car was well gone. It was my own fault, I should have had my ride already fixed up, but I'd just assumed that she was going to get the bus. Still, I had caught her out in two lies, and I was pretty sure that it had been a Thai man at the wheel of the Corolla.

I phoned Terry and told him what I'd discovered, and he said he'd pay me to follow her for another couple of days. He asked me what I thought, and I told him the truth. She was lying to him, and that could only mean one thing. 'But she isn't a bargirl,' he said plaintively. I thought about giving him the 'just because she doesn't work in a bar doesn't mean she's not a bargirl' speech, but I decided against it. I said I'd phone him back when I had something to report.

The following day I was better prepared. I had my own motorcycle guy all ready to go at four o'clock, and when Nam appeared I was on the pillion and he had his crash helmet on. The Corolla turned up at ten past five and we tucked up behind it and followed it a few kilometres through the crowded streets until it parked outside a decent-sized apartment block. The man was in his thirties wearing a suit and tie and the way she touched his arm as they went into the block together suggested that they were, as we say in the private-eye game, 'romantically involved.' I managed to fire off a few digital photographs and I emailed them to Terry later that night.

There was only one more piece of the puzzle and that was to identify the guy. The next day I took a run out to the Car Registration Office at Chatujak, near the famous weekend market, filled out the necessary forms and a twenty-baht fee, and explained to the girl behind the counter as I slipped her a tin of chocolate almonds that I was buying the car and wanted to check that it was owned outright and not under any finance deal. It's a common enough request and the chocolate almonds were the only incentive she needed to offer me every assistance. She punched in the registration number of the Corolla, printed out the details and gave me a copy, along with her phone number, which I thought was quite sweet of her considering she was a good five years older than me and had the makings of a half-decent moustache.

The owner was from Chonburi, the same place as Nam, which suggested the he was a long-time boyfriend, but the surname on his ID was different from Nam's so it didn't look as if they were married. Chonburi is on the way to Pattaya, and as I had a couple of bargirl investigations lined up in Sleaze-By-The-Sea I decided to pop out that way and stop off at the Chonburi Municipal Office to run a check on the guy. I told the girl behind the counter that he had applied for a job with my company and my winning smile, a box of Thai sweets and a 500-baht note got me a look at his house papers. He was married and had a son. Nam was obviously his mia noi, his minor wife.

I guess that Miss Nam was happy to be the Thai guy's mia noi at the same time as she was going out with Terry, and that she was just putting off the time when she had to choose. Maybe the Thai guy would leave his wife, maybe Terry would marry her and she'd settle down with him. To be honest, I could understand why she'd want to keep her options open. Girls marry young in Thailand, often in their teens, and her clock was ticking. For all she knew, Terry might dump her for a younger, prettier girl. It's not as if he'd be spoilt for choice in Thailand. The Thai guy could also trade her in for a newer model at any time. From Miss Nam's point of view, she was simply hedging her bets.

Terry didn't see it that way, of course. He couldn't stand the fact that she'd so blatantly lied to him and he called off the wedding, changed his phone number, and refused to answer her emails and letters. From the day I filed my report, he had no further contact with her. Harsh, maybe, but in my opinion he did the right thing. I've said it before and I'll say it again—lies are like cockroaches, If you find one,. There'll be dozens of others that you don't know about.

So, with two out of two good girls turning out to be bad, I started Mark's investigation feeling pretty confident that Miss Suming had a skeleton or two in her closet. I parked myself at a corner table in Rivas nightclub and knocked back JD and Cokes at 200 baht a throw, plus tax plus service charges plus the odd tip for the very pretty waitresses. I had a good view of Miss Suming and her friends—all thirty-something hi-so Thai women—knocking back bottles of champagne and having a whale of a time. Suming showed no interest in any of the farangs hanging around the bar and no Thai men came over to join them. From the look of it, Miss Suming was enjoying a girls' night out, and fair play to her.

There was a band playing, an American group that could actually hold a tune, and during their break they came over and joined Miss Suming's group and more champagne was swiftly ordered. Miss Suming certainly knew how to enjoy herself, but I suppose it was nothing to her as Mark was paying for everything even though he was out of town for a week on business.

Other than the band, Miss Suming's table remained a man-free zone for the night, but I figured that I ought to hang around until closing time just to check that she went back alone to Mark's apartment. Eventually the band finished and the staff started packing up for the night. Miss Suming and her group were obviously well known there and they seemed in no rush to leave so eventually it was just me and them still drinking. I decided I'd better go so I hung around outside, trying to look as inconspicuous as possible. I was able to keep an eye on Miss Suming through the open doorway.

The band had changed out of their stage outfits and they went over to Miss Suming's table and helped her and her friends finish the last of the champagne. The drummer, a big African American guy with bulging biceps and a massive afro, sat next to Suming and seemed to be hanging on her every word. He was about ten years younger than Miss Suming, with a thick gold chain around his neck and a gold front tooth. One by one most of Miss Suming's friends said their goodbyes and left, and the band members drifted off until eventually there were just four at the table; Miss Suming, the black drummer, one of her friends, and one of the guitarists.

I sat in the corner of the lobby and pretended to read the *Bangkok Post*. Another bottle of champagne arrived at Miss Suming's table, and there was lots of glass-clinking and laughing.

It was two o'clock in the morning when they finally left the nightclub. I was knackered and feeling the effects of the dozen or so JD and Cokes that I'd had drunk at Mark's expense, so I sat in the comfy armchair and tried to focus on the group as they stood in the hotel lobby by the elevators. I expected a bit of air kissing, maybe a handshake or a wai, what I didn't expect was to see Miss Suming link arms with the black drummer and go into the lift with him. As the lift doors closed Miss Suming's friend was giving the guitarist a full-on kiss and a grope between the legs to boot.

I watched as the floor indicator lights blinked. The elevator stopped at the seventh floor and a few minutes later returned to the lobby, empty.

Miss Suming's friend and the guitarist went up to the fifth floor, so if the partying was continuing it was on an individual basis. I waited for another hour but Miss Suming didn't reappear so I headed home to my bed.

The next day I emailed Mark a full report. He was, understandably, livid. He'd invested a lot of time and money in Miss Suming, and had been planning to ask her to marry him. If it'd been me I'd have cut my losses and walked away, but Mark was convinced her infidelity was a temporary slip. He confronted her and she eventually admitted to having a fling with the drummer, but that she'd only been to his room once. That sounded dubious to me. What were the odds that the one time she had slept with the guy, I'd be sitting in the lobby? Pretty bloody slim. And from the way they'd been head to head in the nightclub, I'd say it had been going on for some time.

Anyway, rule number one of the private-eye game is that the client is always right, even when he isn't, and if Mark wanted to pour good money after bad then that was his business. But I did suggest that he install a password sniffer on the computer that they both used in their apartment. Before long he was able to keep a track on her emails and sure enough he discovered that Miss Suming was still very much in touch with the black drummer. Unbelievably, he was asking her for money, which had to be a turn up for the books. Usually it's the Thai girl hitting on the farang for cash, but the drummer wanted a 10,000-dollar loan from Miss Suming, ostensibly to buy new equipment. Mark hit the roof again, and she begged him to forgive her. It was his fault, she said, for leaving her on her own such a lot. She was flattered by the attentions of the young black drummer, but she promised on her mother's life that she would never talk to him again. Anyway, Mark gave her another chance and as far as I know they're still together. I'd like to think he knows what he's doing, but in my experience if a girl fools around once, she'll fool around again. And like I said, generally hi-so girls have the moral standards of alley cats. You're often better off with a bargirl. At least you expect a bargirl to lie and cheat and you won't have your balloons burst. Unless you find yourself in a Patpong show bar, of course, sitting opposite a pretty young thing with a dart gun inserted into her you-know-what.

THE CASE OF THE
RESTAURATEUR'S WIFE

I can probably count my Austrian clients on the fingers of one hand but I was just as willing to accept euros as I was to take pounds and dollars so I was quite happy to offer my services to Helmut when he emailed me from Salzburg. He was in his late sixties and in my experience there's no fool like an old fool, especially when there are Thai girls around. But Helmut had been a frequent visitor to the Land of Smiles over the years and from what he told me he knew how things worked. He'd picked up a Thai wife a couple of decades earlier and together they had set up a Thai restaurant. That was par for the course. Bargirls always seem to think that they can cook and half the Thai restaurants in Europe have been set up by girls who started life dancing around silver poles. In my humble opinion that's the reason why Thai food outside Thailand is generally so bad. Helmut's wife wasn't a great cook, he admitted, and she wasn't a fan of hard work. They'd soon separated and he hadn't seen her for years but Helmut had been bitten by the restaurant bug and decided to stick with it.

He started to recruit chefs and waitressing staff from Thailand and with the missus out of the kitchen the food, and the takings, soon improved. Before long he had a chain of very successful restaurants in Austria and was making regular trips to Thailand to recruit staff. On one of his recent trips he'd met a thirty-something woman called Mem who had been put forward as a possible manageress. She was from Khon Kaen but her husband had walked out on her so she'd moved to Bangkok to work and support her daughter who was a student at one of the city's universities. She's worked in catering for almost a decade and Helmut didn't think twice about hiring her to run one of his restaurants. She was an attractive woman and soon became Helmut's live-in girlfriend and eventually his wife. He emailed me a picture and she seemed a good sort.

Over the years Helmut gave her more of his restaurants to manage and he started spending more time looking after his other business interests. Once Mem's daughter had graduated, Mem started visiting her in Thailand several times a year. It was when she returned from her latest trip Helmut started to smell a rat. He found a receipt for a gold bracelet worth 50,000 baht. Helmut knew that she'd only taken a small amount of money with her and nothing had shown up on any of his credit card statements. Helmut asked Mem about the bracelet—she told him that it was a present for her daughter and that it had only cost 5,000 baht but that she'd asked for a receipt for ten times as much so that she could have it insured for much more. That sounded like nonsense to Helmut, so then Mem told him that the 50,000-baht receipt would give her more face with the staff in the restaurant. That made a bit more sense because face is hugely important to Thais, but even so it was a red flag that something might be amiss so he'd gone trawling through the internet and found my website. Helmut wanted me to pay a visit to the jeweller's store to check how much his wife had paid for the bracelet. That's what he wanted, but of course there was more to it. He wanted to know whether or not she'd lied to him. And if she had lied, that would open up a whole new can of worms.

Anyway, he sent me a scan of the receipt and wired a retainer to my bank account. The jeweller's was a small shop in the Big C department store complex in Ratchaparohp Road. I paid the shop a visit and told the lady in charge that my Thai friend had brought a lovely bracelet there and that I wanted something similar. I showed her the receipt and the woman said that she remembered the sale. The lady had brought the bracelet for her daughter but it had been a one-off and if I wanted a similar one it would have to be made to order and that would take a few weeks.

I told her that I was still a bit confused by Thai money. Had it cost 5,000 or 50,000? The woman laughed and said it was definitely 50,000—the bracelet was solid gold with real diamonds.

I emailed Helmut with the news that his wife had indeed paid out 50,000 baht. He said he'd do a little auditing on the home front and get back to me. A week later he got back to me. There were discrepancies in the accounts of a couple of the restaurants that Mem was managing. And the takings of her restaurants seemed to be well below the levels of the others in the chain. He was pretty sure that she was skimming money, but he wanted to be one hundred per cent sure before he confronted her. He had the number of her bank account in Bangkok—would I be able to get a copy of her statement? I said that in Thailand anything was possible providing you had enough money. Helmut said that money was no object and he wired me the funds.

I had a good contact within the bank that Mem used and for half the money that Helmut sent I was able to get a digital photograph of the screen showing her account. It contained a very modest 30,000 baht, which meant that she was hiding her ill-gotten gains elsewhere.

Then I got another email from Helmut. He had spoken to a trusted member of his staff, who told him that Mem had mentioned building a new home in Khon Kaen. Helmut wanted me to carry on digging and he agreed to send me enough cash to cover me for two more days.

I took a plane to Khon Kaen and hired a taxi driver at local rates once I'd shown that I was fluent in his Isarn dialect. Our first stop was the area municipal office where all housing plans have to be registered. It didn't take long for me to ascertain that Mem was indeed having a new dwelling built. The land ownership office was along the corridor and it only took another fifteen minutes to find out who owned the land where Mem was building the house. It belonged to Mem's former husband. And that was most definitely a red flag that something was rotten in the state of Austria. Or Khon Kaen, anyway.

I got the driver to run me out to the site, expecting to see the usual Thai home being built—a slab of concrete acting as a foundation, a living room and a kitchen with one or two bedrooms and a bathroom, total cost about 100,000 baht. What I found was a mansion under construction with more than a dozen young workers scurrying around under the watchful eye of a middle-aged foreman wearing a Chang Beer baseball cap.

I wandered over and told the foreman that I was impressed by the quality of his work and that I was also thinking of having a house built. Thais are as susceptible to flattery as anyone and he was quite happy to tell me that Miss Mem's mansion had a two million baht price tag. That was quite reasonable by European standards, but it would make it the most expensive house in the village by a long way. The foreman was busy and didn't have time to chat, but he was happy enough for me to take a few pictures with my digital camera. I headed back into town, booked into a hotel and emailed the pictures to Helmut.

My driver picked me up at eight o'clock in the evening and we headed back to the building site with a couple of dozen bottles of Chang Beer and several bags of fried grasshoppers. As I'd suspected, the foreman had gone home leaving his workers camped around the site. My beer and snacks were well received and I sat down with them and started chatting in their native Isarn. They had seen the wealthy Thai woman who was building the house, but didn't know her name. She lived abroad, was married to the village headman and would soon be returning to live in the house with her husband. It looked as if poor old Helmut was being well and truly shafted. I figured that as soon as the house was finished, Mem intended to take as much money as she could from Helmut and hightail it back to Khon Kaen.

I left the labourers with the beer and insects and went back to the hotel to send another email to Helmut. I didn't tell him the bad news about Mem but asked him to email me with any bank details he had for his stepdaughter. I figured that Mem had to be getting Helmut's money into the country somehow, and she clearly wasn't using her own account.

I spent a very enjoyable evening in a local disco entertaining a bevy of beauties at Helmut's expense, and woke with a major hangover at midday, too late to enjoy the hotel's complimentary buffet breakfast. I wandered down to a Dunkin Donuts outlet, stocked up on coffee and carbohydrates, and then visited an internet café. There was an email from Helmut waiting for me. He'd sent money to his stepdaughter's account in Khon Kaen a few years earlier so he had her account details. I went to the branch shortly after they opened and played the part of a dumb farang. I spotted a rather plain middle-aged Thai woman, waied her and gave her one of my winning smiles and a box of imported chocolates. I asked her if she spoke English and she said a little. I said she spoke it really well and we were soon on great terms.

I gave her Mem's daughter's full name, address and account number and explained that my brother had just transferred a large amount of money to the account to pay for the construction of his new home. I said that I had spoken to the site foreman who had complained that his men's wages hadn't been paid. My new best friend dutifully keyed in the details and I saw her eyebrows head skywards.

'How much he send?' she asked me.

I shrugged and took a stab at one million.

'Oh no,' she said. 'There is twenty million baht in the account but no transfer this week.'

Twenty million was a big chunk of change, all right. I gave the cashier another winning smile and said that there was no problem, that she was probably waiting to earn some interest before paying the workers, and that all was well with the world.

I didn't tell Helmut how easy it had been to check his stepdaughter's account, of course. There's no point in letting the client think that the job's easy. And besides, it had been a quiet month. I stayed in Khon Kaen for another day at Helmut's expense and went back to see the cuties at the local disco, and then sent him a full report and a bill for the job that guaranteed I'd be keeping the wolf from the door for a few months.

Helmut was devastated by what I told him. He'd honestly believed that he'd found the perfect wife in Mem, but she'd lied to him and stolen from him. He'd gone back through all the accounts and it was now clear that she had been skimming money from the restaurants from the day that she'd started working for him. She become greedier in recent months, a sure sign that she was planning to leave Helmut for good. He'd always thought that he had a good relationship with his stepdaughter, too, but she had obviously been more than happy to help steal from him.

Looking at it from Mem's point of view, I guess she was just doing whatever she could to make a better life for her family. Her Thai husband was more concerned with his status in the village than what his wife was doing overseas, and he knew that she would be coming back to him one day. Helmut was nothing more than a golden goose, and so far as they were concerned he had more money than sense. What they didn't bank on was him having enough sense to employ yours truly.

According to Helmut, she hit the roof when he confronted her with what he knew. At first she tried to lie about it, but the photographs of the Khon Kaen house and the land ownership records put paid to that. Then she begged for his forgiveness, promising that she really loved Helmut and would happily divorce her Thai husband. When that didn't work she told him that she wanted half of everything he had or she'd have him killed. Helmut just threw her out of his house, changed the locks and hired a good lawyer. Last I heard Helmut was fit and well and hadn't paid her a euro.

THE CASE OF THE
PERSISTENT SPONSOR

When I first set up as a private eye in Bangkok, I didn't run to luxuries like an expense account, an office or even a half-decent pair of shoes, and I certainly didn't have an advertising budget. Not for me the delights of a full-page advert in the *Bangkok Post* or a twenty-second commercial in the middle of a popular Thai soap opera. I made do with a strip of stickers that said 'When You Are Away—Does Your Girl Play?' and gave my mobile phone number and my website address. Whenever I passed an ATM or visited a toilet I'd leave behind one of my stickers. It was one of my strategically placed stickers that brought in Hank, a frequent visitor to the Land of Smiles. Hank was at the airport waiting to catch a plane to New Zealand but he wanted to meet me. He agreed to pay for my fare to and from the airport and for my time so quicker than you could say 'I've an electricity bill that has to be paid by Wednesday or they'll cut off my power' I was in a cab heading for the airport.

Hank was a fairly good-looking guy in his late fifties, broad-shouldered and with most of his own hair and teeth, and he was wearing a decent suit and had an expensive gold watch on his wrist. He gave me his life story in the first five minutes of me shaking his hand and sitting down next to him in the airport coffee shop. He'd set up his own travel agency business in Auckland and had started visiting Asia when more and more of his clients started heading out this way. He was divorced with two sons at decent universities, and like most Westerners who reached middle age he soon realised that he'd have a much more interesting sex life in Thailand than he would in downtown Auckland. As a fellow Kiwi I could only add a heartfelt 'Amen' to that. Hank was a realist, though. He knew that he hadn't become a more interesting or attractive person simply because he'd flown halfway around the world. The fact that every bargirl called him a 'handsum man' and hung on his every word wasn't because he was God's gift to women. It was because he had money and they wanted some of it. Hank knew the rules of the game and was happy to play by them. He started visiting Thailand every few months and was a regular face around Nana Plaza and Soi Cowboy. He made no secret of his desire to 'pay and play' and only smiled when the girls accused him of being a butterfly. That's one of the many contradictions you come across in the Land of Smiles. A bargirl who has sex with several hundred men a year is just doing her job. But if a bargirl catches her client screwing another bargirl, he gets accused of being a butterfly or worse and there are tears and tantrums. Funny old world.

Anyway, Hank paid and played and had one hell of a time. And then, after almost a decade of flying in and out for a bit of the old in and out, he ran into Elle. The girl of his dreams.

Hank held up his hands as I smiled. 'I know, I know,' he said. 'You've heard it a thousand times before. My girl is different, she really loves me, she's a good girl at heart, she doesn't really want to be a hooker, she wants to be with me.'

I shrugged. Yeah, I'd heard it a thousand times before. And it always ends in tears. Hookers hook, end of story. No girl is forced to work in Patpong or Nana or Cowboy. It's a career choice. And girls, especially bargirls, do not give up their career for a man twice their age for love. They might, just might, give up work if a guy is stupid enough to sponsor them, but it all comes down to money at the end of the day.

It's usually tourists who get conned. They arrive in Thailand for a couple of week's hard-earned vacation, meet a pretty young girl and fall for her. They pay to have sex, then it turns into what they laughingly call 'the girlfriend experience.' She takes him out to eat with her friends, shows him where she lives (taking care that her Thai boyfriend's stuff is well hidden), escorts him around a few temples and places of interest, and spins him a sob story about family circumstances forcing her to sell her body. The tourist offers to support her if she gives up working in the bar, and the negotiations start. He'll offer 10,000 baht, she'll say she needs at least 60,000 baht a month to support her family, and eventually they'll settle on 30,000 or 40,000. The tourist flies home and starts sending her a salary every month by bank transfer or through Western Union.

What the tourist doesn't know is that a hard-working go-go dancer can earn upwards of 100,000 baht a month. And that's without a sponsor or two sending her money. Why would anyone with half a brain think that a pretty young girl is going to sit at home for a fraction of their earnings? For love? The girls didn't sign up to dance around a silver pole and have paid-for sex with strangers because they were looking for love. They want money. Lots of it. And the only way to get a girl out of the bar scene is to pay her more than she can earn working. Any girl who claims to be doing it for less is lying. Not that they'd see it as lying. They're just telling the guy what he wants to hear.

Anyway, tourists are one thing, long-time visitors or permanent residents (sexpats, as they're usually known) are another. They should know better. But time and time again I get calls from men who've been in Thailand for years who for one reason or another have let down their guard and opened their hearts to a bargirl. I don't know why it happens, I really don't. Tourists I can understand, most of them check their brains in at the airport on arrival, but guys like Hank should know what they're getting into trying to have a proper relationship with a bargirl.

While I'm on the subject, just because a girl doesn't work in a bar doesn't mean that she's not a bargirl. Being a bargirl is as much of a state of mind as it is a job description. A lot of guys who've married a stunner from Isaan will take you to one side and say proudly 'she wasn't a bargirl, you know.' Yeah, but that doesn't mean that he didn't pay to have sex with her the first few times. Or that he isn't continuing to pay to have sex with her, one way or the other. She might have worked in a hotel or a hairdresser's or a beauty parlour, or even be a student, but she was almost certainly a freelancer who charged for sex with foreigners. Some of the biggest rip-off artists I've come across have been 'regular' girls doing 'regular' jobs. Equally, there are girls who work in the bars who couldn't be described as 'bargirls'. There are waitresses who are working to put themselves through college, cashiers who work in the nightlife industry while a relative takes care of their children and who wouldn't dream of sleeping with a customer. I've even known go-go dancers who won't let customers pay their bar fine. One earned a big salary as a featured dancer and showgirl, plus she got a stack of tips every night. With the commission she got on drinks that guys brought her, she was probably making 40,000 baht a month. Her husband worked as the bar's DJ and they were as happy and faithful a couple as you could meet. So, a bargirl doesn't necessarily work in a bar, and a girl who works in a bar isn't necessarily a bargirl.

Anyway, Hank didn't try to pull the wool over my eyes regarding Elle's pedigree. He'd met her in a bar in Soi Cowboy. She was dancing, he'd paid her barfine, they'd gone to a short-time hotel and he'd given her money for sex. No confusion there, then. She was a bargirl who worked in a bar. Which is why what happened next was so surprising. Hank fell in love with her. Hook, line and sinker. She was, he told me with a perfectly straight face, the love of his life. After their first encounter, he paid her bar fine for ten days and took her to Koh Samui for a holiday. They'd walked hand in hand on the beach, watched the sun go down, eaten sea food and gazed into each other's eyes. He'd told her his history, and she'd told him everything about her life. She had a six-year-old daughter, she supported her aged mother, her husband was long gone, her dream was to open a beauty parlour. That's why she'd started dancing in Soi Cowboy, to get together enough cash to pay for her own business. It was also, of course, why she'd started spreading her legs for strangers, but I didn't say that. Just call me Mister Tact and Diplomacy.

Hank wanted to take care of Elle and her family, and eventually he planned to move to Thailand on a retirement visa and live with her. Elle's story was typical of a thousand you'd hear anytime you sat down next to a bargirl. But for some reason she'd touched Hank. He wanted to help her. He wanted to take care of her. She was a damsel in distress and he was a knight in shining amour. He opened his wallet and took out a photograph, a head and shoulders shot of a rather plain thirty-something Isaan girl with too much make-up. 'Isn't she lovely?' he said.

I nodded. I smiled. I nodded again. She didn't look much to me but Hank was the client and he was paying for my time. If it meant I'd get more money I'd have probably told him that he was a 'handsum man' and stroked his thigh. I know what you're thinking. And you're right. It isn't only bargirls who tell people what they want to hear.

Hank took the photograph back, stared at it with moist eyes for a while, then slid it inside his wallet again. He continued his story. He'd offered to pay Elle a monthly 'salary' so that she could take care of her mother and daughter while she attended a good hairdressing school. Once she was qualified, Hank intended to set her up with her own beauty parlour. Elle was over the moon with the arrangement. She had to work at the bar until the end of the month to collect her salary and drinks commission, but once they had paid her she'd quit and start studying haircutting. It was only when he'd gotten to the airport that Hank started having second thoughts. He was twenty years older than Elle, he only had her word that the husband was out of the picture, and like most long-term visitors to Thailand he'd heard all the horror stories. He wanted me to check that everything was kosher, that she wasn't continuing to sleep with customers, that she did indeed quit her job at the bar at the end of the month, and that she wasn't still married. He also wanted me to find a good hair salon training school. All of it easy work which I figured wouldn't take more than a day or two at worst, but he pulled out a wad of NZ dollars and handed me a week's retainer before I could say anything. I thought about giving him half of it back, but just as quickly remembered that rule number one of the private-eye game is that the client was always right. Rule number two: never look a gift horse in the mouth.

I wished Hank a safe trip and headed back to the city. Coming up with the name of a good hairdressing school was easy. I'd been asked the same question more than a dozen times that year. It was a standard bargirl scam, to ask a sponsor to pay for her to learn hairdressing. Most just pocketed the cash and carried on hooking. Some started the course but quit after a week or so to go back to hooking. Some did the full course and then went back to hooking. So how many bargirls had I met who'd gone on to become hairdressers? Err, let me think about that. Err, none. Zero. Not one. That doesn't mean that it didn't happen, of course. I've never seen Father Christmas, but my seven-year-old nephew says he brought him a bicycle last year. The best schools were in Siam Square, and opposite the Siam Commercial bank on Petchburi road. I already had the names, addresses and contact numbers on my computer but figured I'd wait a few days before emailing Hank. Rule number three of the private-eye game: don't make it look too easy.

Hank flew out on Friday night but I left it until Monday before checking out Elle's bar, figuring it would be easier to talk to her on a quiet night. Her bar was at the Asoke end of Soi Cowboy, small and sleazy, just the way I like them. I wandered in, wide-eyed as if I was a newbie, waied the waitresses and ordered a Jack Daniels and Coke. There were three tired-looking go-go dancers who were well past their sell-by date, up on a podium and another five clustered around a couple of Asian guys in suits, probably Japanese. The girls were probably thinking of the good old Rule of Four when it came to the Japanese: four inches, four minutes, four thousand baht. Okay, that's racist, but then hell, we didn't attack Pearl Harbour, did we?

My drink arrived. The Coke was flat which was par for the course in a go-go bar, but the JD was the real thing. I sipped it and studied the girls. None looked like the photograph that Hank had shown me. He'd given me her number so I squinted at the small circular badges that all the girls were wearing. Each badge had the girl's number, as required by law. It also meant that guys didn't have to bother remembering a girl's name. Hank had told me that she was Number 27. One of the waitresses sat down beside me and started rubbing my thigh. She went through the basic bargirl questions. Where was I from? How long had I been in Bangkok? What hotel was I staying at? Australia. One day. The Sheraton. There was no number 27 in the bar which was either good news or bad news so far as Hank was concerned. Either she'd quit her job early or she was already in the sack with a punter. It turned out to be option three. The track came to an end and the bargirls tottered off to be replaced by a second shift. The middle girl was wearing number 27. She was fairly heavy set and her hair was a bit shorter than in Hank's photograph. The longer that I sat and looked at her, the more I began to question Hank's judgement. She wasn't in the least bit easy on the eye. I guess if pushed I'd have described her as one-bag girl. That's how I rank the dogs I come across. A one-bag girl is so ugly that you have to put a bag over her head to do the dirty. If she's really ugly you need two bags. One for her, and one for yourself so that no one will recognise you. And if she's really, really ugly then you need a third bag, to throw up in. So I guess using that scale, Elle wasn't too bad. Anyway, I smiled and gave her a little wave and she started to dance around the pole a little more enthusiastically.

Twenty minutes later the girls shuffled off the stage and four more not-particularly attractive girls took their place. Elle appeared at my side, wrapping a leopard-skin sarong around her waist. I said hello and offered to buy her a drink. She had a cola, the standard bargirl's commission drink, and within a few minutes she was stroking my thigh and I was getting her life story. She told me that she wanted to open up her own beauty salon and I took a risk by suggesting that she was very pretty and that she must have some guys who could help her. She giggled and said that yes, she had two guys who really liked her but that she wanted to do it herself. She told me about her daughter, and she told me that she lived on Sukhumvit Soi 101, which is the address that Hank had given me. I bought her another drink and brought up the subject of her bar fine and she said sure, she'd love to go with me. I said I didn't think girls could go back to my hotel and she said that was fine, she knew several short-time hotels. I said I was still jet-lagged but that I'd be back the following night and that I'd barfine her then. I got a pout and a quick rub of my genitalia but then it was time for her to dance again. And she went back to the podium.

The waitress came over and asked me if I wanted another drink, so I ordered a JD and Coke and bought her one, too. She sat next to me, stroked my thigh and told me how handsome I was. She whispered in my ear that if I paid her barfine and took her to a short-time hotel, she'd screw me for free. That was a standard bargirl scam, I knew from experience. She was banking on the fact that she'd be so good in the sack or I'd be so drunk that I'd forget the deal and pay her when she left. I told her that she was cute, which she was, but that I really liked Number 27. But I hear she has a few boyfriends, I said.

The waitress nodded sympathetically. Yes, she had a soldier in Germany who liked her a lot and a man from Australia who gave her money. I figured Australia was close enough to New Zealand that it was probably Hank she was talking about, but even so it looked like my client was getting the short end of the stick.

I paid my bill, waved goodbye to Elle and ducked as she blew me a kiss. The next day I emailed Hank with my report. I gave him all the details I had on hairdressing schools, and told him that he could expect to pay about 30,000 baht for a year's course at a good school, or about half that for a six-month course. If Elle were to graduate from one of the good schools she'd have no trouble getting a job in Bangkok. And I told him that he probably wasn't Elle's only sponsor. There was the German soldier, and there could well be other men who were sending her money. And I made it clear that she was still happy to have her bar fine paid.

I got an email back thanking me for my help, and I figured that would be the end of it. Hank wasn't stupid, he'd been around the bar scene long enough to know how it worked, so I assumed that he'd do the sensible thing and just cut his losses. He was a nice guy, too, because he didn't ask for a refund. He'd paid for a week but I'd only worked on the case for an evening. He didn't ask for a refund and I didn't offer. Rules number one and two came into play.

It turned out that I was wrong. Not about the refund, but about Hank's intentions. He phoned me from Auckland and told me that he'd had several long chats with Elle, that she'd left the bar for good, and that he had paid for her mother and daughter to join her in Bangkok. Elle was working in a small hair salon and she was just about to start at hairdressing school. Hank wanted to pay me to check that Elle was being straight with him. He wanted me to check that she had left the bar and that she was indeed going to school. He said that he would send me a week's retainer by bank transfer, so I told him I'd do what he wanted. I figured he was wasting his time, but if he wanted to throw good money after bad then rules number one and two of the private-eye game came into play.

That evening I went back to Soi Cowboy, had a few JD and Cokes and bought a few for my friendly waitress. Elle had indeed quit her job, which was one up for Hank. Elle had told him that she wanted to enrol at a beauty school in Soi 55 and Hank had wired the 20,000 baht for the year's tuition. The next day I headed out there and spoke to a group of motorcycle taxi boys. They knew nothing about a beauty school and that was strange because the motorcycle boys spend all day ferrying people up and down the road and usually know everything that happens in their area. One of them said there was a small place down the road where young girls practised cutting hair, but it wasn't really a school. I gave the guy fifty baht to take me to the place. It was an open air set-up with two chairs for cutting hair and a reclining chair next to a tap, all under a tattered awning tied to trees with lengths of rope. Below the awning was a hand-painted banner offering lessons in hairdressing and sewing with a 'special promotional rate' of 2,000 baht for a six month course. I asked to speak the boss and an old woman stepped forward, her face the texture of old saddle leather.

I gave her my biggest smile and threw in a respectful wai, then told her that my girlfriend wanted to learn hairdressing. No problem, she said, they were open five days a week from nine until five. Girls paid a flat 2,000-baht fee and turned up whenever they wanted. I mentioned that I knew a girl called Elle who had enrolled at the school and the old woman nodded enthusiastically and said that yes, Elle had enrolled but that she didn't turn up very often. I asked her if the girls who completed the course received a diploma and she grinned, showing me a mouthful of bad teeth, and said sure. I doubted that the diploma would be recognised by any decent beauty salon but at least Elle hadn't lied about signing up for a course in Soi 55. But she had lied about the cost, and had obviously pocketed the difference. I asked the old women if it was okay to take a photograph of the 'school' to show my girlfriend and she readily agreed. On the way home I popped into an internet café and emailed a quick report to Hank, along with the digital photograph.

I figured that would be the end of the romance. She'd lied to him about not going with customers, and she'd fleeced him for 18,000 baht. Hank was enough of a realist to know that a girl who lies twice will keep on lying. And that without trust, no relationship has a hope in hell of surviving. I was wrong. Six months later he phoned me again. He was in New Zealand, and he was still very much in touch with Elle. After my second investigation, he'd had several long heart-to-heart chats with her and she had agreed to leave the temptations of Bangkok and to live with her mother and daughter in Udon Thani. Apparently the fact that he seemed to be aware of her every move had convinced her that there was no point in lying to him anymore. He had agreed to give her one more chance, but only on condition that she stayed with her family in her home town once she had graduated from the hairdressing school. I had already told him that the school's diploma wasn't worth the paper it was printed on, but she had attended classes every day and he had phoned her constantly, checking that she was sticking to her word. She was always either at school, or at home, and after six months she'd proudly sent him a photocopy of her diploma and headed back to Udon Thani with her mother and daughter. Hank had paid to set her up with her own beauty parlour and wanted me to drop by next time I was in Udon Thani to check on her progress. He wired me a two-day retainer and we agreed that I wouldn't charge him for travel expenses. I figured he'd already paid me enough, plus I had several bargirl investigations arranged for Udon Thani. The Isaan town is a major source of prostitutes for Bangkok's red-light districts. Probably a third of all farangs who ask for my help have gotten involved with girls from Udon Thani. The girls are pretty, generally, and darker than the Thais think is attractive. Their looks, coupled with the poor farmland and lack of decent jobs, mean that there is a constant stream of young girls on the busses into the capital, eager to work in the bars and massage parlours. Many meet a farang who wants to take care of them and every week dozens head back to Udon Thani with the promise of a monthly 'salary' from an overseas sponsor. A good percentage of them go straight back into the arms of their Thai boyfriend and husband, and once the sponsor starts to get suspicious that his sweetheart isn't being as faithful as he'd hoped, that's when they call me in. I had four Udon Thani investigations ready to go so I added Hank to the list, hired a nondescript Toyota and drove over to Isaan with my wife. She's from near Udon herself and speaks Thai, the Isaan dialect and Laotian so she pretty much covers all bases, language-wise.

Elle's beauty parlour was next to her house, some forty kilometres from Udon Thani. I wore sunglasses and a Singha beer baseball cap just in case Elle were to recognise me from my visit to the bar in Soi Cowboy, and I dropped my wife off outside the beauty parlour. I drove off and parked a mile or so away while I read the *Bangkok*

Post from cover to cover and then drove back to collect the little lady. She'd had her hair cut and washed and her nails done and Elle had obviously studied well because she looked great. My missus and Elle had chatted away, as the girls do when they're getting their hair done, and Elle had pretty much recited her life story. She had a boyfriend in New Zealand who loved her and who was coming to live with her one day. His framed photograph was hanging above her framed diploma, and there were snapshots of the two of them together all around the mirrors in the salon. The man took care of Elle and her daughter and her mother, and he was a good man with a good heart, Elle had said. She even offered to ask Hank if he had any friends who might be interested in my missus, but my missus, bless her, said that she was happy with the farang that she already had. That's what she told me anyway, but I deleted Elle's number from her mobile when we finally got back to Bangkok, just in case.

Elle said that her parlour made her about two hundred baht a day, which was pretty good money for Isaan, and a lot more on days when there was a function or party in the village. She enjoyed the work and loved her boyfriend, she said, and she was finally content with her life.

'She's a lucky woman,' my wife said to me as we drove away from Elle's house. She was right. Elle had been lucky to escape from the bar scene, and she was lucky to have a man like Hank supporting her. Most men would have given up on her long ago, cut their losses and found themselves another girl. But Hank had persisted and by the look of it his persistence had paid off. So maybe Hank was lucky, too. Only time would tell. Time, and maybe another visit from the Bangkok private eye.

'What about you, love of my life?' I asked the wife. 'Do you feel lucky?' She just gave me one of the smiles that the Thais are famous for, and said nothing.

THE CASE OF THE
MISSING MOTOR

D ave was one of my best friends in Thailand. I wouldn't exactly stop a bullet for him, but I'd trust him with my wallet and maybe even my girlfriend. He's from the UK, one of those northern towns where it always seems to be raining, and he made a living as a freelance journalist. He was in his early thirties when I first met him. I was managing a big hotel in Surin and he wandered in with a young bargirl. I kept in touch with him over the years and when I moved to Bangkok he became a regular drinking partner whenever he passed through the city. He was younger and better looking than me so he was a good guy to use on my bargirl investigations. A bargirl who was supposedly not working might turn me down but might well a take a couple of thousand baht to be bedded by the young Adonis.

During one of his frequent stopovers he met Nong, a twenty-two-year-old student at one of the local universities. She quickly became his regular girlfriend, and we'd often go out to Thai nightclubs as a threesome. Nong had an older sister, Sen, who had landed herself a wealthy Japanese guy a few years earlier. She had prised a four-million baht dowry from him which enabled her to buy a nice house in the suburbs, a new car to drive around in, and enough spare cash to be able to send money to make life a little easier for her parents back in

Sara Buri. Sen didn't approve of Dave. I got the feeling she thought that her little sister could do better. The Japanese businessman had gone back to his wife in Tokyo, and Sen had been trying to encourage Nong to land herself a wealthy benefactor. Dave earned enough to get by, but he was never going to get rich working as a freelance journalist. Sen would have been much happier if Nong had landed a rich Japanese, or a rich American, or a rich German. In fact, so far as Sen was concerned, nationality wasn't important but money most definitely was. Their parents were good, middle-class Thais, who owned a small banana plantation in Sara Buri, a town in the centre of Thailand. Once she reached eighteen, the parents had sent Nong down to live with Sen and get a decent education.

After Nong and Dave had been going out for a couple of months, Sen put her foot down and sent her younger sister back to Sara Buri. Dave wasn't too bothered. He was travelling all around the region, and with his good looks he had more than his fair share of female admirers. But before long Nong was back in Bangkok and she soon met up with Dave again. Sen started to realise that she wasn't getting anywhere by trying to keep Nong and Dave apart. She even began to drive her younger sister out to the airport to meet Dave whenever he flew into the country.

Dave used to join me at my favourite stamping ground on the corner of Sukhumvit Soi 13 for a few cold beers. It was during one of these evening drinking sessions that Dave told me that Nong had been asking him to buy her a car. I was surprised because Nong had been really good about not asking Dave for money. In fact the only time he'd mentioned giving her money was when she'd asked him for 5,000 baht for collagen injections to puff up her lips, which was sort of for his benefit, I guess. A car was a big investment, and Dave was having second thoughts. I sensed the hand of Sen and felt sure that she was putting Nong up to it.

Dave said that he was happy enough to spend money on Nong, but he'd rather set her up in a business. Nong had said that a decent secondhand car would cost about 100,000 baht. In fact, Sen was offering to sell Nong her own car. Sen was planning to upgrade to a newer model and rather than trading it in she wanted to sell it to Nong. Dave reckoned that he could rent her a nice shop in Marboon Krong and stock it. He decided to have a long talk with Nong and suggest that she let him set her up in business so that she would be more independent. A business would be an asset that would hopefully grow in value, but a car would be worth less every year.

At the time, Dave was sleeping on the couch in my living room. He was only in Thailand a few days each month so there was no point in him renting a place of his own. If he wanted to sleep with Nong he'd book into a hotel. Not that I was a prude, it's just that the sofa wasn't big enough for two and I wasn't prepared to give him my bed for sex. Anyway, Nong came around to my place to talk things through with Dave. She said that she'd talked it through with Sen, and decided that buying the car was the best option. Nong would learn to drive then she'd be able to drive herself to university, and she and Dave could use it for sight-seeing when ever he was in town. The car was a five-year-old Honda Civic and Dave had already asked around a few dealers and been told that the going rate was between 150,000 baht and 180,000 baht, so it seemed that Sen was giving them a good deal.

Dave figured that if the worst came to the worst he'd be able to get his money back, plus maybe a small profit, so he let Nong talk him into it. They went to the bank together and Dave withdrew the money from his account and gave it to her. He didn't ask for my advice so I didn't say anything, but I couldn't help but think that he was being a bit rash. I've come across countless horror stories where gullible farangs have bought cars, houses, land and even businesses from the relatives of their Thai girlfriends or wives, only to have it all end in tears. Not that Dave was gullible, he wasn't, but he wasn't married to Nong and he only saw her for a few days each month. And why did a student need a car? I didn't even own one, if I needed wheels I hired a car. Anyway, he didn't ask for my opinion, so I didn't give it.

Everything went fine for a while. Nong learned to drive, and she would pick Dave up at the airport whenever he arrived in Thailand. The flat I rented came with its own parking space so when Dave was in town he left it there, and when he was away, Nong used it.

After a few months Dave was sent to the UK on an assignment. While he was away, I went out on the town at one of our old stamping grounds, the RCA, which was where young upper-class wealthy Thais would hang out of an evening. I knew most of the Thai doormen, and on my way into one of the bigger discos one of the doormen pulled me to one side and said that he wanted a word with me. He told me that he'd seen Nong in the disco with several young Thai guys. I wasn't surprised. Nong liked to go out and have a good time, and with Dave away and her driving around in a decent car, Thai boys would be around her like flies around shit. I phoned Dave and told him the bad news. He was philosophical. He said he'd noticed that she was becoming a bit evasive of late and that she'd started switching her phone off late at night. Dave felt that the love affair had just about run its course and was planning to call it quits anyway.

The following week he stopped off in Bangkok en route to Hong Kong. He booked into a hotel so that he could spend some time alone with Nong. Actually, I figured he just wanted a few last shags before calling time on the affair. Anyway, once the sex was out of the way, he got down to some straight talking with the lovely Nong. He told her that he knew about her nocturnal activities at the RCA. She just shrugged and she was there with friends. He knew she was lying, and got the impression that she didn't care whether he knew or not. What really ticked Dave off was the fact that she had been pretty much the perfect girlfriend right up until he'd paid 100,000 baht for the car.

Dave told her that it was best they just go their separate ways. Nong shrugged. Dave said he'd arrange to sell he car and he'd split the money with her, fifty-fifty. Nong shrugged, then left.

Dave called her the next day, but Nong didn't answer the phone. He phoned the sister's house, but no one answered. That really annoyed him. He had to go to Hong Kong so he left a spare set of keys for the Honda with me and asked if I'd take care of the car until he got back. I had a couple of jobs lined up where a car would be useful, so I took a motorcycle out to Sen's house. There was no one at home but the car was in the driveway so I drove it back to the city. I decided not to park it in my space just in case Nong started to get possessive over the car, so instead I left it in the car park of a nearby hotel.

I was watching TV a few hours later when the doorbell rang. I checked the peephole before opening the door. It was Nong. I told her the Dave wasn't staying with me but she kept ringing the bell. I opened the door to give her a piece of my mind but as soon as I did three heavy set Thais in cheap suits charged into the room, followed by Nong's older sister. I made a run for the kitchen, thinking that I was about to get a kicking. My plan was to grab a bread knife and start flailing it around, but one of the men pulled out a badge and started screaming that he was a policeman. I calmed down a bit and looked at the badge. It looked real enough.

Sen began screaming that I was the farang who'd stolen her car, and it all fell into place. Nong didn't say anything, she just stared at the floor. One of the detectives grabbed my left arm. I started talking to the senior office in Thai and asked him if I could talk to him one on one, that I was sure there had been a mistake and that we could easily sort it out. The officer agreed and his two men ushered Sen and Nong out into the corridor.

I offered him a drink and we both sat down with tumblers of Johnnie Walker Black Label and Coke. The detective explained that Sen had returned home to find the Honda Civic had gone and that a neighbour told her that a farang had driven it away. Sen had gone straight around to her local police station and they had asked the police in my area to make enquiries.

I hit the roof. I told him that it wasn't Sen's car any more, that my friend Dave had paid 100,000 baht for it. I explained that Dave had given me the key and that Dave was planning to sell the car when he got back and give half the money to Nong. I was just an innocent party, and I resented the fact that Sen was laying the blame at my door.

The detective shrugged, finished his whisky, and then went outside to speak to Nong. He came back after a few minutes and said that there seemed to be a difference of opinion over who actually owned the car, and that the police would have to sort it out. He seemed like an okay guy so I asked him if we could both go to the police station where the complaint had been lodged and explain the situation to them. I'd feel happier if he was with me. For all I knew, Sen might well be tight with the cops there.

The detective agreed and he drove me in his pick-up truck while Sen and Nong followed in a police car. We reached the station just before midnight and we were all ushered into the duty captain's office. The captain was overweight with short, close-cropped grey hair and a jagged scar across his left cheek as if someone had stabbed him with a broken bottle years ago. He grinned when he saw me and I saw the flash of a gold tooth at the back of his mouth. I could almost see the dollar signs in his eyes as he tried to work out how much money he could extort from me.

As soon as Sen walked into his office she started mouthing off again, that I'd stolen her car and lied to her sister, that I'd told Nong's boyfriend that she was sleeping around, that I was a liar and a thief and that I should be sent to prison.

I turned to my new-found detective friend for support but as soon as he started to speak the captain jabbed a finger at him and told him that he was out of his jurisdiction and that he might as well go straight back to Bangkok. My detective hurried out, clearly embarrassed. Sen launched into another verbal attack, pacing around the room as she accused me of stealing her car, lying to her sister, having bad body odour, and everything else she could think of. When she finally ran out of steam, the captain picked up a toothpick and began jiggling it between his front teeth as he waved at me to speak.

I spoke slowly and clearly, in my very best Thai, with lots of smiles and nods. My fate was totally in the captain's hands. If he decided there was no case to answer, I'd be tucked up in my bed within hours. If he decided I was guilty or didn't like the look of me I'd be in a prison cell for up to a year waiting for my case to come to court. I explained that the car belonged to my friend Dave, that he had paid 100,000 baht for the car, and that I had the keys. I took them from my pocket and waved them over the captain's desk. If Sen wanted to give back the 100,000 baht, she could have the car.

The captain grimaced, tossed the chewed toothpick into an ashtray, and told us both to make written statements. That took the best part of two hours. Then we were back in the captain's office. He read through the statements while Sen sat in the corner, glaring daggers at me. Eventually the captain tossed the statements into a metal tray on his desk.

'You must tell us where the car is, then we can decide how much money you owe,' he said.

Sen let out a sharp yelp of triumph, but the captain silenced her with a cold stare.

I offered to go and fetch the car but the captain said no, under the law he couldn't let me go until the car was returned. I knew that I had no choice other than to give him the keys and tell him where I'd left the car. I said that the apartment car park was full so I'd left it at the nearby hotel. Two uniformed cops took me upstairs and I was placed in a small waiting room while the captain sent one of his men to fetch the Honda. It was three o'clock in the morning. Two hours later the captain came upstairs. The older sister had taken possession of the car, he said.

I hit the roof and shouted that it wasn't her car, that she'd been paid a 100,000 baht for it.

The captain said that the car's papers were in order and showed Sen as the owner. And that for the moment, I was to remain in police custody. With that, he turned and left. A uniformed officer gripped my arm and took me to a holding cell. There were twenty men in there. No bunks, no pillows, no blankets, just a bare concrete floor, a foul-smelling bucket to piss in and a tap with a short length of hosepipe attached for washing. Several of the men already there were curled up on the floor, trying to sleep. The overhead fluorescent lights were on. Rats were scurrying around the edges of the cell, and there were cockroaches all over the walls.

A couple of Thai men with tattoos came over and asked what I'd done. I told them about the car. They were in on drugs charges. One had been caught with several kilos of amphetamine tablets in his truck and would almost certainly get the death penalty. I squatted against a wall and cursed the day I'd offered to help Dave out.

At eight o'clock in the morning there was a change of shift and two uniformed officers arrived with a small plastic bowl of rice for each of us, a bowl of hot, rancid soup and a bottle of water. I asked one of the guards if I could talk to the duty captain but I was told that he'd gone home.

'Who else can I talk to about my case?' I asked, scratching one of the dozen or so mosquito bites I'd acquired during the night.

'Only him,' said the guard.

'When is he back?'

'Ten o'clock tonight.'

I cursed. I'd have to stay in the hellhole for at least another fourteen hours. I asked if I could phone the New Zealand Embassy but was told that I wasn't allowed to make any phone calls. I drank from the bottle of water and gave the bowl of soup to one of the scrawnier-looking prisoners. It was going to be a long day.

There was nothing to do but talk to the other guys in the holding cell, so during the course of the day I got to hear most of their stories. One young guy who was in for attempted rape kept telling everyone that his father was rich and that he was paying 50,000 baht and that he would be released that afternoon. He was, too. Others were shackled and taken away to be sentenced. Most were there on drugs charges. I felt really sorry for one guy. Gung his name was. He couldn't have been more than twenty years old. He was almost in tears. He'd been in the holding cell for almost a week and reckoned he was going to go to prison for at least three months. He had no money so he hadn't even been able to phone his mother to tell her where he was. He gave me a scrap of paper with his mother's name on it and begged me to phone her when I got out. He said I was his only hope.

I had a few hundred baht on me so I was able to buy a can of Coke and a packet of crisps. I tried to sleep but it was almost impossible on the hard concrete floor, even using my trainers as a makeshift pillow. One time I opened my eyes to see Gung scoffing the last of my crisps. I screamed at him and he burst into tears, telling me that he was starving. I ripped up the piece of paper he'd given me. I was damned if I was going to call his mother after I'd caught him stealing from me.

I waited until five minutes after ten before asking one of the guards if the captain was in yet. He frowned and said it was the captain's weekend off and that he wouldn't be back until Monday. I almost passed out. Monday? I had to spend another forty-eight hours in the holding cell for no other reason than that the captain was away playing golf or snooker or shagging his minor wife.

My T-shirt and jeans were already caked in dirt and sweat and I itched all over. I couldn't bear the thought of two more nights. I wanted to shout and scream but I knew that there was nothing I could do to change the situation. I forced myself to stay calm. *Jai yen yen*, as the Thais are so fond of saying. Cool heart.

As it happened, the duty captain put in an appearance the following night. Manacles were slapped on my wrists and I was taken down to his office. He seemed to be in a good mood and he listened patiently as I said that it was the older sister who should be behind bars, that I was an innocent third party, that I wanted to speak to my embassy and to my lawyer. When I finished speaking, he cracked his knuckles, picked up a toothpick and flicked it with his thumbnail as he outlined the case against me. The case he would be presenting the judge. The car wasn't mine. The paperwork for the car was in the older sister's name. She had not given me permission to take away the vehicle. And the money that I was claiming was payment for the car was in fact a dowry that Dave had paid as an engagement gift.

That stopped me in my tracks. What?

The captain said that Dave had been sleeping with Nong's younger sister and the 100,000 baht was to compensate for the time she wasn't studying, for her university fees, for her food and her keep. As an act of good faith, the older sister had lent Dave her car.

I started to appreciate just how much trouble I was in. And that maybe, just maybe, Sen had been telling the truth. It could well have been the case that Nong had been too embarrassed to tell Dave that the family was demanding a dowry, and that she'd spun him a line about the money being a payment for the car. And even if it wasn't the truth, in my experience Thai courts tend to take the word of Thai nationals over the word of a foreigner. Plus it would be two against one, their word against mine. And as things stood, I had stolen the car.

The captain smiled at me sympathetically. 'I know you are not a thief, Khun Warren,' he said, He shrugged. 'The problem is, I have already done the paperwork. I would be very difficult to make any changes at this late stage ...'

He looked at me expectantly. I knew exactly what was happening. He was giving me the chance to buy myself out of the hole I was in. 'I don't have any money on me,' I said.

'But you have an ATM card,' he said.

I did a few quick calculations in my head. I figured I probably had about 40,000 baht in the account. I told him that I was a teacher and that I had hardly any money, but that I could probably get him 30,000 baht.

'Fifty thousand,' he said.

I told him that all I had left in my account was 40,000 baht, and that he could have it all. I pulled out my wallet and took out my ATM card. 'If you take me to the nearest machine, I'll withdraw all the money.'

He held out his hand for the card. 'You have to stay here while you are charged,' he said. 'Give me the pin number and I will see what I can do.'

I wrote the pin number down on a piece of paper with my manacled hands and the captain told one of his men to take me back to the holding cell.

I was dog-tired and I sat down with my back against the wall, my knees drawn up against my chest. I closed my eyes but stayed awake, hoping and praying that my name would be called and that I would be let out. The call never came. I dozed, and when I woke up I was sprawled on the floor and it was daylight. Breakfast had been served while I was asleep and someone had eaten my rice and soup. When a guard appeared I was told that the captain had gone home and wouldn't be back until the evening. Now I was really worried. The captain had taken my card and probably emptied the account, but I had no way of knowing whether or not he would honour the agreement. I don't think I've ever been so scared in my life. I've had guns pointed at me, I've had guys pull knives on me, I've had bargirls threaten to cut off my private parts and feed them to ducks, but none of that compared with the terror of knowing that I was facing months if not years in a Thai prison. People die in Thai prisons. Lots of people. They get sick, they get knifed, they get raped, they commit suicide. And if they survive their incarceration, they're never the same. My three days in the holding cell had been just a taste of what lay ahead of me if the captain didn't keep his end of the bargain.

I kept looking at my watch and prayed that the captain would come back. He did. And at eleven o'clock I was taken to his office. The manacles were removed and a bottle of Thai whisky appeared from his desk and he poured two glasses. We toasted each other. Then he waved a typed report in front of me. 'I have made a small alteration,' he said. 'A small but important alteration. It now says that you borrowed the car from the older sister. Borrowed and not stole.' He picked up another typed form and slid it across the desk towards me. 'This is a release form. You will sign it. It says that you have been well and fairly treated here, it says that we have not asked you for any money. And it says that you will not bother Khun Nong any more.' He handed me a ballpoint pen. 'If you give me any problem in the future, I will cross out "borrow" and write in "steal".

Do you understand?'

I nodded. Yeah, I understood. I had paid him a 40,000-baht bribe and was now signing a piece of paper that said I hadn't bribed him. I signed. The papers were taken away to be counter-signed, photocopied, stamped and filed. I was even given a copy of both papers, and the captain slipped me an envelope containing my ATM card then the captain told that I was free to go.

I stumbled down the stairs in a daze. It was just after midnight. I felt like the guy in *Midnight Express*, staggering out of prison, not believing that I was actually free. I kept thinking that at any minute the cops would come running after me to slap the manacles on me again. I was hungry, I was thirsty, and I stank to high heaven. I needed a bath, I needed a steak and I needed my bed. And a woman would be nice. But first of all I needed a taxi, because I wanted to put as much distance between myself and the police station as possible.

I saw a blue and red cab with its light on and I flagged it down, jumped into the back and barked out my address before he could complain about the smell. Thailand was never the same for me after that weekend. It had been sullied. Spoilt. And I had seen for myself how easy it was for things to go horribly wrong in the Land of Smiles.

AFTERWORD

They say there's a book in all of us, be it fact or fiction, and in my case, working as a private eye in Bangkok, I had many clients telling me I should one day publish my memoirs. This might never have happened. However, thanks to a chance meeting with Stephen Leather, an idea became reality, and rough scribbles in tatty notebooks, together with random recollections, were, through Stephen's mastery, woven into what I trust was the entertaining book you have just read.

Everything in this book is based on fact. Some cases were a little too sensitive to include and of course many were repetitious. Over the years, the success of my business grew largely by word of mouth, and this was due to the fact I became involved personally—most clients treated me as a confident, a friend, perhaps even a psychiatrist! I would take their calls day or night; they were several continents away waiting on the results of my investigations to shape their future life plans.

In order to protect all parties, the names, nationalities, and in some cases locations, have been changed but the stories are basically as they happened.

Reading through the book, you may feel that Thailand, and the local women in particular, are something to be wary of. That is certainly not the case. I have been fortunate to have travelled extensively, especially throughout Asia, and in my opinion there is not a country in the world where the people are friendlier, where the women are more graceful.

If you are going to become involved with Thailand, especially with Thai women, I would strongly suggest that you take time to learn something of the people, the culture and the language. Thais will greatly appreciate any effort you make to understand their country and their culture. You must take into account a different way of thinking, a different upbringing, a country where it is common for females from the large, poorer section, not be able to go to secondary school, and where by and large, pensions, unemployment benefits, childcare payments to single parents, or even fifty-fifty asset splits in divorce cases, do not exist.

I have seen Thai girls accept large sums of money without a second thought from foreigners they have recently met, displaying very little gratitude or showing no remorse when they don't honour their end of things. And a few weeks later, when the money has gone and they are destitute, these same girls are genuinely grateful that I would give them twenty baht for food. Many girls working in bars are depicted as cold and calculating, yet these same girls would dote on my young daughter if they saw her out with me, and would rush off to buy her some fruit or a toy.

In my own case, my wife is Thai, and much younger than I am, plus she is from a poor family and although bright, had a limited education, yet, perhaps against the odds, I have to say I could not ask for a better wife or a more devoted mother. It has not been easy for us, but we both realized that as a family we would be better off living in New Zealand and we made the decision to leave Thailand. I am now completing a Masters in Strategic Studies, instead of sitting in bars, chatting to lovely ladies and getting paid to drink Jack Daniels! My wife cares for our daughter, and braves the bitter local elements in search of Asian supermarkets, instead of sitting in our Bangkok apartment eating somtam and playing cards with her friends. But we are together, and our daughter Natalie, the love of our life, is growing up healthy and wise, and fortunately appears to have inherited some of her fathers brains, and all of her mothers good looks!

So, relationships with Thai women can work but it does not come easy, you have to work on it, and don't alienate them from their families, their culture or beliefs. Perhaps as you read this book, apart from outlining some of the many pitfalls one can encounter, you may come to get a little more understanding of things Thai, perhaps your eyes will be opened a little more, and should you develop a relationship with a Thai at some stage, there maybe some things here that help you make the right choice, or help smooth the way. It is my hope this book does accomplish that, just as much as it entertains.

My thanks go out to those many, many people who contacted me over the years as a Thai private eye; I can honestly say I always tried to do my best for you—I just hope that in most cases it was enough. If some of you recognize cases, and feel you have been poorly portrayed, my apologies, as those who know me can testify, I always tend to say things as they are—or at least as I see them.

To the many good friends I made during my years in Thailand, to all those who were happy to help, assist or recommend a struggling PI my heartfelt thanks and best wishes for your respective futures in the Kingdom.

Thanks also to those good friends over the years, the likes of PK, Cookie, Bruty, the gang from the 'X' forum, all of whom helped provided the genuine friendship one needs when domiciled in a country far from home.

To the Thai people in general, nothing but thanks and admiration, always willing to help when they could. A classic example: Khun Moi, the dear old drink seller who no doubt still sets up nightly on the corner of Sukhumvit Soi 13, a real treasure. When times were tough, she happily supplied TPE (Thaiprivateeye) with a bottle of Sangthip and some Coke on tick!

Similarly, most officials I had to confront were always helpful and understanding, and I did my best to show them respect and some appreciation when I could.

My time spent in Thailand, espcially as an investigator, was a wonderful chapter in my life. Perhaps not always as easy or successful as it may appear in the book, but nonetheless a part of my life I would never change, and it certainly helped me develop a better understanding of life in general. I was fortunate to leave Thailand not only with great memories, many of which I have shared here with you, but also with a jewel in the form of our daughter Natalie. This book is for her for she is my motivation and perhaps my saviour—an investigator needs plenty of luck to remain unharmed, I think I had just about used all mine.

Warren Olson
2006